Foxglove

Foxglove

Seasons of the Veil – Book One

Written by Aaron McQueen

Illustrations by Jennifer Lange
Editing by Kara Bernard

Book One of the Seasons of the Veil series by Aaron McQueen

Copyright © 2019 Aaron McQueen and McQueen Serial Fantasy

All rights reserved

ISBN: 978-1-7343646-1-3

This book is a work of fiction. Any resemblance to actual events, locations, or persons, living or dead, is entirely coincidental.

For Jeannie

The Appointed Time

Morrow hid in the shadows, stifling the rage that filled his heart as he watched his mistress's candles sputter in the dark.

Her voice filtered into his ears like a breath of cold wind.

"Come over here."

Shivering, he took up his gloves and buckled on his sword. It was one of few left in the city, given to him by his mother on her deathbed. These days, it was easier to steal weapons from humans: knives, brass knuckles, and guns. They were poor substitutions for a culture that once lived in moonlight.

His mistress spoke again. "Now, little prince!"

Though he despised the pet name she'd given him, there was no point in arguing and little to be gained from petulance. She was in control, and the truth of it sat like rotten fruit in his gut. He trudged over, scraping his boots across a floor covered in slime.

The Erlkin had become strays, roaming the human sewers and alleys hunting for scraps, swimming in runoff and stinking of excrement. The vaulted halls that once stood as symbols of their way of life were lost, the underways to the old cities were shut, and the great studios of the masters had all been boarded up. They lived like rats, mounded on top of each other in the catacombs beneath the human metropolis.

Chicago. The very name was bitter on his tongue.

The contents of the cauldron oozed black and smelled of blood and sulfur. The acrid smell clung to the back of his throat, and he felt his stomach turn. Were he not so accustomed to the odor, he would have vomited on the spot.

His mistress handed him a jug with a broad mouth and said, "Hold this."

Morrow obeyed. His mistress picked up a ladle and filled the container. The liquid moved on its own, curling and folding over itself, clawing at the sides of the vessel as it struggled to escape. Once it was filled, Morrow stuffed a thick cork stopper in the mouth of the jar to trap it.

"Must we do this?" he asked.

His mistress gave him a stern look. "Of course we must. It is the only way."

"But it's murder."

"The Foxglove is not a person," she replied with icy indifference. "It cannot be killed like some . . . mortal creature."

"She's an innocent woman, mistress."

She giggled. "And?"

Anger swelled in Morrow's chest. It didn't faze her at all that they were about to ambush a 19-year-old girl in the woods. He said, "And it's wrong!"

His mistress turned, grinding in place like a mill wheel. "Is it?"

A dark weight dropped heavily behind her words. Morrow tried to take a step back, but his legs froze in place. The witch's gaze held him like the coils of a constrictor snake. She put out a hand, clutching, and his sight dimmed. His body weakened as invisible fingers closed around his throat.

"I didn't mean…" he said, raking in a breath.

"Didn't mean what?"

Morrow's eyes fluttered shut, and he coughed, writhing under the weight of her will. "I'm sorry!"

The pressure eased. Morrow found himself on the floor, too disoriented to recall when he had fallen. He struggled to his knees as his mistress stood over him. She planted a bare foot his shoulder.

"You belong to me, little prince," she said, pressing him back down to the floor. "Never forget that."

Her hollow eyes peered down the slim bridge of her nose. Her skin was like wet paper, thin and pale, revealing the fair lines of her bones. Once, she would have been indescribably beautiful. Morrow's knees trembled at the mere memory of her former self. Now, she loomed like a marble statue, smooth and cool and laced with black.

Gwynedd, dark witch of the fair folk, queen of the evening and the night. Among the Erlkin, there were none as old or as powerful. Withdrawing her foot, she reached into her robes and produced a long knife. The blade was ancient, chipped from stone by her own hand in a time long before the fair races came to the Earth.

"Open your mouth," she said, setting the point against her palm.

Morrow strained against his body's impulse as it rose to meet her hand. One half of his thoughts cowered, terrified to the point of tears; the other half ached for release. His jaw relaxed, and his mouth watered as black blood fell from the witch's palm and dropped onto his lips. His eager tongue collected every drop.

When she took her hand away, Morrow fell against the cool, silken flesh of her thigh, resting his cheek against her skin as the fearful half of his mind fell away into silence. Gwynedd scooped the heavy jug up with one arm and tucked it into her robes. The knife disappeared into her sleeve.

"Now, we must go," she said. "I've waited five-hundred years for this night to come, and I do not intend to be late."

Uptown Girl

There was a knock at the door, and Maddie jumped awake. Sunlight streamed into her bedroom through half-closed blinds. Rubbing her eyes, she leaned back in her chair and wrestled with the cords to pull them shut, except she yanked the wrong string. The blinds flew open and the afternoon came blazing through. Cursing, Maddie covered her face with one arm and flailed, falling away from her desk as her chair tipped and fell over backwards. She landed on the floor with a thump.

A familiar voice spoke through the door. "Miss Foster? Are you alright?"

"I'm fine!" She called back, wincing. "I'm up!"

There was a brief pause. "Have you finished your breakfast?"

Maddie looked around, disoriented. The tray was still on the bed. She hadn't touched it.

"No," she answered.

Footsteps retreated down the hall as Maddie crawled to her feet and stared down at her desk. A puddle of drool had spread across her papers. It was no big deal. They were only college forms. "What a bunch of crap," she grumbled as she grabbed a tissue to wipe them off.

She picked up her phone. It was 4pm. She'd slept through more than half the day.

The last thing she remembered was James dropping off her breakfast. He was her butler, or more to the point, he was her *mother's* butler, hired the day after her dad passed. Even now, months later, the memory stung, because it was on that morning, when her new caretaker came through the door, that Maddie realized that it wasn't just her father that was never coming home.

Breakfast was eggs on toast. Maddie grabbed a cold piece and nibbled, sipping water from a sports bottle she kept on her nightstand. James had left her mail on the tray, and she picked up the first envelope. It was marked international and had a Chinese return address. Maddie tossed it in the trash.

Joanna-Lynn Foster was a Booth woman: University of Chicago, class of '73, back when Booth was still called the Graduate School of Business, something she was quick to point out whenever the opportunity came up to reference her degree. She worked out of a high-rise in Hong Kong, brokering deals between big internationals and, as of last month, had not set foot in the United States in five years.

Truthfully, it wasn't her mother's absence that bothered Maddie. She and her father had certainly enjoyed the fruits of her labor. He used to say that big people needed big dreams, and that her mother liked knowing that she could look after so many people: her family, her employees, and her clients. It was an idea that Maddie grudgingly accepted. Nevertheless, it just didn't feel right that her whole life was just another line in a day planner.

On the other hand, her mother's inattention had also kept her at least temporarily unaware of the fact that Maddie hadn't *actually* enrolled in college.

At first, the problem was a curiosity. Honestly, Maddie had never given it any thought. After all, it was the dumbest, simplest question in the world. What do you want to be when you grow up? It had never occurred to her that someday someone would actually be *asking*. And so here she was, nineteen years old, with a 4.0 grade-point average, a fistful of AP credits, and no idea what the hell she was going to do.

She got up and changed into shorts and a sports bra. Her legs tingled from too much sleep and too little activity. Maybe after a run, Maddie hoped, she would be able to clear her head, finish filling out the forms, and get on with the rest of her life.

James was by the door, watering the houseplants, as she came thumping down the stairs.

"Heading out?" he asked.

Maddie forced a smile. "Yeah. I'm gonna blow off some steam."

He gave her a little bow and said, "Enjoy your run."

The pavement cracked in the heat. Maddie cursed the local weather service for having the gall to refer to the sky as "partly cloudy." It had to be a hundred degrees in the shade. Her father had taken her all over the world when she was a kid, but there was no place on earth as unforgiving as Chicago in the summer. She stretched, popped in her headphones, and headed for the park.

After a few blocks, she passed a group of students relaxing in a broad pavilion, enjoying the sunshine now that the long, cloudy months of the school year were over. Maddie looked away. The crowd only served to remind her of the uncomfortable truth that, for the first time in her life, she was falling behind.

At least Tammy would be in town for the break, visiting from her dad's place in Aspen. She was even nerdier than Maddie was, and Maddie considered herself a connoisseur. They'd been planning a meet up for weeks, and they had a whole library of video games to get through. The marathon would continue until they either passed out from exhaustion or killed each other over whether or not infinite-hit combos were legal.

She headed for the woods, where the path led into what was — as far as Maddie was concerned — the crown jewel of the Chicagoland area: the Cook County Forest Preserve system, 70,000 acres of bona fide green space smack in the middle of one of the largest urban centers in the country, complete with parks, picnic benches, nature trails, and more than a hundred miles of well-lit bike path. Maddie brought in a deep breath of contentment as she jogged through the shade, taking in the tweeting of the birds and the soft buzz of the insects. The pollen was so thick she could practically brush it away from her face with an open palm, and yet her heart ached. Before her father's accident, these woods had always made her feel at home; now they only made her feel like running away.

It was an old story, and a short one. It began downtown with a drunk driver at the corner of Michigan and East Adams; it ended with her father in the trauma ward of Mercy Medical on Polk. She didn't even get to say goodbye. The doctors said it was quick and that he wouldn't have felt any pain. Small comfort. He deserved better.

Her mother paid for the funeral, but she didn't come back for it.

Her assistant had called. There was a big deal at stake, and she couldn't get away. Something about a bridge.

Things went downhill pretty fast after that. Conversations rapidly became arguments, then shouting matches, until, in the end, Maddie stopped picking up the phone. They hadn't spoken in eight months.

Maddie turned onto an unpaved trail, and it carried her into the forest. The woods became a sea of ferns and patchy sunlight as Maddie's heels pounded against the earth. She'd forgotten how much she loved running on dirt. It felt more natural, and didn't have the plastic quality that seemed so inescapable in modern society. There were no lamps, or concrete, or curbs, and certainly no people. She was alone on the planet as she sprinted down the trail, lost in her own little piece of the world.

The world became a blur of green. Sweat beaded on her brow and ran down her back, darkening the orange of her tank top. She forgot about her mother, the application forms, and college. There was only the rush of the wind, the glare of the sun, and the soft cushion of leaves beneath her feet.

Eventually, her breath gave out, and she leaned over onto her knees. She reached for the water bottle on her hip, panting as she realized that it was still in her room on the nightstand. Cursing under her breath, she trudged back up the trail towards the parking lot. How far had she gone? A mile? Two?

She stopped when she heard the sound of running water. Maddie left the path and shouldered her way through the undergrowth to find the source of the sound, skin prickling as she wobbled on her feet. The thickness of the brush parted after a dozen yards, and she found herself standing in a field painted over with the dazzling color of tall wildflowers. Stumbling through the rainbow display, she came to a pool fed by a natural spring. Clear water drained into it, emerging from a cleft between two huge gray stones, smooth from age and weather.

She knew all about the dangers of drinking untreated water, but at this point, sweltering in the heat, she didn't give one hot damn. Throwing dignity to the wind, Maddie thrust her face into the pool and drank. The cool liquid was like ice in her throat. When she felt her belly would burst if she drank any more, she rolled over and lay in the flowers.

The wind was warm, the sun flooded in red through her closed eyelids, and for the first time since her father passed away, she felt at peace.

Alone in the Dark

When Maddie woke up, it was dark. The pool lay beside her, still bubbling softly, but the flowers had all closed. A thin crescent moon hung in the sky. Its reflection cut like burning silver across the surface of the water.

Crap, she thought.

She checked her phone. It was eleven o' clock. She was five hours late for her evening with Tammy. James had probably already called the cops, and the last thing she needed was for her mother to hear she'd had a run-in with the Chicago PD. She'd never let her leave the house again.

Tammy would know what to do. If she got a hold of her right now, maybe the two of them could work together and come up with an alibi. Maddie heaved herself off the ground and went to call.

No signal. Perfect. How could there be no signal in the middle of the suburbs?

Maddie started back towards the trail, growling in frustration, phone held high in a useless attempt to snag a connection. She plunged into the brush, eyes locked onto the little screen hovering over her head as her mind raced. What did they do to you if you mobilized the whole police department in the middle of the night for no reason? Would she be fined? Arrested? She wasn't a kid anymore. Would there be jail time involved?

A twig snapped under her feet.

Maddie jumped and looked around, realizing that her surroundings were no longer familiar. She'd never been out in the woods at night before, and it took on a whole different persona. There were no comforting rays of sunlight, nor seas of soft green ferns. Instead, she found only darkness and tangled branches, cold and sharp in the porcelain moonlight.

It was the quiet that disturbed her the most. Maddie always imagined that walking through the forest at night would be frightening in some kind of active way, like one of those cautionary videos they showed in high school about the importance of traveling in groups and covering your drinks at parties. Instead, the darkness muffled the landscape like a black woolen blanket, and the silence was penetrating as she squinted to scan the ground between the trees.

Where the hell is the trail? she thought.

Maddie decided to double back, hoping that she missed it, and that there was nothing to worry about. The trail was still there, right where she'd left it. Eyes on the ground, she picked her way through the bushes, searching for the narrow line of packed earth that would lead her home.

Her confidence slowly fell as the minutes ticked by. By the time 11:30 rolled around, she was forced to admit that she was hopelessly lost. All she could do was pick a direction and walk. The forest preserve was big, but it didn't go on forever. Eventually she would hit a road, and

she would either make it home or the cops would pick her up and take her.
Stupid forest, she thought. *Stupid field. Stupid flowers. Stupid pool.*
She tromped through the brush. By the time she got back, she would probably be covered in poison ivy.
The forest came at her with all the tenacity of a pack of wild dogs, tearing her top and scratching at her legs. Mosquitoes bit at every inch of her exposed skin, and it felt like the temperature had dropped fifty degrees.
All she could think about was getting home to a warm bath and a soft bed, but deep down she knew that, more likely, the night would end in back seat of a patrol car. Desperate for comfort, she reached for her headphones, hoping that a little music would lighten the mood.
As she fumbled with the cords, the ground dropped away and she fell down a steep, damp slope. Her phone went flying, and she landed with a wet smack in ten inches of stinking mud.
"Craaaap," she groaned, flinging it off her hands. She tried to stand, but her feet slipped out from under her and she splattered face-first in the muck. Sputtering as she rolled over, she wiped her fingers across her eyes.
This, she thought, *is as bad as it can possibly get.*
Stifling the urge to cry, she took a deep breath, crawled to her knees, and prepared once again to get to her feet.
But as she lifted her head, a pair of dark figures descended the slope across the bog.
Her eyes could barely make them out. They seemed to blend into the moonlight, shifting rather than stepping as they moved. One of them was a man, tall and thin like the skeleton of a long-dead tree. A narrow braid of white hair hung down to his waist, bright against his dark clothing. Renaissance-style boots rode up his calves, and a sword

hung from his belt. The woman was paler than wedding fabric, with a shock of coal-black hair worn short at the top of her head.

Maddie froze. Something deep in her soul began to scream as her eyes fell on the woman's chilling features. A well of fear churned in the center of her chest, and a vine of terror coiled around her heart, strangling as it squeezed.

She had to get away. She didn't know how she knew, but Maddie's blood raced in her veins as she looked around wildly, eyes darting around the swamp as she searched for some avenue of escape, but before she could get to her feet, the woman turned. Her gaze swept across the stagnant pool and settled on Maddie's face as she brought up her arm and pointed.

The man began to move.

Maddie ran. She hurled herself across the ground, plunging through dirt and rotting leaves. As she heaved herself forward, she heard heavy squelching behind her, and the sound of boots charging through mud.

She glanced back and saw the man, sliding through the muck with unnatural speed as the mire parted in front of him. Maddie threw herself to the edge of the slope and climbed. Dirt slipped between her fingers and crumbled under her feet. Her fingers stung and bled as she clawed her way up the muddy incline, scrambling with every ounce of her strength until she caught hold of a dangling root sticking out of the ground. She started to haul herself up.

Another yard, another foot, another inch. Her thoughts raced as she pulled herself out of the bog. The sloshing was louder now. He was close.

Move, Maddie! Go! Now!

A gloved hand closed around her ankle.

Maddie screamed as the man dragged her back down the muddy slide.

"Get away from me!" she shouted, kicking wildly.

As they landed at the bottom, the man let go of her and leaned down, reaching for her arm.

Maddie thrust her foot into his groin. He grunted and doubled over, sinking to his knees in the thick, murky water. Maddie scrambled backwards before turning and throwing herself back onto the slope. She gritted her teeth and rammed her fingers into the dirt, forcing her way up.

Who are these people?! She thought. *Drug dealers? Rapists? Murderers?*

The thoughts flashed through her head alongside a thousand terrible ends to her life. She reached up, and her palm smacked against dry earth.

As she crawled over the top, the ground suddenly lurched. Like a great serpent writhing awake at the bottom of the sea, the earth swelled and broke, flinging Maddie up and back through the air to splash down into the wet. Her head struck a rock beneath the surface, bursts of light broke across her vision, and she sank, dizzy and limp.

The man stood over her. His expression was like stone as he said, "Running won't do any good."

Maddie tried to lift her head, but she could barely move. She brought her arms up weakly as the man took her by the shoulders. Her thoughts swam, lost in a cloud of pain and confusion, and when she tried to speak, her words came out in gibberish. Blood oozed from her temple as the man dragged her across the mud hole and dumped her in front of the woman.

"I've been waiting a long time to see you again," she said, looking down.

Maddie's mind shrieked as the other-worldly terror seized her again. She forced her mouth to form words. "Who are you? Why are you doing this?"

"Who am I?" the woman said, giving a little smile. "I'm surprised you don't remember. I was with you when you were born, and when you were lost. I was even there when you received this . . ." She pulled Maddie's collar down gently, revealing the birthmark slashing down from her neck. "You were mine once, Foxglove, and now you will be mine again."

The man whispered harshly, "Will you get on with it?" His eyes flicked across the darkness between the trees. "We don't have time. The others will be coming."

The woman's face twitched, and she took a long breath. "Patience," she said. "When the time comes, I will know."

Maddie tried to sit up.

"Don't fight," the woman said, pressing her down.

Maddie pushed against her. The strength was returning to her legs and arms.

The woman turned to her companion and said, "Hold her."

The man looked down at Maddie. For a moment, a ghost of sympathy passed across his face.

"Sorry," he said.

Kneeling down and resting his hands on her shoulders, he pressed her into the mud. As Maddie thrashed, the man grunted and put his whole weight against her. Maddie hurled her voice out into the night, praying desperately that someone would hear her screams.

The woman gave her a disappointed look.

"You needn't bother with that," she said. "There's no one here to help you. I'm afraid you've come a long, long way from what you know."

Maddie shouted until her throat burned. The woman calmly reached into her robes and drew out a jug of black liquid. Vile odor flooded the air when she pulled out the stopper, and Maddie gagged. With her other hand, the woman pulled out a knife. The blade was broad and fat and chipped from black stone.

Maddie shrieked.

The man glanced up at the trees again. He looked afraid. It was only then, in her wild-eyed fear, that Maddie noticed the trees. They were enormous! The trunks were like skyscrapers, their branches spreading out in a canopy of leaves that blotted out the sky.

Her bones quaking, Maddie slowly turned her eyes back to the woman.

"Where am I?" she asked.

The woman slid the knife down Maddie's collar and answered, "One step closer to home."

The blade sliced open the fabric of Maddie's tank top, cutting down through the sports bra covering her chest. The man looked away and shut his eyes. His mouth moved noiselessly, repeating, *I'm sorry. I'm sorry. I'm sorry.*

Maddie shouted again, screaming into his ear. "If you're so sorry, then HELP ME!"

He held her down, but he strained as though his own muscles were working against him. The woman cracked a smile, and his neck went taught, pulling his head around to face her as his eyes pressed themselves open.

"I . . . can't!" he said, forcing the words through his teeth.

The woman closed her eyes as she lifted the jar and drank. The smell forced its way into Maddie's nostrils and down her throat, a combination of rotting meat, old grease, and blood. She gagged as the woman swallowed the entire contents of the container, and exhaled a sigh of disturbing pleasure. Maddie's stomach heaved, and she threw up. The woman took no notice. Instead, she tilted her ear skyward as if listening for a distant signal.

"Don't do this!" Maddie shouted, wrestling. "I don't understand! Please, stop!"

A choked rattle emerged from the man's throat as his paralyzed expression tightened to the point of tearing.

The woman's eyes opened, revealing empty pools of penetrating, seamless black. Maddie froze in terror as the woman's veins grew darker, blackening like they were filling up with soot. The darkness grew until it spread across her face, flooding down her neck and shoulders until it covered her body like a shawl of ebony lace.

"It's time," she said, setting the point of the knife against the mud-encrusted skin of Maddie's chest.

Maddie pressed herself into the mud, a final, futile effort to escape. The woman lifted the knife and stabbed her through the heart.

Fear and anger. Desperation and regret. The shock blew them all away. Maddie felt a tugging motion as the woman sawed the blade back and forth. She felt . . . strange, like she was draining out of herself. The woman murmured softly as the world began to fade. Maddie couldn't understand the words, but the language was somehow familiar.

Her eyes drooped and fell shut.

Dead. Missing. Was that all? she asked herself.

Her last thoughts were of a dim epitaph, a few faded lines on a crumbling headstone. *Here lies Madeline Foster . . .*

And there was nothing else. Had she the strength, she would have wept.

The man's weight lifted, and in the final moments, Maddie heard the sound of steel ringing against steel. A shout broke through the dark as the lights went out and the world slipped away.

Into the Woods

"She's waking up."
"Hold her still."
"How can she be awake?"
"She shouldn't even be alive. Just hold her."

Maddie felt a weight on her shoulders and warm wood against her back as gold light poured, burning, into her eyes.

Hot . . . so hot. Water.

Her mind was swimming as a rhythmic thumping brought her attention back to the voices in the room.

"Is this even going to work?"

"There's no way to know, but we have to try."

So many voices. Maddie rolled her head to the side. A woman with long blond hair stood nearby in a bright green robe. Something in her hand dripped with cloudy water. Maddie tried to focus on it, squinting through the light, when she became aware of a discomfort rising in her chest.

At first it was dull, more like an ache than a pain, but as the seconds passed it grew sharper and hotter until it felt like she'd been doused with boiling water. Her muscles tensed and she writhed, struggling to crawl away.

The weight on her shoulders shifted, holding her tight.

"The shock is wearing off."

The woman came to the table. Dark eyes stared down at Maddie, and blackened veins showed through her skin. She said, "Then we have to hurry."

Maddie winced. The pain beneath her ribs burned like hot coals as she lifted her head and looked down.

A bloody hole lay open in the middle of her chest.

The world swirled away into blurred spirals of light and color. She screamed as searing pain rolled over her and her back wrenched up into a bridge.

"There she goes!" someone shouted.

"Hold her!"

Light crashed down like an avalanche of fire as the woman pressed her hands into Maddie's gaping chest. Maddie's eyes rolled back, and the room disappeared in a wash of gold and white.

When she woke up, the room was gone. Only the blond woman remained. Maddie found herself lying in a bed wearing a soft linen nightgown, the front of which was undone, revealing a long, bloody scar running down the center of her chest. The woman dabbed at it gently with a brush soaked in thick, brown paste.

She looked up at Maddie.

"It wasn't a dream," she said.

The soft grain of wood met Maddie's bleary eyes as she glanced at the walls, ceiling, and the floor. It was like the whole room had been carved from a single piece. Maddie could even see the lines of tree rings running along its surface. Warm, orange light filled the air.

Maddie let her eyes drift back to the woman. She asked, "Am I dead?"

The woman let a smile slip out through the golden waves of her hair. Her eyes glinted playfully, and there was a kind of humor in her expression that put Maddie at ease.

"If you were dead, you wouldn't have a scar," she answered.

Maddie tried to sit up, but a jolt of pain raced up her chest and she gasped.

The woman put a hand against her shoulder. "Lie down. You've got a lot of healing left to do."

"But who are you? What happened to me?"

"My name is Maeve," the woman said. "What's yours?"

"Maddie. Maddie Foster."

The woman kept dabbing at her chest. "What happened is a question for another day," she said. "For now, you need to rest."

She reached out and put a hand on Maddie's forehead.

Maddie's eyelids drooped. The bed was so soft, the pillows felt like they'd been stuffed with clouds, and the light warmed her like a softly burning flame. She shut her eyes and drifted off to sleep.

When she woke again, the room was empty. She tried once more to sit up, only to discover the same shooting pain she'd felt before. She lay back against the pillows and examined her surroundings.

The room was tiny. The furniture barely fit: the bed, a nightstand, a narrow wardrobe, and a short dresser with a little round mirror, all carved from bare, natural wood. Across the room, a wooden lattice led out to a small balcony. Maddie's gaze drifted over the bed to where the room's dim light bloomed out from a huge orange mushroom protruding from a cleft in the wood.

Maddie stared at the over-sized fungus, and memories of the night before bubbled up in her mind like wisps of steam from a pot of warming water. She remembered the huge trees with leaves that covered the sky. She remembered the woman, black-haired and pale-skinned. She remembered the man, compliant but also terrified. And she remembered the knife . . .

Maddie fumbled with her shirt, pulling open the fabric and looking down. The scar lay like a snake on her chest. She yelped and felt a churning in her stomach. She leaned over the bed and puked, crying out in pain as her chest throbbed and her muscles spasmed.

The door opened. Maddie heard a shout, and a pair of strong hands propped her up as she finished emptying her stomach. When she looked up, soft brown eyes met her own. A girl not much older than she sat down on the edge of the bed. Deep brown hair fell in loose tangles over her strong, narrow features, spilling over the shoulders of a brown linen dress bound tightly with a thick, green belt. And her skin . . .

Maddie pulled away.

At first glance, the girl appeared perfectly ordinary. The deep tan of her skin did a fine job of concealing the peculiar detail that had drawn Maddie's attention. Pale rivulets of green ran along her arms, through her wrists, and along the edges of her brow and temples. Her veins were the wrong color. Maddie looked down at her own. Pale blue. Pale blue was correct. Green was not.

Maddie watched the girl in bizarre wonder as she helped Maddie back onto the pillows before leaning down to clean up the mess. Her almond-shaped eyes were long, and in the dim light of the room they seemed to glow.

"What are you?" Maddie said.

The girl straightened up. "My name is Rain. I'm a friend."

"And where am I?"

The girl pursed her lips, hesitating for a moment before she stood up and took a step back.

"I'll get Maeve," she said.

And then she left, leaving Maddie staring after her, dumbfounded.

Maeve returned a short while later, carrying a tray with her medicine bottle and brush. Fragrant steam wafted up from a shallow bowl beside them. Maddie's stomach rumbled as the woman set the tray down on the nightstand and sat down on the edge of the bed.

"Are you hungry?" she said.

Maddie took a long look. Maeve's veins and eyes were the same as Rain's. She winced as Maeve leaned forward and fluffed the pillows behind her so she could sit up. Picking up the bowl, Maeve filled the spoon and held it to her lips.

Maddie hesitated.

"You think I would save your life just to poison you?" Maeve asked with a little smirk.

Cautiously, Maddie leaned forward and sipped. The soup was warm and smelled of onions. The sweet liquid flowed smoothly down her throat. She could have drained the whole bowl at once, but even in her disoriented state she knew that if she ate too fast she would end up having another date with the floor. So she ate patiently as Maeve fed her, spoonful by agonizing spoonful. When the bowl was empty, Maeve set it aside.

"You'll have to forgive my bedside manner," she said. "I don't normally do this sort of work."

Maddie lay back. "Is anyone going to tell me what's going on?"

Maeve reached for her medicine cup, and leaned forward.

"Open your shirt, please," she said. "I have to check your wound."

Slowly, Maddie nodded and undid her nightgown. Maeve dipped her brush and began dabbing it onto Maddie's chest. "Explaining your situation is the queen's prerogative," she said. "She'll be here shortly."

Maddie furrowed her brow. "Queen?"

Maeve gave a quiet nod, painting Maddie's scar with the brush..

"What is that?" Maddie said.

"It's called a poultice. There are many varieties. Don't worry, you won't need it for much longer."

Maeve put the medicine away.

"How long have I been recovering?" Maddie asked, buttoning up her nightgown.

"About three weeks. A speedy recovery, considering your circumstances."

Maddie's eyes went wide. "Three *weeks?!*"

She took a few short breaths, forcing herself to remain calm. James would have called her mother. She was going to go ballistic! And Tammy . . . She probably thought she was dead! Maddie's mind raced. Three weeks? Would they even still be looking for her? They would have to be, right?

Breathe. Just breathe, she thought as she said, "What circumstances?"

Pity crept across Maeve's features and her eyes flicked down to Maddie's chest and back. "Your heart was cut out," she replied. "I'm sorry. I would have said something, but when you sicked yourself I thought you had remembered."

Maddie felt another wave of nausea break over her. She leaned over the side of the bed. Maeve stood up and took a step back as onion broth splattered on the floor. When the heaving stopped, Maeve gingerly stepped forward and supported Maddie as she sat back up, dabbing her chin with a cloth from the tray.

"I was able to save you using a . . . specialized technique," she said, picking her words carefully. "You were lucky. We weren't sure the graft would hold."

"Graft?" Maddie asked. "You mean like an organ donor?"

Maeve gave a little chuckle. "Of sorts. I was able to replace your heart with a knot of heartwood from our city. It's an advanced spell, but one I've done before, though never on a human."

Maddie gawked at the woman. "You expect me to believe that?"

"Believe what you wish," Maeve said, standing up with a casual shrug. "It will work either way. You can thank me later if the mood strikes you."

The door swung open and a little girl with short, blond curls poked her head inside.

"Miss Maeve?" she asked.

Maeve turned. "Yes?"

"Rose is on her way."

Maeve nodded. The girl stared at Maddie for a moment before shutting the door. Maeve reached into her robes and drew out a necklace made from dark metal. A thick glass bauble hung from it, filled with a mixture of black sand and seeds. She hung it around Maddie's neck.

"This is for you," she said.

Maddie lifted the pendant and looked at it closely. The sand wasn't sand. It was some kind of dried powder.

"What is it?" she asked.

"A ward," Maeve answered, gathering her things. "It's for your protection, so please don't take it off. The queen will be here soon to answer your questions. Afterwards, try to get some rest." She balanced the tray on her hip as she pulled open the door, glancing over her shoulder. "I will be back to check on you in the morning."

Her footsteps gave a muffled echo in the corridor as she left and the door swung shut.

Maddie took a deep breath as she struggled to collect her cluttered thoughts. Fragments of explanation lay scattered through her mind like mis-matched puzzle pieces as she lay back and stared at the glowing mushroom on the wall.

Maybe when this "queen" arrived, she would finally get some answers.

Night and Day

Maddie was drifting off to sleep again when the door opened and the queen entered the room. She was tall, with dark hair and tanned skin. There was something imperial about her beauty and the way she walked that made her look imposing, but her eyes shone with the brightness of the morning and her smile was like a spring breeze. She wore a long, deep red dress with a tall bodice embroidered with intricate vines of black and gold thread. The metal caught the light and shimmered as she passed before the lattice of the balcony door. A delicate wooden circlet rested humbly on her brow.

Attending her was the same young girl Maddie had glimpsed earlier. From her round, sunny face, Maddie guessed she was about eight. Short, blond curls bounced with her every step, and green ribbons fluttered behind her dress.

The queen sat down at the foot of the bed. The girl arranged the woman's dress and left quietly, sneaking a backward glance at Maddie, who was slowly realizing that she was the only human in the room.

Maddie regarded the woman warily. "You're the queen?" she asked.

The woman leaned back, resting against against her arms, and casting off her royal posture with an abruptness that made Maddie want to giggle.

She said, "My name is Rose, and you don't have to call me your highness. I've never been wedded to formality, and after everything you've been through, I'm hoping you can think of me as a friend. You must have a lot of questions. I'd like to answer them if I can."

Maddie took a moment to frame her thoughts. There was no reason to believe that these people meant her any harm. In fact, their attitudes and actions so far suggested the opposite. But that didn't change the fact that she'd been attacked in the woods, and had undergone surgery, and that so far the only explanations she'd been given were absolutely preposterous.

"Where am I?" she said.

"You are in Amaranth," Rose answered. "The Veil-city of Chicago."

"Veil-city?"

Rose stood up and asked, "Can you make it to the balcony?"

Looking down, Maddie realized Maeve hadn't said anything about moving. Maddie felt a twinge of pain throb in her chest as the queen gently lifted her out of bed. but it was dull and tolerable.

Rose steadied her as Maddie limped across the room. The queen pulled open the latticework, and the sight took Maddie's breath away.

She was in a tree. A *huge* tree. The balcony protruded from a thick limb in the upper branches. An extravagant structure, carved into the trunk, extended up above her head. Its contours hugged the tree, hanging from the bark like clusters of Victorian bee hives. Below, a network of thick limbs and leafy foliage filled the sprawling canopy.

A whole city rested on the branches, linked to the forest floor by a pair of spiraling ramps that ran up and down the trunk, each one the size of a two-lane road. Long streets and narrow alleyways ran along the branches alongside buildings fashioned from leaves, sticks, and mud. From them, bright colors flew into the air in the form of awnings and canvas shades. The vibrant flashes caught the light of the sun as it fell through the leaves.

And there were people! From her perch, Maddie saw thousands of them just . . . going about their lives: walking, running, trading, and playing. There were no railings, but they didn't seem to mind, strolling across bridges stretching from branch to branch — with nothing to protect them but open air — like it was the most natural thing in the world. An array of cable-cars hanging from heavy cables joined the city to the palace high above.

"What is this place?" Maddie asked.

Rose led her to two chairs teetering on the edge of the miniature overlook and sat across from her.

"This is the Veil," she said. "It is the name my people give to our world, and to the barrier that separates it from yours."

"Your world?"

The queen's eyes looked down on the teeming city. "My people are the faerie. Millions of us live in communities just like this one. We call them Veil-cities. They are forests, of a sort. They grow where humans have built cities of their own."

Maddie's chest tightened, twinging beneath her skin. She winced.

"How did I get here?" she said.

"We don't know," Rose answered. "Insects and birds pass through the Veil all the time, but for humans and higher animals to wander across is extremely rare. I have my staff looking into it. For now, I want to stress that you are safe, and I will take care of you for as long as you are here."

Maddie paused as the big question reared its ugly head. "And how long will that be?"

The queen's face fell.

"Your body has healed," she said. "But yours was not an ordinary injury."

Maddie felt a lump forming in her throat.

"I know it must sound impossible," Rose said, laying a hand on Maddie's thigh, "but at this moment, a knot of the city-tree's youngest wood beats inside your chest. Only the magic of the Veil sustains it. If you were to go home . . . you would die."

Maddie's heart sank and she took a long, slow breath. Whether it was wooden or not, the hurt felt real enough.

"Who attacked me?" she asked.

The queen stiffened. "An enemy of my people. She is called Gwynedd, queen of the Erlkin."

"The Erlkin?"

"Another race of fair folk, similar to us but not nearly as populous. They once lived in beautiful cities deep within the layers of the Veil, in a place where the forest is filled with moonlight and stars. Their art and culture enchanted the soul, but under Gwynedd's poisonous leadership, decades of neglect and endless conflict have eroded their society. Now they live at the surface of the Veil, in the sewers beneath Chicago."

"I don't understand," Maddie said. "Who was the man that was with her? Why did they attack me? And what did they want with my heart?"

"The man with Gwynedd was Morrow, crown prince of the Erlkin and the source of her political power. Long ago, Gwynedd used forbidden magic to save his life. Since then, he has been bound to her dark will, and his family and people with him. When his mother passed, Gwynedd seized control of his kingdom."

"And my heart?"

The queen hesitated. "I'm afraid we can only guess at the witch's intentions."

"You mean you don't know."

"You have to understand," the queen said. "On this side of the Veil, the spirit and the body are one. Our souls are intermingled with our physical forms. The substance of who we are runs through our veins like living water. We call them the humours, and the heart contains the greatest portion. With your heart, Gwynedd can perform all manner of terrible works. Had my wardens not interrupted her, she might have cast a spell to steal your life to extend hers, curse you with disease or disability, or even control your mind."

"And what's stopping her from doing that now?"

The queen gestured towards the necklace resting against Maddie's chest. "The ward you now wear will keep you safe, shielding you from Gwynedd's eyes and ears, as well as her magic, so long as she does not come near. You must always wear it. For obvious reasons, the less she knows about you and your whereabouts, the better."

"And who are the wardens?" said Maddie.

"Soldiers of mine," Rose answered. "They watch over the forest. You were fortunate that they found you and were able to drive Gwynedd away. I know it doesn't feel like it right now, but you were very lucky. It is a shame they weren't able to recover your heart at the same time."

Maddie hung her head. "But why me?"

The queen sighed. "I wish I knew the answer. Humans are rare in the Veil. Perhaps she thought you were special or had some kind of experiment in mind, but until we find out what her motives were, I want you to stay here in the city-tree, where we know it's safe. My staff will see to your needs." She paused. "You're not a prisoner here, Maddie. If you believe nothing else I've told you, please believe that."

Maddie slumped in her chair.

"I guess I should be grateful," she said.

Rose placed a hand on her shoulder squeezed. For a moment they sat in silence. Maddie stared out at the city. The buildings, painted in browns and greens and speckled with sunlight, shook gently in the breeze. It was like standing in the middle of a giant's garden, splashed with flashes of yellow, pink, and white. As she watched the people below, a sparrow the size of a mid-sized van zoomed by. There was a woman in a saddle strapped to its back. Maddie watched in awe before a disturbing thought wormed its way into her mind.

"Rose...?"

The queen watched the bird fly up through a gap in the treetops. "Yes?"

"How tall am I right now?"

The queen laughed. "Don't worry, you're the same size, but you'll find that quite a few things are different here."

Maddie leaned onto her elbows as a wave of dizziness swept over her, and she swayed in her chair. Rose held her arm and took her back to bed.

"It's not so bad. I promise," the queen said. "Amaranth is a beautiful city, and our people are kind. You'll enjoy your time here once you're up and about. I'm sure of it."

Maddie lay back against the headboard, and Rose turned to leave.

"If we can get my heart back," Maddie said, "will I be able to go home?"

Rose didn't answer right away. She only frowned and shook her head. "I don't know."

Maddie's heart sank. "Thank you again for all your help," she said.

The queen bowed and left. Maddie lay alone, staring out the balcony door at the sunlit shadows of the otherworldly city.

Sitting up, she put her head in her hands, and cried.

Old Magic

All power comes at a price, and for the oldest and most powerful sorceries, there was only one currency. More than a dozen prisoners had been bled dry to fill Gwynedd's reflecting pool, the latest of countless others before them. Morrow stared down into its cloudy depths, a grim frown fixed upon his face as red light filtered out into the room, painting the walls with the flickering shadows of the dead.

Gwynedd leaned on the edge of the pool, eyes barely open. She'd been at it for weeks, barely stopping to eat or drink. Her frail features quaked with the weight of her fatigue.

"They'll never let her leave the city, you know," Morrow said.

His mistress's arms buckled, and her shoulders drooped. She caught herself and straightened as she took a breath. "We'll see."

The liquid shifted over a murky image of corridors and people. Their indistinct forms were impossible to identify.

Morrow said, "Well, right now, it doesn't look like you're seeing much of anything."

Gwynedd's eyes flicked up, and he flinched. The wards around the faerie city had always been difficult to penetrate, and they seemed to have equipped the human woman with a double measure of protection. They knew his mistress would be watching.

"We would already have her if it weren't for your incompetence," she said.

Morrow curled up his nose and scowled. "What incompetence? You were the one who refused to bring soldiers. If we hadn't been alone, maybe we could have made a fight of it." He leaned down. "Perhaps then you wouldn't have been denied your prize."

Gwynedd ignored his answer and kept her eyes on the pool. Morrow glanced at the jar hanging on her hip. The human woman's heart still beat inside. A bubble rose to the surface of the pool and burst. The image cleared, offering them a fleeting glimpse of their victim. She was in bed, weeping.

Morrow clenched his fists and asked, "Why do you need still need her? You have her heart. Isn't that enough?"

Gwynedd's voice dropped to a low murmur. "She is very special. That is all you need to know."

"That's not good enough. I can't help you if you keep me in the dark. Tell me, what makes her so important?"

His mistress looked up. "Do not press me, little prince. This girl is not as she appears. She is the Foxglove, and I must have her."

The image clouded over again and Morrow knelt down. "What will you do now?" he said, eyes scanning the thick liquid.

His mistress's lips settled into a smooth, thin line. "We will wait. Sooner or later the fear will fade, and a weakness will expose itself."

"I doubt that," Morrow said. "Amaranth's neighbors already envy its position and wealth. If it had a weakness, it would have been exploited long ago."

Gwynedd laughed softly. "I'm not talking about the city."

The image cleared a second time, and Morrow glanced down. The girl still wept.

He looked to his mistress. "What is the Foxglove?" he asked.

Gwynedd's eyes glimmered with anticipation.

"A weapon."

A Change of Heart

Maddie kept telling herself that recovery took time, but as the days wore on and her grip on hope grew weaker, she learned it took much more than the quiet comfort of a warm bedroom, hot soup, and waiting.

Don't cry, she thought over and over. *Not anymore.*

Crying only made her angry, but whenever she held it in, she ended up screaming into her pillow and clenching her hands until her fingers were too week to make a fist. When she wasn't doing that, she lay on her back and counted the rings in the wood of her ceiling.

The searches would have been called off by now. James had probably been let go. For all she knew, the house had been sold and her mother was back in Hong Kong, assuming she'd gone through the trouble of coming back. After all, there was no body to bury and no ashes to spread, and her mother wasn't the type of woman to grieve publicly. Even during the investigation, the police would have been able to reach her by phone. Only Tammy would have benefited from a memorial service, and she and Maddie's mother had never met.

Rain visited three times a day with food and water. For the first few weeks, she'd been cheerful, but over time, Maddie's curt responses had put an end to that. These days, she came in quietly, set the tray down, and left.

Maddie kept wishing that one day she would wake up to a fully-functioning human heart, and that Rose would come in and say "Maddie! Great news! We can send you home!" But that day never came, and each new morning brought closer the dreary realization that it never would. There were probably still a few missing-persons signs taped to lampposts around town, but soon those would disappear, and people would move on. They would have to. But Maddie never would. The Veil was her world now, Amaranth was her home, and there was no going back.

Maddie rolled over and cried into her pillow. Some days she just couldn't help it.

The door opened, but Maddie didn't have the energy to look up. It was probably Rain with her breakfast. A hand touched her shoulder.

"Maddie?"

Maddie's eyes snapped open.

"Your majesty!" she said, sitting up in a panic. "I'm so sorry! I didn't know it was you!"

The queen's face glowed in the dim light of the room. "It's okay, and you can call me Rose. I just came to check on you. You've been in here a long time."

"I don't know what to do," Maddie said, rubbing her eyes. She pulled up her blanket and dried her face.

Rose sat down beside her. Her dress flowed like a blood-red river over the sheets.

"I know," she said. "But you can't give up. You never know what tomorrow might bring."

Maddie sniffled. "Will it bring me home?"

Rose folded her hands in her lap. "Probably not," she said. "Maeve's still working on it, but so far she hasn't turned anything up. I wish there was more that we could do."

"I'm dead," Maddie said, slumping back into her pillows. She covered her face with her hands, fighting tears that were already welling up again.

Rose took her hands and pulled her gently back up. "You're not dead. You're breathing, and you can walk and see and feel. That's enough for a start."

"I don't want to start," Maddie said, her voice ragged. "I want to go home!"

Rose came in and gave her a hug. Maddie felt the warmth of her body as the queen whispered in her ear.

"I'm sorry," she said. "Sometimes things happen to us that we can't change, but you have to keep going. You have to hold on to hope."

Maddie coughed, and the dam broke. She cried for what seemed like forever, tears running down her face, until Rose's shoulder was wet with her grief.

"I don't know what to do," she said, as the tide began to ebb. "I don't know anything about this place."

Rose leaned back, making a long reach to a glass of water from the nightstand. "Well, what did you study in school?" she said, handing it to Maddie.

Maddie gave a bitter laugh as she wiped her eyes and looked up at the ceiling.

"Right," she said, sipping the water. "School. I have no idea. Rose, I couldn't even pick a major for college."

Rose stood up, held out a hand, and said, "Maybe I can help you with that."

Maddie sighed and stared at her outstretched palm. "Do I have to?" she said.

Rose gave a wry smile. "It's a royal order. Come on. You'll like it."

Maddie climbed out of bed. Until now, the furthest she'd bothered to go was the chamber pot near the door, a concept that had floored her when Rain brought it in.

Rose moved to help her up, but these days Maddie could stand and walk on her own. Her wound had healed and the scabs were gone. She wore only a pale, glossy scar under her bedclothes. Time had, at least, managed to accomplish that.

"Where are we going?" she asked, moving slowly.

Rose took Maddie to the door and opened it, gesturing through. "It's a surprise."

She led Maddie into the corridor and up a dark, narrow staircase. Maddie marveled at the expansive interior of the city-tree. It seemed to go on forever, but the tight quarters and sparse lighting lent a kind of cozy atmosphere to the place, even if it meant barely being able to walk side-by-side. A trail of orange mushrooms lit their path as they passed bedrooms, conference rooms, dining rooms, and all sorts of other chambers until they came to a little wooden door. The image of a man and woman working a loom had been carved into it.

"This is my personal parlor," Rose said, leading Maddie in. "I come here when I need to unwind."

A huge, flat mushroom grew across the room's low ceiling, covered by a wooden cage. The lattice flowed down seamlessly from the wood, carved meticulously to form a scene of children running through the forest. Enormous pillows of red, green, and brown lay heaped against the walls, which were overflowing with old books bound in leather and thick cloth. A fire burned in a gallon-sized stove in the center of the floor. Its small flames flickered quietly as they warmed the room. The smoke escaped through a pipe set into the wall.

Maddie gasped, staring up at the sculpture. "This is beautiful."

"It took me years to finish it," Rose answered with a smile.

Maddie wandered to the wall, running her fingertips over the books. "You did all this?" she said in wonder. "Yourself?"

The queen walked over to a pile of pillows across the room and sat down. "My husband and I worked on it together for a long time. He never did get to see it finished."

She pointed to the carving covering the mushroom. "Those are our children. The girl on the left is Theresa, our oldest. The boy behind her is our son, Finn. The others . . . we never had, but when my husband died, it just didn't seem right to change the sculpture, so I carved them the way I always pictured our family would end up: three girls, two boys."

Maddie looked back at the artwork with renewed reverence. Two children. Five in the piece. She'd never thought about having kids. She always imagined there wouldn't be time, and the last thing she wanted was to end up like her mother, having a child and no time to raise it. But for the queen, it must have been such a disappointment.

"Do you mind if I ask what happened?" she asked.

Rose's face tensed, tortured by the dull ache of an old wound.

"Gwynedd killed him," she said. "Many years ago."

Maddie hurried over and sat down beside her to take her hand. "I'm sorry. I didn't mean to . . . you know."

Rose forced a smile and drew a fingertip under her eye to catch a tear. "There are many who have lost loved ones at her hands," she said. "You are not alone among those she has hurt."

She took a long breath and leaned back into her cushion, staring at the carving on the ceiling. "A lot of my plans changed when my husband died. For a while, I felt like nothing would ever be the same. In the end, I realized that my life was going to have to change. I knew that he wouldn't want me to live the rest of my life in mourning." She put her hand down on Maddie's knee. "Do you understand?"

Maddie covered the queen's hand with her own. It was a hard truth to face.

"I think so," she said.

Rose gave her hand a squeeze, cheer slowly returning to her expression. "A life is something you build," she said. "It was up to me to find something else to give me purpose, so that I could cherish the dreams my husband and I *did* achieve. I still had a city to care for, and my two children. It was strange at first, knowing I wouldn't have the large family that we'd planned, but over time, the city and its people became my family."

"And then you became queen?"

Rose laughed and lay back on the pillows. "No, I was the queen already. Amaranth was always my city, even before there *was* a city. I built it with my husband from the ground up."

Maddie leaned back, doing the math.

"But wouldn't that make you—?"

"Very, very old," Rose finished. "Faeries are long-lived. The oldest among us have exceeded a thousand years." She got up and picked her way along the wall of books. "Leadership of the city came to me naturally as it grew, though if truth be told, I never really committed to the role until after my husband died. It was easier to let my counselors handle most of the work. When I took up the reins, I found that I could dismiss nearly all of them. Now, there's only one left."

"Which one?" said Maddie.

Rose slid a heavy book from the shelves and returned to the pillows. "His name is Cedric. He's my librarian, and also my son's teacher, which brings me to why I brought you here."

Maddie tensed and sat up. "What reason is that?"

"I'd like you to take lessons here at the palace," the queen answered. "If nothing else, it will give you something to do, and maybe with some time you'll start to feel a little less—"

"Dead?" Maddie interrupted.

Rose pushed the book gently into her hands. "I was going to say lost."

Maddie read the title: *Fair Folk of the North American Realms*.

Rose knelt down in front of the stove. "The author is from one of the European city states," she said, closing the vent to snuff it out. "I thought an outsider's perspective might help you."

Maddie ran her fingers over the binding. It was dated 1909. The pages inside cracked like dried leaves as she opened it. All the textbooks she'd ever read had come in full-color glossy paper, but there was something appealing about the worn out tome, an antique magic that spoke of old stories and ancient mystery.

The queen had certainly found the right bait to lure her out of her slump. After all, how many chances would she get to study a magic realm? And if she stayed cooped up in her room forever, it was only a matter of time before she withered away or went mad.

"The Veil is a place of dreams," Rose said. "You just have to find your own."

Maddie thought for a long moment and shut the book. "I guess it's somewhere to begin."

"Good!" Rose said, clapping her hands. "You'll start tomorrow. I'll have my staff draw up a lesson plan. In the meantime . . . "

She paused and blushed. Maddie smiled as she watched the queen's face turn a deep shade of green.

"What?" Maddie said.

Rose covered her mouth with her hands. "I don't know how else to say this," she said, muffled. "But you need a bath."

Maddie's face paled with embarrassment as she sniffed herself and grimaced. She smelled like . . . well, like someone who hadn't left her room in three weeks.

"Come on," the queen said, helping her to her feet. "Let's get you cleaned up."

Back to Life

Rose handed Maddie off to her handmaid, the same blond girl Maddie had seen twice before. She had on a green cotton apron embroidered with yellow flowers. A tight braid secured with brown ribbons held her curls in place. Rose introduced her as Ebba, and she started talking the moment the queen was out of earshot. Maddie discovered that there was no interrogator more ruthless or intimidating than a curious eight-year-old girl. And of course, she wanted to know about "human stuff."

"Have you ever kissed a boy?" she asked.

Maddie blinked at the question. "That's not your business."

Ebba groaned. "Boring! I've kissed lots of boys."

"At your age?"

The girl nodded affirmatively.

"It's easy if you tackle them first," she said. "You should try it."

Maddie's face flattened. "Uh huh. I think I'll pass."

"Suit yourself," Ebba said, skipping down the hall ahead of her. She pirouetted around. "But you're going to need my help if you want to learn to be a faerie. I'm an expert."

"Are you, now?"

Ebba stomped her foot. "I am! I've read books and everything! And I'm going to teach you so that you can tell Rose how knowledgeable I am. Then she'll put me in charge of all the other handmaids in the palace."

Maddie couldn't stop herself from smiling. This was going to be an interesting relationship.

"I'm sorry I doubted you," Maddie said. "I'll try to be a good student."

Ebba eyed her for a long moment before saying, "Okay."

The bathroom's huge, metal door was only a few yards away from her own quarters. A thick brass ring hung in the center. Rain was leaning against the wall beside it when they arrived.

"Feeling better?" she asked.

Maddie looked down at the book Rose had given her. "A little bit, yeah."

"I thought you might be," Rain said, giving her a little punch on the shoulder. "Rose has that effect on people. Come on. I've got the water hot."

Ebba bounced off down the corridor, returning to her own duties, but not before Maddie promised to comply with her own "top secret" portion of the coming lesson plan.

Rain said, "You'll have to forgive her. She's really harmless."

"She's certainly enthusiastic," Maddie replied. "Are all faerie children like that?"

Rain shook her head. "Absolutely not. Ebba is an anomaly, but we love her, and she'll mellow out once she gets to know you. Remember, she's never met a real human before."

"I guess that's fair," Maddie said. "Before I came here, I'd never met a real faerie."

Rain said, "It's actually pronounced 'fay-ree.' And it's only natural for her to be curious. She's lived in the palace practically her whole life."

"Doesn't she have any parents?"

"Died in a windstorm when she was four," Rain said, taking hold of the door handle. "Rose took her in. Actually, she started taking care of me at about the same age. The queen has a soft spot for lost souls."

Maddie looked down the corridor after Ebba and said, "I guess I'll fit right in."

Rain yanked on the door and it groaned open. Heat washed over them as a cloud of steam billowed out. A low warm light flickered inside. Maddie peered into the room, squinting to see a deep, clay tub sitting over a fire in an iron bowl. Smooth, flat stones covered the floor, and, through the gloom, she glimpsed a tall cupboard against the wall.

Rain pulled a little wooden step stool over over to the tub.

"In you go," she said.

"Um…" Maddie chewed her lip. "Is there a screen or something?"

It took Rain a moment to realize what she meant. "Oh, of course."

She turned her back while Maddie disrobed. As she got out of her clothes, Maddie looked down and grimaced at her scar. Her chest looked like it had been to the morgue and back.

"Ready?" Rain said, still facing the wall.

A fine mist rose up from the tub, carrying with it the soothing fragrance of lavender and exotic salt. Maddie pulled her eyes away from her scar and climbed over the rim of the tub, sliding down into the fragrant water. The heat turned her muscles to jelly.

Maddie stared up at the wooden ceiling, idly remembering all the lonely hours she'd spent in the tub at home, examining calcium deposits between the ceiling tiles.

Rain fetched a handful of cloths, sponges, and rainbow-colored soap from the cupboard.

Then she held up a brush.

Maddie couldn't help but think of her mother. She swore by domestic staff. Living in Hong Kong, or perhaps just as a consequence of being rich, she employed an army of servants to perform all manner of tasks and services: manicures, pedicures, massages. They even helped her get dressed. It all sounded very luxurious, but it was just so . . . medieval. Maddie felt that the things domestic servants did were things everyone ought to be doing for themselves. Bathing was at the top of that list.

"I don't mean to be rude, but . . . " Maddie said, trailing off.

Rain handed her the brush. "You'd rather wash yourself,"

"Yes, please."

Rain popped over to the wall and dragged a tall, spindly table to the edge of the tub.

"I'll be just outside," she said, depositing the shampoo and sponges on the table. "If you need anything, just call."

After she washed, Maddie spent a few minutes soaking, staring up at the ceiling and inspecting the calcium deposits. Some things never changed. She closed her eyes and drifted away, grateful for a moment of relaxation and peace. The popping of the fire warmed her senses, and the back-and-forth of the palace swaying in the breeze gently rocked her to sleep.

It was peculiar, yet strangely calming, to be inside a living building. Maddie could almost feel the water being drawn up the trunk that formed the walls, the slow crawl of roots digging down into the earth, and in the distant corners of her mind, the soft whispering of the city and its people.

"Maddie?"

She felt the water ripple.

"Maddie?

Rain touched her shoulder, and the peaceful haze disbursed like a summer fog vanishing in the sun. Maddie looked up at Rain, blinking, and yawned.

"Did I fall asleep?" she asked, eyes still half-closed.

Rain held out a towel. "I would have left you, but I didn't want you to overheat. Let's get you dried off, then we'll find you some coffee and something to eat."

The water sloshed as Maddie sat up and took the towel.

"Coffee?"

Creature Comforts

Rain helped Maddie dress and led her down a long, sloping tunnel that spiraled through the center of the tree. It was like navigating an anthill, if ants had mastered architecture and had a penchant for turn-of-the-century decor. A tantalizing aroma of meat, vegetables, and wood smoke crept into the air as they descended, and running through them all was the most intoxicating smell in the world: coffee. Maddie considered it the drink of the gods, and there were few problems it couldn't solve.

She fidgeted with her dress. She'd discovered the wardrobe in her room was filled to bursting with them. Maddie didn't question the faeries' generosity, but she'd never been a fan of dresses, preferring blue jeans and sneakers to skirts and slip-on shoes.

"Sorry about the clothes," Rain said, noting her unease. "The dresses belong to Princess Theresa, but she never wears them. She said you could use them while you're with us."

"No, it's fine!" Maddie said, scrambling. "I'm just not used to it, that's all."

She straightened the fabric over her hips. The dress wasn't the only thing she wasn't used to. None of the outfits came with underwear, and there wasn't any in the dresser either. Either the faeries went commando or there simply hadn't been any extra sets available. Maddie couldn't figure out a good way to bring it up.

They emerged beside a huge, clay structure, fastened to the trunk at the foot of the palace. It resembled a wasp nest. A sign hung over heavy leather curtains covering the door. It read: *Rose's*.

Maddie's mouth watered as Rain drew the curtains aside. A blast of heat, dripping with savory spices, practically knocked her off her feet. She could almost taste the food in the air.

Years of baked-on soot and grease blackened the low, clay ceiling. Huge ovens lined the walls, yawning open with red-orange light, while strangely-shaped roasts turned on iron spits. Long tables ran along the center of the room. A small army of faerie chefs and their diligent assistants surrounded them, shouting and barking out instructions as they buzzed from station to station, busily preparing the meals for the day.

Maddie paused as she looked around. "They're all women."

"Of course," Rain said, taking her hand. "Not many men in the palace."

The faeries working the line glanced up, staring at Maddie as they passed. The work began to slow.

Rain stopped and swept her gaze over the room. "Hey! Back to work!" she shouted. "Lunch is in an hour!"

They snapped back to their duties.

"Don't mind them," Rain said. "They've never seen a human up close."

Maddie looked around warily. "Right . . . "

Rain led her to a little door at the back of the room. It opened into a pint-sized kitchen at the bottom of a short stairwell, far homier than the first. Rain sat Maddie down on a stool next to a tall table opposite the stove. Soft light fell across its pitted surface, shining down through a tiny, street-level window near the ceiling.

Rain opened the pantry and began to lay out breakfast.

"Rose and her husband opened this place as a restaurant when they came over from Europe," she said, grabbing a cast-iron skillet from a hook on the wall. "His name was Amaranth. She named the city after him when he passed. The main kitchen used to be the dining room. This is the old kitchen. Eventually she added a trading post, a hotel, and a stable, and the city grew around the establishment. Once she started having kids, she converted the original businesses into the royal residence, but she kept this room the same. She doesn't come down often, but I think it helps her to know it's still around."

The door opened and a woman crept in holding a ladle filled with orange soup.

"Is this alright, matron?" she said.

Rain put out a hand. The woman stepped gingerly over and handed her the ladle.

"One second," Rain said to Maddie, tasting it. She handed it back to the cook. "Needs more paprika."

The woman scuttled off. Maddie watched her go before she slowly brought her head back around.

"You're not just a servant girl, are you?" she said.

Rain laughed and put the kettle on to boil. "Technically, my title is matron, but I only make the kitchen staff use it.

Keeps them on point. I oversee the queen's household. Don't worry, you can still call me Rain. Rose asked me to make sure you were comfortable, but I'd like us to be friends."

"I'd like that too," Maddie said, trying not to gawk. Rain couldn't have been more than 20. "How do you get a job like this? I mean, you're so . . ."

"Young?"

"Well, yeah."

Rain returned to the pan and sprinkled the contents with salt and pepper. "I've lived here almost my whole life. No one knows the palace like I do. There were other applicants when the old matron retired, but she picked me to be her replacement. Her name was Heidi. She was a great woman. Very strong."

"That's amazing," Maddie said.

Rain bowed. "Thank you."

There was a brief pause in the conversation.

"Hey, speaking of applicants, where are all the male faeries?" Maddie asked. "Don't any of them work here?"

Rain opened a cupboard by the sink and grabbed a plate.

"A few," she said. "They aren't really suited for it, though. I mean, there's a lot of pressure, and working at the palace is pretty prestigious."

"You mean they're not allowed?"

"No, they're allowed, but they have more submissive personalities. It's kind of a quirk of our species. It's not common for faerie men to reach higher positions. Even experienced leaders have a hard time maintaining control once there's a woman in the picture."

"What about kings? Mayors?"

Rain gave a slow shrug. "I'm not aware of any."

Maddie was floored. Talk about a glass ceiling, or rather, a glass floor.

"Do they mind?" she asked.

Rain kept her eyes on the sizzling pan. "I've never met one that did. I'm sure some do, but most don't seem to care. It's natural."

Maddie didn't buy it. She'd taken too many social studies classes not to recognize the traditional arguments, albeit applied in reverse. For the moment, she decided not to press the subject. It was a different world, after all. For all Maddie knew, the men around here were all as meek as field mice.

Maddie sat quietly and watched Rain cook, feeling a little jealous of her talents. She could cook for herself up to a point—eggs, toast, chicken fingers—but she'd never really invested in the skill. Rain handled the ingredients with ease, slicing and frying like a master chef. Maddie appreciated the old-fashioned image. Looking at this world was like viewing an old oil painting, rich in color and enchanting in its simplicity.

"I hope you're hungry," Rain said, emptying the pan onto a plate as she turned around. She set the meal in front of Maddie. "Bon appetite."

As the kettle started to whistle, Rain spun around and snatched up a couple of mugs for coffee.

Maddie's stomach rumbled as she looked down at her plate, but something wasn't quite right.

"What is it?" she asked, picking up her fork.

"Steak and eggs," Rain said. "I thought you might enjoy something familiar."

Maddie gulped. The egg yolks were pale and slightly translucent, and the steaks, which looked more like slices of ham, were white and had a glossy sheen that reminded Maddie of calamari.

"Steak and eggs... from what?" she said, poking at the yolks.

Rain sat down across from her, pointing at the food. "Those are ant eggs, and that's pan-fried grasshopper. Try it! You'll like it."

Maddie took a deep breath. She'd gone with her father to visit her mother in China once, and they'd all gone out to a fancy restaurant that served sea cucumber and fish with the heads still on. Her twelve-year-old self was not quite prepared for the experience, but her parents scolded her for turning her nose up. Once she tried it, the food turned out to be delicious. Since then, she'd made it a policy never to judge a culture by its eating habits. Only one worry lingered in her mind. If you could eat their eggs for breakfast... how big were the ants?

The grasshopper tasted like Canadian bacon. The eggs tasted, surprisingly, like eggs.

Rain poured Maddie a cup of coffee. She drank it and sighed in contentment.

"So, what's it like being a matron?" she said.

Rain started washing the dishes. "Busy. I have staff to handle most of the legwork, which is why I can spend time with you, but organizing the assignments can be a real pain. There are over 300 people working here."

"Sounds like a big job."

"It is, but I love it. I like knowing that Rose can depend on me, especially now."

Maddie finished her breakfast. "What's so special about now?"

Rain took Maddie's plate and brought it to the sink. Maddie stood up and walked over to help her dry the dishes.

"There's a big festival coming up," Rain said, handing Maddie the skillet. "People from all over the Veil will be coming into town, not to mention about a hundred VIPs from other cities, all of whom will be staying at the palace."

Maddie grunted as she hefted up the iron pan and dried it. "Where do they come from?"

"All over the Veil," Rain said, passing Maddie a plate. "Usually deeper."

Maddie dried the dish and set it aside. She was still having trouble wrapping her head around the Veil. "What do you mean, deeper?"

Rain pulled the stopper on the sink, turning to lean against it as it drained.

"Deeper in the Veil," she said. "It's not just a wall between us and the humans. The Veil is also a place. Amaranth was built near the surface. Some communities are even closer to the human world, but most faeries live deeper. The farther down you go, the more the world becomes a kind of untamed wilderness, filled with huge flowers and strange plants. It's very beautiful, but things are different even where we are. The trees of the Veil-city are larger, as you've seen, along with the animals and insects. We can't see Chicago or the suburbs, but if you go to the real surface of the Veil, you can walk right down the city streets."

After everything Maddie had seen and experienced, it wasn't hard to imagine that such a construct might exist, even though it was completely outside the realm of physics. She put researching it at the top of her to-do list. If she was ever going to find a way home, she would need to know as much about the Veil as possible.

They finished putting the dishes away and sat back down at the table.

"How big is the Veil-city?" Maddie asked.

Rain squinted at the ceiling. "Maybe 25 square miles? You can walk it if you have to. Most of the people live in the main city-tree, but there are dozens of smaller settlements all around us, scattered throughout the layers of the Veil like . . . I don't know, raisins in a cake.

"Personally," she added, "I prefer to visit Chicago. It's very exciting, and the food is *great*. Maybe someday Leoh and I can take you."

"And who's Leoh?" Maddie asked.

"My boyfriend," Rain replied. "He lives in one of the Chicago settlements, where he runs a business importing human goods. He's actually making a delivery today. If we hang around for a bit, you might get to meet him."

Maddie screwed up her forehead. "How does that work? Isn't the Veil supposed to stop, you know, everything?"

Rain paused, struggling to explain. "No," she said. "Higher animals can't get through the Veil, but objects can be pulled through easily as long as no one is looking at them."

"Looking at them?"

"It's all part of the magic," Rain said with a shrug. "But the important part is, once something is on our side, it can't go back."

Maddie's face fell.

"Sorry!" Rain said as she realized the implication. "I didn't mean to say it that way."

Maddie stared down at her reflection in her coffee. "It's alright," she said. "I'm just trying not to think about it. What sort of stuff do you take? From our side, I mean."

"Little luxuries mostly," Rain said. "Soda, food, vaccinations. We prefer a natural way of life. Our ancestors used to take more, but these days, we produce almost everything we need, although human goods are still a popular trade for city faeries."

Maddie quietly said a prayer for every city faerie in Chicago. Anyone who could bring pizza and carbonated beverages to a place like this was basically an angel.

"And Leoh is coming now?" she said.

Rain stood up from the table and looked out the little window. "He should be here any minute. He doesn't know you're here, by the way. Rose wanted to keep it quiet until you got settled. But don't worry, I'm sure the two of you will get along great."

A few minutes later, a set of knuckles knocked on the window. Maddie looked up and saw a pair of bare feet standing outside. Rain undid the latch, and a thin, sun-faced boy slid down into the room. It was the first time Maddie had laid eyes on a male faerie. She wasn't quite sure what she'd been expecting.

A shirt, probably.

He was short— no taller than Maddie— and cute, in a Huckleberry Finn sort of way. Chestnut hair sprang out in all directions in a mass of cowlicks on his head. He carried a bag over his shoulder on a wide leather strap. Dried dirt and grass stains covered a pair of denim jeans, which he secured to his waist with a length of knotted rope. Lean muscles tightened along his arms and across his shoulders as he swung down over the sink and planted his bare feet on the floor.

Like the other faeries Maddie had seen, his eyes were long and almond-shaped. Cast in silhouette by the light from the window, they seemed to softly glow.

Rain slipped a hand around behind his neck and pulled him into a kiss.

"Wait! Rai—!" he blurted out, muffled.

Bottles clinked in his satchel as he fell back against the sink. When Rain let him up, he wore a dazed grin.

"Good morning to you too," he said, holding up his satchel. "I have the queen's delivery."

He opened it up and took out a square cloth bag. It thumped heavily against the table as he set it down and glanced at Maddie.

"I'm Leoh," he said. "Are you a new employee . . . ?"

He stopped, staring.

"Ho-ly crap."

Maddie waved. "Hello."

Leoh raced around the table. "I'd heard the rumor," he said, "but I didn't believe it. But it's true! You're here!"

He stuck out his hand. "I'm Leoh. I run the Triple-C."

"Triple-C?" Maddie said, shaking his hand.

He struck up a proud grin and thumped his chest. "The Cook County Caravan. Fine human commodities at affordable prices. Catchy, isn't it? We operate mostly in the north suburbs. I've got a storefront in the Spiral Market."

"What's the Spiral Market?" said Maddie.

"It's the main market in Amaranth," Rain cut in. "At the top of the ramps where the trunk meets the city."

Leoh winked and clicked his tongue in his cheek.

"Prime real-estate," he said. "Pretty cool, eh?"

Maddie chuckled. *Faeries said "cool." Weird.*

"Sounds great," she said.

Leoh closed his satchel and hefted it up onto his shoulder. "Well, I've got to be going, but feel free to swing by the shop if you're looking for the comforts of home."

"She doesn't have any money, Leoh," Rain reminded him.

He paused. "Oh, of course." His hand went into his bag and came out with a green glass bottle, tightly sealed with a shiny aluminum cap. "Then consider this a gift. Welcome to the Veil. Mountain Dew, 2019. Very good year."

Maddie practically drooled as she took it and twisted open the cap. The liquid burned like lemon-lime fire in her throat, and she let her head fall back, staring at the ceiling in rapture.

"I think I love you," she said.

Leoh made his way to the door.

"Staying over tonight?" Rain asked.

His face took on a green tint. "If you've got space on the couch."

Rain took his cheek and locked him into a kiss.

"Oh, you won't be on the couch," she said as she let him go.

His knees were practically wobbling as he went up the stairs and out the door.

Maddie's emotions churned as she sat in the little pioneer kitchen. She wasn't sure if she wanted to laugh or cry, but as she reveled in the joy of her pilfered soda, a small part of her entertained the hope that maybe the worst was over, and that spending a little time living with the faeries wouldn't be so bad after all.

First Mover Advantage

Morrow stepped quietly into Gwynedd's chamber. Weeks had passed since the human woman slipped through his mistress's fingers, and they were no closer to recapturing her. Morrow hoped in vain that she had abandoned the pursuit and turned her thoughts to other matters.

The sight of the bodies in the middle of the floor crushed that feeling. Morrow stepped around them as he walked. Gwynedd sat quietly, combing her hair in front of his mother's mirror. Pure white porcelain framed its silver surface, casting back the harsh electric light that filled the room.

Like Morrow's sword, the mirror was one of few objects left that bore the artistry of the old Erlkin society. Morrow had never been able to figure out why his mistress had taken their people from their home in the deep Veil. The human city didn't suit them, and in only a few short years, their culture and history had all but bled away.

But perhaps that was the whole point. A prosperous nation would not kneel so easily to her madness.

"What do you want?" he asked, coming to stand behind her.

She set down her comb. "I have need of you, little prince. The time has come for us to make our next move."

She walked to her bed and slid a heavy wooden box out from under it.

"What's that?" Morrow said, following her.

She opened the box and drew out a thin vial made from black glass.

"Drink," she said, handing it to him.

He held it up in front of his face. "What is it?"

"A spell, of course," she said. "It will allow you to get close to the girl."

Morrow removed the stopper and looked inside. Threads of black and red mingled on the surface of the green liquid. The aroma of his mistress's blood slithered into his nostrils, and he fought the urge to drink. Sweat beaded on his brow as he struggled against the dreadful thirst that had plagued him all his life.

He was too young to remember, but to his mother, it must have seemed a fair arrangement at the time: a royal appointment in exchange for saving her son. Gwynedd healed him using her own vile humours, and he had been addicted to them ever since.

"It had better make me invisible," he said. "You know, the war was only 20 years ago. Our people aren't exactly welcome in Amaranth."

Gwynedd shut the box. "It will accomplish far more than that. Its magic will make you appear as one of the faeries."

Morrow glanced over his shoulder at the bodies on the floor. All faeries, all women. Their worn boots and leather garments marked them as hunters. No doubt his mistress had taken them in the woods.

"Do I have them to thank for this?" he said.

"Don't be squeamish. Their sacrifice was necessary," his mistress answered. "Now, drink."

Morrow felt a pressure on his neck as the witch's will pressed down on him. He lifted the vial and poured it down his throat.

His mistress walked back to her chair to watch.

Morrow's stomach turned as the magic took hold. Shooting pain ran down his legs and through his arms. He convulsed and collapsed onto the ground. It was like he'd been tied to a wrack and pulled to the point of tearing. His bones broke. His ribs cracked. He screamed in agony as he twisted and contorted on the cold stone floor. Gwynedd laughed at the spectacle, and Morrow saw her smile as she watched him writhe. His vision blurred red as the magic clawed its way across his face.

As the pain subsided, he pulled in a quaking breath. "Did it work?" he said, shuddering.

Gwynedd beckoned him to the mirror. "Look."

Morrow crawled over and hauled himself to his feet. His face flushed with anger as he stared into the silvered glass. A woman's face stared back at him.

"What have you done?!" he said, putting a hand to his cheek.

His mistress laughed. "I should think that would be obvious."

Morrow staggered back, struggling to control his transformed body. He was taller than before. Dense muscles packed themselves around lean limbs, and hair the color of crows fell to his waist. His foot slipped out from under him, and he hit the floor with a thump.

Gwynedd gave a disappointed sigh and crossed the room to a cupboard in the corner.

"I combined the humours of nine women to create that body," she said. "Try not to break it."

"Why not use *male* hunters?" Morrow shouted.

Gwynedd opened the cupboard and returned with a heavy leather backpack and a pair of boots. "The faeries have so few, it would have taken weeks to gather them," she said, dropping the items at his feet. "Idiot."

She retrieved the box from the wall and brought it over. "The backpack contains a few changes of clothes and some money. Use them to get yourself established. There is enough potion to last you eight weeks. Each spell will last 24 hours. You would do well not to miss a dose, unless you relish the thought of undergoing the transformation a second time."

Morrow grumbled and returned to the mirror. This was going to take some getting used to.

Gwynedd slapped his cheek. "And don't gawk. Try to act naturally."

Morrow put a hand to his face, running his fingers along his new, sharp features. Hard skin like tanned leather answered his unfamiliar touch.

"Why only eight weeks?" he asked.

"That is when the summer will reach its peak. After the solstice, it will be too late."

"And how do I get close to the girl?"

Gwynedd drew a leaflet from her robes and handed it to Morrow.

"Through her friends," she said.

Morrow mumbled as he read. "Fine human commodities . . . affordable prices . . . " He looked up from the paper. "A job?"

"The human girl is alone in this world," his mistress said, moving to the door. "I have been watching her. The wards cloud much of my vision, but she longs for the luxuries of her old race. It's only a matter of time before she grows homesick, and you will be there when she does. In the meantime, I will work to gather allies."

Morrow lifted the backpack onto his shoulder and picked up the box of potions.

"What allies?"

"You said it yourself: Amaranth is envied. There are many who might be convinced to help us if they believe we can succeed. You must not fail."

She pushed the door open and stepped aside.

"Now, go."

Old School

Maddie folded up her class schedule and stuffed it in her pocket. It was her first day of school, and despite the fact that it had been a long time since she was a freshman, she wanted to come across as nonchalant as she made her way across the palace. The queen had come through with a lesson plan, and Ebba had been reassigned to serve as Maddie's guide.

The young girl skipped along the dim corridors, humming to herself as she led Maddie to her first class: antiquities. Maddie assumed it had something to do with history. Most of her lessons were to take place in the palace library with Finn.

Make that Prince Finn. Ebba had reminded her.

Somewhere deep in Maddie's subconscious there was a 12-year-old girl bouncing up and down. Maddie gave her a time out. While the notion of a faerie prince did have a certain appeal, as she approached the narrow door to the library, she found herself speculating as to the kind of person he would turn out to be.

Would he be intelligent? Charming? Handsome? The movies of her childhood predicted as much. On the other hand, real royal families tended to be made up of stuck up, arrogant, overbearing brats. It was anybody's guess which would turn out to be true in a literal fairy tale.

Concerns aside, Maddie was excited to begin her new education, and genuine excitement was a feeling she hadn't experienced in a long time.

Ebba had insisted she dress up, just in case the prince fell hopelessly in love with her. Maddie had grudgingly consented to a brown ankle-length dress patterned with pale yellow vines, though she'd drawn the line when her guide had offered to braid her hair. All of this was in exchange for a guarantee that Ebba would find her a pair of jeans and a regular shirt within 24 hours.

A carving of desks and books coated every inch of the library door. Ebba pulled it open, and the two of them went inside.

A fire burned unattended in the hearth, spilling warmth over a pair of hefty desks that took up the middle of the floor, hemmed in by stacks of books. Neat rows of wooden, metal-tipped fountain pens and dark glass inkwells rested on the desks' freshly polished surfaces. Maddie pushed a rolling cart aside as she and Ebba made their way into the room. Her eyes wandered to a huge oak desk in the corner, piled high with still-more books and papers. Its surface was worn, pitted and scarred from decades of use. A tall blackboard stood beside it on a wooden frame. Maddie smiled at the cramped space: equal parts sitting room, rabbit hole, and fire hazard.

Ebba scanned the room in disappointment.

"Aww, he's not here yet!" she moaned, smacking Maddie on the leg. "I told you to let me braid your hair."

Maddie suppressed a smile and glanced above the fire, where an old-style cuckoo clock hung from a peg on the wall. They were indeed early. Maddie dismissed the crestfallen Ebba, who only left after Maddie promised to provide a detailed report when she came back to take her to her afternoon classes.

Maddie went to the desks, but she hesitated before sitting down, unsure of which was hers. She examined both stations, hoping to find a clue. The desks were identical: papers, bottles of ink, pencils, erasers, and stacks of soft cloth for blotting the papers dry. She leaned over and began rooting through the desks' deep drawers.

"Looking for something?" a voice asked behind her.

Maddie froze. She hadn't even heard the door open. Cursing inwardly, she straightened up and turned to face the door. It was the prince, whose first image of her, now and forever, would be her butt bent over a desk. Fantastic.

She'd expected him to be older . . . and less cute. He was slightly shorter than she was, with spiky blond hair roughly combed over a lean face. A red doublet with slitted sleeves hugged his shoulders, revealing a flash of black fabric underneath that matched his boots. There was a playful spark in his smile that drew Maddie's attention to his eyes, which glowed a piercing blue.

Handsome? Check. Human? Not quite. But her instincts told her he was close enough.

"There should be some candy in the second drawer of that one," he said, pointing to the desk on the left. "I have a supply for emergencies. Don't tell Cedric."

Maddie looked between the desks and the prince. "No! I mean . . . I wasn't looking for anything. I was just trying to find my desk. You have candy?"

He walked over and slid open the bottom drawer. It was empty.

"They took my candy," he said, sighing.

Maddie felt her heart break. "I'm sorry."

He went to the chalkboard and wrote, *You owe me 12 maple drops.*

"There should be a law against it," he said.

Maddie watched him. "There isn't?"

He drew the chalk along under the message in a determined swipe and set it down.

"Evidently not," he said, squaring off to her. He bowed, one arm held out to the side and the other offered forward, palm down like a lady's in an old movie.

"My name is Finn," he said. "You must be Madeline."

He waited. Maddie stood for a moment, confused, before she remembered Rain' comments about the faeries' matriarchal nature. Gingerly, she took his hand and leaned down, mimicking the old films. She kissed his fingertips, and he straightened up.

"First time?" he said.

Maddie gave a polite nod and folded her hands in front of her. "It's just a little backwards. And you can call me Maddie."

The prince went back to the desk. "Maddie it is," he said. "I suppose my people must seem very strange."

Maddie said, "No. Just different."

He sat against his desk. "Well, hopefully I can make a good impression."

Doing pretty well so far, Maddie thought.

The door opened and an older man stepped through. His hair was ashy gray and the wrinkles on his face suggested the beginnings of old age, which in faerie terms probably meant he was ancient beyond description. He wore a long, burnt orange western overcoat that went to his ankles like a robe. Thin, gold-rimmed glasses framed a pair of shimmering amber eyes.

He bowed and offered his hand to Maddie in the same fashion as Finn.

"My name is Cedric," he said. "It's a pleasure to meet you, Miss Foster."

Maddie took his hand and he straightened up, skipping the kiss.

"Are you ready to begin?" he asked.

"I think so," Maddie said, taking a breath as she looked nervously around the room. "Thank you for having me."

The corners of his eyes creased as he smiled and walked to the blackboard.

"It's the least we can do," he replied, taking up an eraser to wipe away Finn's note.

The prince grumbled.

"Our first topic for today is antiquities," Cedric went on. "Then we'll move on to art history, literature, and government. Please take your seats."

Maddie followed Finn to the desks. The prince hesitated a moment as Maddie started to sit down.

She caught herself and paused, thinking for a moment before she decided to ask, "Who's supposed to pull out whose chair?"

Finn smiled and came around to her side of the desk. "You, technically," he said. "But in the spirit of inter-species diplomacy . . . " He pulled out her chair. "Allow me."

Maddie sat down.

Charming? Check.

Cultural Differences

Intelligent? Not so much.

"How can you say that?!" Maddie shouted. "Our democracy is *not* a farce!"

Finn sat back in his chair and crossed his arms. "It's not a democracy; it's a republic, and it *is* a farce. Your legislature is slow, your election system is flawed, and half of your politicians end up in jail."

"It is not *half!*"

"Well, it should be. And by the way, your court system is a joke."

Maddie leaned across her desk. "I suppose you'd prefer to just throw out the whole thing and establish a monarchy . . . have some king throw anybody they want in jail!"

"Queen," he said, cracking a smarmy grin. "And our people are freer than yours."

Maddie had never been so infuriated in her life. After four hours of class, Maddie's patience had reached its end.

If she weren't certain that it would get her banished or executed, she would have taken her fountain pen and stabbed it into Finn's smug, arrogant little faerie face. And what the hell happened to the submissive personality of faerie men? It was bullshit!

She turned to Cedric. "Would you say something to him?"

"I'd say the two of you are doing fine by yourselves," Cedric replied with amusement.

"But he's wrong!"

Finn put up a hand. "I am not."

Maddie grabbed her pen.

"Alright," Cedric said, putting up his hands as he got to his feet. "That's enough for today. Both of you study up tonight. We'll have a debate in the morning and get this settled before it turns to bloodshed."

Maddie cracked her knuckles and fixed the prince with a hard stare.

"I'm going to destroy you," she said.

He didn't even blink. They gathered their things and left, but Finn didn't stay. He had fencing lessons to get to. Maddie watched him go, stewing as she waited for Ebba to come and get her.

Fencing lessons, she grumbled in her head. *Well lah dee dah.*

Ebba demanded a full report when she arrived.

Maddie gave it to her straight: the prince was a jerk.

Ebba was devastated, but only for a moment. Within a dozen steps, she was convinced Maddie had simply failed to recognize his obviously positive qualities. Maddie rolled her eyes and let the matter drop as Ebba led her to the stable for her final course of the day: animal studies. Like every other route through the palace, their path wound around the interior of the tree. A cool draft blew in as Ebba opened the door and led her out. Maddie made it halfway through before she threw herself backwards and latched her fingers onto the door frame.

"What?" Ebba asked, stopping to turn around.

Maddie gave a mad laugh. Ebba was standing on the edge of a two-foot walkway nailed to the outside of the palace wall. The wooden ledge hung open—no railing—and the spaces between its boards yawned to reveal a drop of hundreds of feet to the ground. That was assuming she didn't crack her skull on the city rooftops in the lower branches. The wind threatened to shove Maddie off even as she maintained her death grip on the door. Ebba swayed gently in the breeze like it was nothing.

"I-Isn't there another way?" Maddie asked.

Ebba grumbled and stomped back towards her. "Come on. It's easy!" she said, taking hold of Maddie's belt with a tug. "You're not going to fall."

Maddie's fingernails dug into the wood. Any lingering thoughts she had about classroom lectures and frustrating princes were blown away by the rising terror of gravity and death. She squeezed her eyes shut and shrank back into the corridor.

Ebba held firm, and her voice became stern.

"Maddie, you have to come out. It's just the outside. We're almost there, and I'll be with you the whole way."

Ebba pulled on her again.

Maddie's tendons strained in protest as she slowly released her grip on the door.

"You're sure it's safe?" she asked.

Ebba let go and huffed. "Of course. See?" She jumped up and down on the planks before sticking her hand back out. "Now, come on."

Maddie trembled as she reached out and took the girl's hand. Ebba slowly led her along the path, which wound around the palace wall for a dozen yards before breaking off to run along a branch. Maddie locked her eyes onto the back of Ebba's head as she forced her brain to ignore the deadly drop only a few inches away from her feet. One of the boards creaked. Maddie snapped an eye shut and winced as they passed through a cluster of leaves, and their destination sprang into view.

Her eyes rose skyward.

It hadn't occurred to her that the stable wouldn't be for horses.

"Oh my God," she said. "It's an aviary."

The building perched on the outer limbs of the tree, a towering scaffolding of wooden floors and spindly metal supports. Spiraling stairways connected the airy layers alongside broad ramps, cargo lifts, and elevators, while an enormous platform spread out over the top like the flight deck of an aircraft carrier. Bursts of color and movement fluttered and flashed as the pilots came and went, riding on the backs of giant birds too numerous to count.

A chorus of voices filled the air, calling, crying, and singing until the sound blended together into a single, awe-inspiring roar. Maddie clamped her hands over her ears as the noise filled her head, but the power of the aviary's occupants rattled through her skull all the same.

Her knees buckled, and she sank down. Ebba reached into her pocket, pulled out a pair of cotton earplugs, and stuffed them into Maddie's ears. Helping Maddie to her feet, she led her across the remaining distance to the entrance.

"I'll come back for you at the end of the day!" she shouted, pointing to the base of a broad ramp. "Head up that main walkway. You can't get lost. Just keep going up. When you get to the top, ask for Kidhe. He's your teacher. Everyone knows him, so you shouldn't have any trouble."

Maddie looked up, remembering the first time her father took her into downtown Chicago. The buildings had retreated into the sky as though they were holding up the clouds. She found herself falling backwards from the sensation, a mix of vertigo and wonder. Ebba planted her hands on the middle of Maddie's back and pushed to steady her.

"Are you okay?" Ebba asked.

Maddie forced a breath as she regained her balance, bracing herself as she stared through the open door.

"I'll be fine," she said. "I've got this."

Flyboy

I do not have this, Maddie thought.

The aviary was a zoo. From the outside it was only bare layers of wood and scaffolding. Up close, Maddie was blown away by the frenzy of people and animals racing around inside. Cardinals, starlings, and blue jays the size of horses flapped and bounced on wooden perches as thick as tree trunks.

Meanwhile, enough people to staff a small hotel rushed and shouted, barking out instructions as they tended to the animals. Maddie found herself staring at the beady black eyes of the birds and their dazzling plumage as she passed. Between the sights and the sounds, it was almost enough to overload the senses.

Maddie pressed her fingers into her ears, forcing the cotton plugs in as deep as she could as she marched up the aviary's huge central ramp. The floor rumbled as cable-driven platforms bearing food, people, and equipment rose and fell through the center of the aviary's flying layers.

It didn't help that the whole place was covered in bird crap. Maddie shifted a hand to her nose as she followed Ebba's instructions and made her way up. It was certainly the most crowded place she'd been to since she came to the Veil, and the first time she witnessed male and female faeries working together.

She tried to remain inconspicuous as a chickadee the size of a small sedan hopped by, led by a boy who couldn't have been more than 14 years old. Maddie skirted around them, shaking off the culture shock. She wondered if the faeries bothered with high school, and since his-annoying-royal-highness was being privately tutored rather than institutionally educated, she suspected the answer was no.

She was still steaming about their debate, but Maddie's intellectual side was slowly kicking in as she analyzed and re-analyzed their interaction. She was used to being right, and she'd never met anyone she couldn't convince. While she refused to classify the prince as a worthy opponent, she was willing to privately admit that their shouting match might not have been completely his fault. Finding someone capable of debating her on even terms was a new experience, and it was damned unnerving.

That said, she was still planning to sharpen her pens.

The floor swayed under Maddie's feet as she approached the top floor, and glimmers of sunlight began to creep in through the cracks in the floors above. Maddie stopped as she caught a glimpse of the open air over the flight deck. It was time to ask for directions.

She walked up to a woman grooming a sparrow and asked, "Do you know where Kidhe is?"

Maddie stumbled over the name. She'd only heard Ebba say it once and the pronunciation was weird: Keedah, except the two syllables ran together. She was sure she didn't get it right.

The woman's brush stilled as she looked at Maddie. An awkward moment passed while the woman quietly took her in, then she pointed down a long line of perches.

"At the end," she said.

Maddie gave a little bow and said, "Thank you."

The interior walls disappeared as she neared the outer edge, giving way to open racks loaded with rope and strangely shaped saddles. Maddie passed a dozen sparrows perched in little stalls, tweeting idly to each other as they waited for their riders. On the far side, she came upon an open work area set with tables and tools, but there was no one there. A black, speckled starling sat on a perch near the wall.

Maddie approached it tentatively. She could hear the air in its chest as it took huge breaths beneath a massive harness that had been fastened to its body and neck. Mesmerized, Maddie put out a hand to stroke the smooth, black feathers of its face.

"I wouldn't do that."

Maddie pulled her hand away and turned around as a man climbed down through a hole in the ceiling, descending a ladder on the wall.

He was taller than she was, and his broad shoulders and facial hair suggested he was a probably a little older as well. The ghost of a beard cut along a sharp jaw, framing a bright expression beneath a shoulder-length mass of windblown hair. Cords of muscle packed his sleeveless arms, though despite his frame, the man maintained the same wiry build that seemed common among faerie men. A brown leather vest, weathered and green from age and use, fell loose around his chest. His deep green eyes flashed with furtive light in the shade of the aviary ceiling.

Maybe, Maddie thought, *animal studies won't be such a bad subject after all.*

The man jumped the last few feet to the ground and walked over. He did not bow.

"You can pet them, but you want to go in from the side like this . . . " He maneuvered around the bird's head and approached it from behind, resting his shoulder against its neck. Reaching up, he stroked its feathers gently. "Instinct is a powerful thing. They'll peck at anything that might be food. If you're not careful, you could lose a hand."

Maddie followed his path and came around beside him.

"Now you try," he said, moving out of her way.

Maddie brushed her fingers across the bird's feathers. They were rougher than she'd expected. She could feel every coarse fiber under her palm.

"This is wild," she said, grinning from ear to ear.

The man took a step back and held out a hand, palm to the side, human-style.

"I'm Kidhe," he said. "It's great to meet you. Madeline Foster, right?"

His name swept like breath over the end of his tongue. The nerdy part of Maddie's brain couldn't help but wonder about the root language.

She stuck out her palm and shook his hand. "Maddie."

He hopped up onto one of the tables and sat. "I'll be handling your practicals: animal studies, wilderness survival, and botany."

He leaned down to pick up a bag of tools, but the sack slipped out of his hands and spilled on the floor. Scrambling, he cursed, jumping off the table as he got down on his knees to pick them up.

Maddie leaned down and picked up a pair of strange, curved pliers. "Aren't you a little young to be a teacher?" she said, holding them out.

He blushed green as he took them. "I thought I would use big words to make up for it. How am I doing?"

Maddie cracked a smile and crossed her arms. "They're not that big," she said.

He sat back on his heels. "I guess I'll have to have a word with my elementary school teachers."

Maddie laughed and they set off, walking past the birds until they came to a line of empty stalls.

"Most of our work will be here at the aviary," Kidhe said, setting down his tools. "I've never been one for textbooks. I've always preferred hands-on. What about you?"

Maddie looked over the stalls. They were filthy, covered with soiled straw and shit.

"I've always been more of the classroom type," she said.

"Well, I'll try to ease you in," Kidhe said, taking a pitchfork down from the wall. "Speaking of which . . . " He put it in her hands. "Lesson one."

Practical Experience

Lesson one turned out to be bird shit.

Lots and lots of bird shit.

Maddie held her breath and drove the pitchfork into the nearest pile, lifting with her legs and shoulders the way Kidhe had taught her. She shoveled the dirty straw and crap into a wheelbarrow, feeling like her arms were about to fall off.

Her back cracked as she straightened up and tightened the knot on the cloth she wore over her face to keep out the smell. It was soaked in oil and camphor and smelled like cough syrup. Kidhe sat a short distance away, watching her work as he explained the finer points of bird care.

"A clean bird is a healthy bird," he said. "And a healthy bird is a well-behaved bird, which we're counting on because none of them are fully tame."

Maddie scraped up another mound of crap. "How can they not be tame?"

"They're wild animals," he said, yawning as he put his feet up on a crate. "And they're not that smart. Lord knows I love them, but you can only suppress so much instinct."

Maddie finished with the last pile and leaned the pitchfork up against the wall.

"You love them?" she said.

Kidhe reached into his pocket and pulled out a handful of peanuts. "Sure," he said, shelling one and popping it into his mouth. "I've known most of them their whole lives. We raise them from birth. They're like, I don't know, my nieces and nephews."

"Aww, that's kind of sweet."

"I do my best," Kidhe said as he popped another peanut into his mouth. He tossed Maddie a broom. "Sweep. Once we're done here, we'll wheel it all downstairs. The staff will take it to ground level and bury it."

"Bury it?"

Another peanut. Another crunch. "To prevent the spread of bird-borne illness."

"How clinical," Maddie said. "I'm surprised."

Kidhe raised an eyebrow. "Why?"

"I don't know. This whole place just seems so low tech."

"I guess it's a little counter-intuitive," Kidhe said, "but our way of life is something that we choose. It would be pretty difficult to live alongside humanity and not learn to care about germs."

"Fair enough," Maddie said, wincing as a spasm shot down her back. She limped to a crate and sat down. "I think I'm done with this one."

Kidhe pointed. "Missed a spot."

Maddie fixed him with a death glare and stood back up. "You know," she said as she swept up the last scraps of straw, "if it turns out that you used our class time to make me do your chores, I'm going to be really upset."

Kidhe laced his fingers together behind his head and leaned back. "We all start at the bottom."

Maddie brandished the broom and said, "I'm armed, you know."

"I'm petrified."

Maddie dropped the broom and grabbed the pitchfork. She lifted a huge lump of shit from the wheelbarrow and dumped it into his lap.

"Hey!" he exclaimed, standing up.

Maddie stood in front of him and stared hard into his eyes. "You were saying something about the bottom?" she said.

He stared back at her for a long moment before something softened in his eyes and he stepped back. He took the pitchfork from her.

"Fine, I'll help," he said, brushing himself off. "I should give you detention, you know."

Maddie was a little surprised at his reaction. She'd expected him to at least raise his voice.

She squared her shoulders triumphantly and said, "You can't. You're too young."

He laughed at that, and they spent the next hour cleaning a dozen more stalls. Maddie's spine was ready to snap by the time they finished and put their tools away.

"Why do I smell pine needles?" Maddie said, massaging her back.

Kidhe sniffed his armpits. "That's me. Sorry."

"Your sweat smells like a car air-freshener?"

He gave her a wounded look and said, "Don't make fun."

Maddie chuckled. "It's weird. My whole body aches, but I don't feel winded at all."

"It's the heart," Kidhe said, thumping his chest.

Maddie's eyes flicked over to him. "You know?"

"Maeve told me. The magic is strong. The replacement is probably tougher than the original. No offense."

Maddie looked down at her chest. "None taken, I guess."

His face suddenly fell and he put his hands behind his back. "I should apologize," he said, staring at the floor.

"Why?"

He pointed to a patch on his arm. The image was of a bird's silhouette flying across the horizon. "I'm the captain of the wardens. Keeping the forest safe is my responsibility. The attack should never have been allowed to happen, and I'm sorry."

Maddie felt a surge of anger rise in her chest. Images of the attack flashed across her vision and she clenched her jaw.

Kidhe must have seen it on her face. "If you want another teacher, I can arrange it," he said. "It just didn't feel right not to tell you."

Maddie crammed her feelings down. "No," she said, forcing calm into her voice. It wasn't fair to be angry with him. "It's alright. I'm sure you did your best, and I was rescued, after all."

Kidhe kept his eyes on the floor and said, "Thank you."

He hefted up the wheelbarrow, and they headed for the elevators.

"There just aren't enough of us," he said. "We've got the whole Veil to look after, and it's a lot bigger than the surface of the earth. It makes true law and order impossible, and the Erlkin have been more active in the last eight weeks than in the past five years. Theresa's convinced they're planning something big. She's got all the wardens on high alert."

"Except for you?"

He gave her a weak smile. "I guess I drew the short straw."

Maddie put a hand on his shoulder as the angry chemicals in her brain slowly disbursed.

"Well, thanks for your help," she said.

Kidhe set the wheelbarrow down and lifted up a rickety gate that sealed the lift. They stepped inside, and he grabbed a little cone on a wire.

"Down, please," he said. The lift shook into motion.

"You'll get used to the Veil," he said. "We're all pulling for you. With the vote coming up, you could end up being very important."

"Vote?" Maddie said.

Kidhe leaned up against the wall. "We've always had trouble with our neighbors. Never know when one of them will come poking around, trying to stake a claim on our territory. Amaranth is a new nation, relatively speaking. It's only a hundred years old. Not all the other nations are prepared to recognize our independence, and at least one of them thinks we should still be paying them taxes and tribute."

The lift shook. Maddie steadied the wheelbarrow. "How many are there?" she asked.

Kidhe did a quick count on his fingers. "Lots," he said, giving up. "Faerie nations are more like the city states of ancient history, with systems of fealty and homage tying them together. The largest on this continent is Aster, in Pennsylvania. Their influence covers the eastern seaboard all the way into Canada. Amaranth used to be a part of it. We're the first city to seek independence in hundreds of years, and we're still waiting to see how it turns out."

Maddie tilted her head. "You make it sound like you're under threat."

"I suppose we are. Rose asked for independence a century ago. Aster didn't want to do give it to us, but Rose is one of the oldest faeries alive, which in our culture means what she says goes.

"Aster decreed that she could rule Amaranth independently for a hundred years. After that, representatives of the city-states would all meet here to review our progress and vote on our claim. Rose took the deal. The centennial is in a little over a month, and some of the ambassadors are already here."

The lift clattered to a halt.

"What if they vote you down?" Maddie said.

Kidhe lifted the gate. "There'll be a war, I suppose. I doubt the people here will be willing to give up their freedom. That's why you're so important. Demonstrating that we can care for our people is a big part of the politics."

Maddie blinked. And here she was, thinking that Gwynedd and a wooden heart were all she had to worry about. She was about to ask what their chances were when a woman came rushing down a nearby flight of stairs.

"Captain," she said, saluting.

Kidhe saluted back. "Yes?"

"They're back. We need you on the deck."

Kidhe pulled the wheelbarrow out of the lift and pushed it up against the wall. "Alright, we'll take the lift up," he said, returning to the elevator as he shot a grin at Maddie. "Want to earn some extra credit?"

Maddie heard boots thumping and looked up at the ceiling. The cries of birds rose as excitement built in the air. Maddie felt a tremor in her chest, and her shoulders tensed.

"Do I have to?" she asked. "We've been working for hours."

A look of disappointment flashed over Kidhe's face.

"Nah, you're alright," he said. "You can head out if you want."

Maddie felt her muscles ease as Kidhe reached up to close the elevator gate, shoulders straining as he lifted his arms. They'd been breaking their backs all day and he was out of gas, but he was still going back to work.

It had been a long time since she'd felt that kind of dedication. She used to feel it every time she stayed up all night to finish a calculus assignment, and wondered how long it had been since she'd really forced herself to do anything. Kidhe reached for the little cone to call the lift attendant before Maddie grumbled and ran up to the gate.

"Alright," she said. "Count me in. What kind of student would I be if I let my pint-sized teacher do all the work?"

"Pint-sized?! I'm taller than you!"

"Whatever you say, peach fuzz."

Kidhe lifted the gate and let her on as the elevator rumbled into motion. "I'll have you know most faerie men can't even grow a beard," he said.

The wind whistled over the top deck, and Maddie gasped as they emerged into the glow of the evening sun. She stared, watching a drift of cloud pass over the forest, which extended out in every direction for miles. The sunset bloomed across the trees, a wash of orange and red dust shifting in the wind. Far in the distance, the dim outline of Chicago rose into the sky, barely visible through the amber haze of the Veil's fading light.

"You'll be able to visit after you learn to fly," Kidhe said.

Maddie said, "Learn to fly?"

"Sure. Why else would they send you to me? You'd still be on our side of the Veil, but that doesn't mean you couldn't enjoy it."

"But wouldn't I not be able to see anything?" said Maddie.

Kidhe clapped his hands together in front of her and said, "Think of it like a one-way mirror. You can see and hear them, but they can't see or hear us. It takes a little getting used to, but you could still catch a movie or go to a baseball game or get a hot dog. You know, regular stuff."

"Get a hot dog?" said Maddie.

"Well, steal a hot dog. Not exactly the moral thing to do, but if you *really* wanted one . . . "

The staff began to point at the horizon, where a flock of birds emerged from the light.

"Here they come," Kidhe said.

Maddie squinted into the brightness as the birds approached. On the deck, a dozen faeries grabbed lengths of rope, blankets, and poles with loops of string on the ends. Kidhe took up a long cord and slung it around his shoulder.

"Look sharp," he said, addressing the group. "This is Theresa's patrol, and they've been out for 18 days. The pilots will be tired, so don't expect much help handling the birds. This one's on us."

Maddie kept her eyes on the birds. "Is that a long time? 18 days?"

"Very long," Kidhe said. Then he leaned down and whispered to her. "Theresa's convinced the attack on you was a prelude. With the centennial around the corner, she thought it would be a good idea to take extra precautions. The last thing we need is for another innocent civilian to get ambushed in the woods." He leaned back up. "It's a shame, really. I was going to go camping next weekend."

The birds started to circle the top deck. Kidhe grabbed a blanket and called out to the others. "Get ready!"

The faeries tensed, knuckles cracking around their tools. Maddie braced herself as the flock swooped in.

"You'll be fine," Kidhe said, taking her by the wrist. "Just stay close and do as I do."

The first birds alighted on the deck, and the faeries scrambled. Maddie and Kidhe sprinted after them. The faeries caught the harnesses as the pilots dismounted, taking the reins before throwing blankets over the animals' heads to keep them calm while they were escorted inside. Maddie jogged to a halt behind Kidhe, bewildered by the flurry of activity.

"It's alright," he said, reaching out to take her hand. He led her to a bird. "Do you want to hold him or throw the blanket?"

"I guess I'll hold him," she replied nervously. She didn't want to throw the blanket and miss.

The pilot unstrapped herself and vaulted out of the saddle, landing on the deck in front of Maddie. She thrust the reins into her hands and staggered away with a tired nod. Maddie's eyes followed the reins up to the knotted harness and the enormous bird to which it was attached.

She held on tight.

The animal chirped and tossed its head, yanking Maddie six feet into the air. She shut her eyes, screamed, and held on for dear, sweet, precious life. A moment later she felt a pair of arms clamp around her legs as Kidhe ran around from the bird's front and jumped, pulling her down.

"Stay calm," he said.

Maddie opened her eyes. "Calm?"

"And pull down. Gentle but firm."

Maddie leaned down, putting her weight into her grip as she hung onto the rope. The bird hunkered down onto the deck and she took a deep breath.

Kidhe moved around beside its head. "You're doing fine. Just keep him steady."

"How?"

"Talk to him."

He unslung the rope from his arm and swept it around the bird's neck. The animal flicked its head away.

Maddie inched in alongside the bird and stroked its feathers, murmuring. "Pretty bird. Pretty bird."

"Pretty bird!" it answered.

Maddie jumped back. The bird chirped and fluttered its wings.

"Hold him!" Kidhe said.

"But it's talking!"

He reached up and grabbed the bird's harness, grunting as he struggled to hold it. "Yeah, the starlings do that. Help me, please."

Maddie pulled down on the rope again, and Kidhe threw the blanket over its head. The bird calmed down and Kidhe handed the rope off to a pair of attendants who took the animal inside.

"See?" he said, dusting himself off. "Easy."

"You think that was easy?!" Maddie shouted.

"Well, easy for a start. You should see the big birds."

Maddie hit him in the shoulder. "Jerk."

It took almost an hour to get all the birds tucked away in their stalls. Other faeries took over the process of brushing and feeding them. When it was over, the sun was already down and Maddie felt like she'd just finished a tug-of-war with an Olympic wrestling team. She went to the edge of the roof and flopped down on the deck to cool off.

The last pilot walked over with Kidhe, and Maddie stared up at her, framed against the sky. The moonlight fell across her like a monument in a courtyard. Her shoulders were square, wrapped in the folded steel of a heavy breastplate etched with a pattern of long, thin flowers. Muscles like carved rock held up a round metal shield in her right hand and an eight-foot spear in her left. A long, thick braid of silken black hair, woven through with bright red ribbon, hung down to her ankles.

She bent over at the waist until her face was right over Maddie's.

"First day?" she asked.

Maddie tried to sit up, but her body was limp with fatigue. The woman set her gear aside. Taking her by the shoulders, she hefted Maddie up like a bag of groceries.

"I'm Princess Theresa," she said, shaking her hand as she steadied Maddie's exhausted body. "You must be Madeline. I've been looking forward to meeting you."

Maddie wobbled on her feet. "I'm honored."

"You look a little worse for the wear."

"Kill me," Maddie said, groaning.

"I don't think I can do that," Theresa replied, picking up her gear. "You're under the queen's protection."

Maddie waved a hand at Kidhe. "Then kill him instead."

"That would be ironic," Theresa said, supporting Maddie by the shoulder as she steered her back to the lift.

"Why?" Maddie asked.

"Well, think about it," the princess said. "Saving someone's life only to have them order your execution? It's pretty funny."

Maddie tripped, and Theresa caught her.

"Kidhe . . . " she blurted out. "Saved me?"

The princess looked back at Kidhe and then to Maddie. "You mean he didn't tell you?"

Civilized People

"Look out!"

Morrow jumped back, pressing himself against the tree as an enormous produce cart rolled past, drawn by a team of brown rats. The driver waved apologetically but made no effort to slow down as she cracked her whip and carried on up the ramp.

Morrow grumbled as he straightened his new long hair and resumed his climb up the spiraling slope. With all their prosperity and resources, he would have thought the faeries of Amaranth would have put in an elevator.

He looked up the ramp. After walking for more than an hour, he was finally nearing the top. The sounds of the market clattered in his ears, and shouts of local merchants filled the air with promises of fine produce and over-the-top savings. Morrow wanted to wretch. These people didn't know how good they had it. Even the poorest among them could count on at least one reasonable meal a day, some kind of work, and the shelter of the branches over their heads. There were those in the Erlkin catacombs that barely managed a blanket and a few morsels of rotten bread.

A pair of city watchmen in polished breastplates waved him through as he neared the top of the ramp. Morrow smiled as he passed, a gesture that drew a coy blush from one of them. It seemed his mistress's potion was effective. This was probably the closest anyone of his kind had been to the faerie city in two decades, and he was being welcomed with open arms.

The ramp emerged into a broad market, three times the length of a human football field. The roar of the crowd was matched only by the complaints of the animals and the banging of tools. Morrow gritted his teeth, tightened his grip on the strap of his pack, and marched into the throng.

The people pushed and shoved. Morrow immediately longed for the cities of his childhood, where the nights were long, the music was soft, and the voice of every person was but a whisper to the waiting ear. It sickened him that, more and more, his people were beginning to resemble these crass faeries, scrambling to accumulate wealth as they shouted at each other for attention. The indignity of it soured his stomach as he made his way to the edge of the market in hopes of finding a little room to breathe.

A woman in a leather apron shoved a bundle of arrows into his face.

"Fine oak!" she shouted. "Guaranteed to fly true! Only five branches!"

"No, thank you," Morrow replied.

"Fresh fruit!"

Morrow felt a shove as a passer-by knocked him into the next stand. The man behind it held out an apple.

"Just picked this morning," he said, taking a deep breath in through his nose. "You can practically taste it. Half a dozen for three leaves. What do you say?"

Morrow waved him off. "I'm fine, thank you."

He pushed forward, shouldering his way through a pack of faeries shouting orders at a baker across a wooden table.

"Sugar rolls! Fruit tarts! Fresh-baked bread!"

"Two of the walnut loaves, please!"

"I need a dozen donuts!"

Morrow clamped his hands over his ears and stumbled ahead. A hand emerged from the crowd and closed around his shirt, pulling him into the middle of the street. He found himself standing in front of a brown-haired man in worn denim jeans.

"Are you alright?" the man asked.

Morrow took a moment to gather himself before speaking. "Yes, thank you."

"Not used to the crowds?"

Morrow looked the man over. His sunny expression and soft features put him in his early twenties, and the satchel over his shoulder, not to mention the state of his hair and clothing, marked him as a messenger, or possibly a vagrant.

"Something like that," Morrow said.

The man tightened a rope around his waist. "Well, you'll want to keep to the middle of the market. The crowds are thicker the closer you get to the shops, okay?"

Morrow glanced around. He was right. The market was full to bursting, and there was no sense of order to the traffic, but in the middle of the broad street, the vehicles and people were at least moving, jostling against each other like fish in a crowded stream. The man began to walk away.

"Wait!" Morrow shouted, digging in his pockets as he ran to catch up with him. "Do you know this place?"

He fetched out the slip of paper Gwynedd had given him.

The man looked at it and smiled as they walked. "The Triple-C, eh? Looking for some human food?"

"Looking for a job, actually," Morrow said, folding the paper and putting it away. "I used to live in downtown. With the festival coming up, I was hoping there might be an opening."

"You don't look like a city faerie."

Morrow examined his clothes. "You mean my outfit? This is just for the road. I thought I would travel light."

"You mean you're broke," the man said.

Morrow adjusted his pack and conceded with a shrug. "Almost. My parents didn't leave me much when they passed. Now that they're gone . . . " He allowed the words to hang for a moment before he finished. "I just thought it was time for a change."

"And you think the owner's just going to hire you off the street? No experience? They work in Chicago, you know. That's Erlkin territory. What if you get kidnapped? Or killed?"

Morrow glared. This man was becoming annoying. "Hey! I can handle the Erlkin. I told you, I've lived in Chicago my whole life."

"Is that so?"

"It is! Now, can you tell me where the Triple-C is or can't you?"

The man turned and crossed his arms, pointing a thumb back over his shoulder. A tall red and white sign with lettering in the style of a human fast food chain marked the front of the Cook County Caravan.

"You're here," he said. "I'm Leoh, the owner."

Morrow's shoulders dropped. "Well, shit."

"Uh huh."

"I guess that was my interview."

"Only one question left."

"And what's that?"

"You put ketchup on a hot dog?"

Morrow had never eaten a hot dog in his life. He took a guess. "No?"

Leoh extended a hand. "You're hired. What's your name?"

Morrow took it and answered, "Moira."

Warrior Princess

"You're too modest, captain," Theresa said, leading Maddie and Kidhe through the palace. "I can't believe you didn't say anything!"

Maddie glanced back at Kidhe. "Me either."

"The princess did most of the work," he said, starting to blush. He looked away and covered his face with his hand.

Theresa cackled with glee. "Don't be fooled. The crazy bastard dove right in when he saw you, and by the time the rest of us got there, it was almost over. Bless his faint little heart. I would have told you right away. Hell of an ice breaker."

Maddie turned around and walked backwards, facing Kidhe. "Is that true?"

His face turned greener than a granny smith apple.

"They mostly ran away…" he said.

Theresa opened a door, revealing a steep staircase, and began to climb. "Well, you can tell her all about it at dinner.

Mom's hosting a quiet get together for the ambassadors. The early arrivals, anyway. They're all friends, and she would want you to meet them."

"But, but . . . " Maddie stammered. "Aren't there rules for that sort of thing?"

"What sort of thing?"

"You know, state dinners and stuff. I mean, look at us. We're a mess!"

Theresa glanced back over her shoulder. "It's not a state dinner. More like a family meeting, and we've got plenty of time to clean up and get dressed. Relax. You'll be my guests."

The narrow stairs spiraled upwards until they came to a modest, wooden door.

Theresa opened it and led them inside. "Here we are."

Maddie's mouth fell open. They were standing on a landing halfway up a wall, suspended in a hollow column of smooth, carved wood. Stairs swept and spiraled throughout the space, riding the walls and stretching across the air like the fibers of a spider's web.

Deep alcoves dug into the wood to form rooms. Maddie could see a dining area, a kitchen, and a study from where she stood, but there were dozens of other chambers, as well as passages leading out. Below, the stairs landed in a cramped sitting area. Couches, piled high with thick cushions, circled a cluster of low tables beside a stone fireplace. A hanging log set with fist-size clusters of glowing orange fungus filled the room with light. And of course, there wasn't a railing in sight.

"The men's washroom is that way," Theresa said, pointing to a nearby passage. It was dark and turned sharply after a few feet. "Kidhe, there should be a spare robe in the closet. If you lay out your clothes, we'll have them laundered while we bathe. Maddie, you can follow me."

Kidhe bowed low and disappeared down the corridor, casting a nervous glance back at Maddie as he vanished around the corner.

The princess led Maddie down another flight of stairs and into a hall that ended in her bedroom. It was smaller than Maddie expected, not much larger than her own quarters. Roughly hewn depictions of wild animals and flowers covered the walls, and in the spaces between, iron hooks held up the glinting steel of swords, daggers, and a dozen other weapons. Furs covered the bed, and there was a desk beside it, stacked with papers.

The princess ditched her saddlebags on the floor. "You'll have to forgive the mess," she said, hanging up her spear. "The centennial review is coming up."

"Kidhe told me about it," Maddie said, running her finger along the hilt of a long sword. The leather was worn and soft with oil. "He said there might be a war."

The princess waved the comment away and tossed her shield on the bed. "That's not going to happen. Amaranth is doing fine, and we're pulling out all the stops to make sure our visitors have a good time." She went to the desk and started leafing through the papers. "Of course, that hasn't stopped every lord and diplomat from here to Moscow from going absolutely crazy. Everyone thinks my mother is going to retire. Do you know how many marriage proposals I get a month now? It's maddening. Consider yourself lucky your culture left all that business behind."

She set the letters down and pointed to a door partly hidden by a green curtain. "The bathroom is this way."

Maddie was expecting another misty spa with smooth stones and aromatherapy candles, but in retrospect, she didn't know why. Those things didn't really fit the princess's personality. The tub took up the whole room, barely leaving space for a trunk beside it, filled with bottles of shampoo, washcloths, and hefty blocks of soap. Used towels covered the floor. Theresa picked them up quickly and threw them into a hamper in the corner. Her breastplate clattered to the floor as she began to undress, revealing scars that cut across her skin from head to toe.

Maddie turned away and stared up at the ceiling nervously. "Um . . . I can go after you. I'll wait outside."

"Nonsense," Theresa said, undoing her trousers. "It's just a bath. Go ahead and get in. The water's warm."

Maddie shook her head and stammered. "I-It's really okay."

Theresa laughed. "You humans are so insecure," she said, pitching her clothes into the hamper. "Haven't you ever been in a group shower? At camp? At school?"

Maddie kept her eyes averted. "I never went to camp."

It didn't help that her bathing partner looked like a contender for middle-weight boxing champion. It wasn't that Maddie had ever been especially insecure about her body. She just resented it. She had her father's eyes, but the rest came from her mother. She had a great figure. As a gift, it was a hand-me-down that Maddie grimaced at every time she looked herself in the mirror.

Theresa grabbed a bar of soap and a scrub brush and hopped into the tub.

"Oh, man," she said, letting out a satisfied groan. "I've been looking forward to this all week. There's nothing like a bath after a long stay in the woods."

Maddie glanced at the water. Her muscles ached so much that she could barely stand up straight, and the steam filling the room was turning the layer of dirt on her skin to a film of sticky mud. A bath was exactly what she needed. She hesitated for only a few more seconds before giving in.

"Alright, fine," she said, peeling off her clothes. "Just don't laugh at me. Not all of us can be Wonder Woman, you know."

Theresa kicked a foot up from the water and scrubbed her leg. "Well, you have to work at it." She added, "Interesting birth mark you've got there."

Maddie's hands flew to her collar to cover it up. "Oh, this? I hate it."

"Really? I think it gives you an edge. Looks like war paint."

"Or like someone poured mud over my shoulder," Maddie said, grabbing a brush as she climbed into the tub. The hot water soothed her aching muscles and she groaned.

Theresa kicked up her other foot. "Better?"

"Uh huh."

Maddie sank down until only her face was above the water.

"Told you," Theresa said, tossing her the soap.

Maddie caught it and turned it over in her hands. It was bright green and swirled with white. The stamp was worn off but Maddie knew the smell by heart.

"My dad used to use this brand," she said. "Don't faeries have their own soap?"

Theresa chuckled and reached for a bottle in the trunk. The contents were black. She dabbed a little onto a cloth and began massaging it into her puffier scars. "Sure we do, but you humans make some great stuff when it comes to toiletries."

"Like that?" Maddie said, pointing to the black sludge.

"No, this comes from Maeve. It's supposed to help flatten them out. Can you get my back?"

Maddie sat up and took the cloth.

"Just the puffy ones," Theresa said.

Maddie started to rub it in. "How did you get all these, anyway?"

"Here and there. Military life and all, but most of them aren't from fighting."

"Then what are they from?"

"Hunting," Theresa said, pointing to her various wounds. "The animals in the Veil get pretty big. This one was from a rat… These were ants… This one was from a grass snake." She leaned back and looked up at the ceiling, smiling. "Man, now *that* was a fight. They had to carry me back to the city. I was technically dead for 22 hours. I just wish I could tell your book-of-world-records people."

A circle of pale, gnarled flesh wallpapered a third of the woman's chest.

Maddie stared at the scar and said, "Big snake."

Theresa grabbed a bottle of shampoo and soaped up her hair. "You're telling me. Fang impaled my heart. Left ventricle. I'd have been down for the count if it weren't for Maeve. She fixed me right up. Just like she did you, actually."

Maddie sloshed around to get in front of Theresa. "You've got a wooden heart too?"

"White oak," she said, thumping her chest. "It was a little weird at first. I'm sure you know the feeling—kind of numb, no real pulse—but now it's a part of me like all the rest. Truthfully, I don't even notice it anymore."

Maddie was stunned by the casual dismissal of the trauma.

Theresa pointed to the soap in her hand. "You should get started."

Maddie realized she was staring. She began to wash, struggling to recover an idle conversation.

"Did you always want to be in the military?" she asked.

Theresa dunked her head in the water. "Actually, I kind of fell into it. When I was a teenager, I wanted to be a professional hunter. Active, outdoors, lots of excitement. But the kingdom needed me. I still find time when I can . . ." She dunked her head again. "But not as much as I'd like."

Maddie inwardly confessed to being a little jealous. "It must be nice to know what you want to do," she said.

Theresa lay back against the edge of the tub. "We all do, really."

Maddie grabbed the shampoo and grumbled. "Not me."

The princess scoffed. "I'm sure you do. What do you like?"

"I don't know," Maddie said, massaging her head. The suds ran down her face, and she dunked to rinse off.

Theresa snorted. "Of course you do. What do you do the most? How do you fill the hours?" She climbed out of the bath, sloshing the water as she grabbed a towel.

"All I've ever done is study," Maddie said, propping her elbows on the edge of the tub.

Theresa dried her hair. "Professors study all the time. You could be a teacher."

Maddie thought it over. It had never occurred to her, but it didn't feel like a good fit.

"I don't know," she said. "I'm not so great with people. Plus, what would I teach around here?"

Theresa wrapped her hair in a massive towel turban. "Let's see. Lots of studying, no good with people . . . Don't worry, it'll come to me." She paused, rooting through the trunk. "All the towels are in the hamper. Let me find you something to dry off with."

She hopped to the next room and started searching her drawers. "I really need to keep this place tidier," she said.

"It gets so cluttered. I swear, I could have the Foxglove in here and never know it."

"That's the second time I've heard someone say that," Maddie said, climbing out of the tub. "What are you talking about?"

Theresa pulled a woolen blanket out of the dresser, and tossed it to Maddie. "There Foxglove? It's kind of a folk tale. Where'd you hear about it?"

"From Gwynedd," Maddie said, looking down at the scar on her chest as she dried off. "She mentioned it when she attacked me. She called me a foxglove."

Theresa straightened up suddenly and stood in the doorway, shoulders square and tight. She was still smiling, but something about her posture told Maddie that her stress level had jumped.

"Did I say something wrong?" Maddie asked.

"A foxglove . . . or *the* Foxglove?"

Maddie fidgeted with her towel. "I don't really remember. Is there a difference?"

Theresa stepped forward and laid a hand on her shoulder. "Yes," she said, drawing her thumb along Maddie's birth mark. "I'm sorry, Maddie. I'm afraid there is."

Ancient Animus

Maddie sat by the fire, across from Rose and Theresa at the bottom of the royal apartment. Kidhe had been sent home.

"Try to remember," Rose said. "Tell me her exact words."

Maddie pressed her eyes shut and thought back, but the night of the attack was a blur.

"I don't remember," she said. "I'm sorry."

Maeve came down the steps with a cup of tea. "Drink this," she said, offering it to Maddie. "It will help your memory."

"Is it magic?" Maddie asked, staring down at it.

"It is," Maeve said as she sat down. "Drink."

Maddie turned to Rose with a distressed look.

"Please," Rose said. "It's important."

Maddie took a long breath and brought the cup to her lips. The tea tasted like orange blossom soap, and she gagged. A tense moment passed. The flavor turned to steam in her head. She inhaled a harsh breath as a hot, airy sensation splashed across her face and seeped into the space behind her forehead.

"Now, try again," Rose said.

Maddie thought back. "She was standing over me," she said. The fog was beginning to clear. "I asked her who she was. She said that she was with me when I was born. She called me 'Foxglove,' like it was my name, and said that I belonged to her." She set the cup down on the table. "What does it mean?"

Maeve reached into her robes and withdrew a heavy, leather-bound book, which she handed to Rose.

"It's a very old story," Rose said, opening it. "It has a lot to do with our history and, perhaps, a little to do with yours."

"Go on."

Rose ran her fingers over the leaf-like pages. "Our people are from Iris, a world of wilderness and natural beauty, not unlike the Earth in its infancy, but the people who lived there were menaced by a terrible evil. Its true nature was never written down, but we know that the six races of the fair folk spent a hundred years secretly gathering powerful elements from every part of nature as part of a plan to defeat it."

"Six races?" Maddie said.

"We are only aware of two," Maeve replied. "The Faerie and the Erlkin. We don't know what happened to the others."

"But when their task was complete," Rose continued. "Gwynedd and the old queen used what they had gathered to create a weapon."

Maddie's chest tightened. "What kind of weapon?"

Theresa leaned forward. "We don't know, but it was connected to every part of nature: to every creature, every mind, every breath of air, speck of earth, and blade of grass.

It was a construct of unlimited power, capable of safeguarding all of creation."

"They called it the Foxglove," Rose said, "Gwynedd and the old queen planned to use it to destroy the evil that had taken over their world, but something happened that they didn't anticipate. It manifested a consciousness of its own, possessing infinite knowledge and intelligence, and it refused to carry out its purpose. We don't know why, but instead of vanquishing the threat, it created the Veil, and brought our people here."

Maddie shook her head in disbelief. "How do you know all this?"

"The queen of the faeries wrote it down," Rose said. "Her name was Bronwyn, and this diary is all that is left of her."

A tear slid down her cheek.

Maddie peered forward at the pages. "What language is that?"

"We call it the Old Tongue," Maeve answered. "It is the original language of the fair folk, and not even our most powerful magic reveals its meaning. I've spent decades researching it and have only managed to translate a tiny portion."

"Why would you have to translate it?"

"It's difficult to explain," said Rose. "But when we arrived in the Veil, we had no idea who we were or where we came from. Our memories had been washed away."

"Washed away?" Maddie said. "How?"

Maeve answered. "In the deepest parts of the Veil, there exists a barrier made up of a mist we call the World Curtain. Any creature that touches it is robbed of their memory: their ideas, their thoughts, their skills, even their language. The magic that brought us here carried us through those mists, and we arrived in the Veil with no memory of our past."

"My husband and I only knew we were married from these," Rose said, holding up her hand. Two gold bands carved with alien-looking leaves circled her wrist. "They matched."

"That's awful," Maddie said.

"As far as we know," said Maeve. "There is only one person in the world who fully understands the Old Tongue."

The letters flowed in strands down the page, unraveling like fabric. Maddie had a feeling she knew who Maeve was referring to.

"Gwynedd," she said. "She remembers? Everything?"

Maeve gave a sinister nod and said, "She does."

"We received the diary from Bronwyn, long after we arrived," said Rose. "We didn't find out she was the queen until just before she died."

"She died?"

"Murdered by Gwynedd in a dispute over the Foxglove. Before she was killed, she gave her diary to me and my husband, along with a warning: never to reveal that we had it to anyone, because one day, Gwynedd would come in search of it. After that, we fled."

"According to Bronwyn's story," Theresa interjected, "the Foxglove was stabbed with a knife, right here . . . " She gestured to her collarbone.

Maddie's hands drifted to her birth mark.

"All of this was before I was born," Theresa said. "And before the city was founded."

"We encountered Gwynedd again many years later," Rose went on. "At the time, she was working as the royal practitioner for the queen of the Erlkin, Morwena, having gained her position by saving the life of Morwena's infant son."

"Morrow," Maddie said.

"In the years that followed, Morwena's health steadily declined, and Gwynedd's influence grew. When the queen passed, Gwynedd assumed the throne. It was only then that she approached us concerning the Foxglove." Rose shut the book. "I'm afraid that we can't trust the rest of the story."

"Wait, why not?" Maddie said, straightening up. "What's the rest?"

"I've been able to translate some of the diary," Maeve answered. "And Rose knew Bronwyn personally. That's how we know what you've heard so far. What comes after was never written down. We heard it from Gwynedd herself, and we can only assume that her version of events cannot be trusted."

Maddie set down her tea. "Still, I'd like to hear it."

Rose and Maeve exchanged glances.

"Very well," Rose said, setting the book aside. "We don't know how Gwynedd learned we possessed the diary, but 20 years ago, she tried to convince us to help her locate the Foxglove. She claimed that it was imperfect, and that, over the years, she had developed a spell to strip out its consciousness and control its power, but she needed our help. According to her, the old queen feared the Foxglove's power, and in an act of cowardice, sent it away."

A lump formed in Maddie's throat. "Sent it where?" she asked.

"According to Gwynedd, the human world," Maeve answered. "Perhaps she was indeed afraid of it, or perhaps she simply believed that the Foxglove was acting in the best interest of her people when it brought them to the Veil.

Either way, she must have hoped it would lie dormant as it passed through the ages, never to return."

"But that's not all," Theresa added. "By this point, I was in my twenties, and the city was in the middle of its quest for independence. Gwynedd told us that the Foxglove would soon return to the Veil, and that she wanted our help to capture it."

"She also wanted the diary," said Rose. "Claiming that it contained the spell she would use to snare its power. Once she had both, she planned to use the Foxglove to open a gateway back to our homeland, and command it to destroy the evil it was created to defeat. Then, we could take our people home."

"That doesn't sound so bad," Maddie said.

"True," Theresa replied, "and we might have believed it, were it not for the old queen's warning."

Rose took over. "We don't know what really happened, but Bronwyn and I were more than simply friends. I loved her, and I trusted her, and I knew better than to trust Gwynedd's story. I declined her request for help, and in response, she gathered her army and tried to conquer the city to obtain the diary. There was a war. The Erlkin were defeated, but during the final battle . . . "

Her voice fluttered to a halt.

"Rose's husband, Amaranth, was killed," Maeve said, taking her hand. "Since then, Gwynedd has descended deeper and deeper into madness, leading her people away from their homes and into a life of desperation and depravity."

Rose drew in a slow breath to recover herself. "The worst part is that in the end, it wouldn't have mattered if she were victorious or not. I destroyed the pages containing the spell when Bronwyn gave me the diary, and my spies report that in the years that followed, she rediscovered the magic on her own. My husband died for nothing."

"Not for nothing," Theresa interjected. "He died fighting for us all."

"I'm sorry," said Maddie.

"It's alright," Rose replied, pausing to swallow a knot in her throat. "These days, few believe the Foxglove really exists, even among the Erlkin, who were taken to war over it, but if Gwynedd truly believes that you are what she seeks, she will never stop hunting you."

Maddie stayed quiet for a long moment as she struggled to process the story. She looked into Rose's luminous eyes and popped the million-dollar question.

"Are you saying I'm not human?"

Rose did her best to smile. "We're not sure. We'll have to find out."

"And if it's true? If I am this . . . Foxglove?"

"Then a great power lives inside you," Rose said. "And it has been with you your whole life."

"So how do we find out for sure?"

Maeve reached into her robes, drew out a long, stone knife, and placed it on the table. "With this."

The Witching Hour

The ant's shell crunched as Maddie brought down the cleaver, splitting its skull in half.

"Separate them," Maeve said, standing behind her.

Maddie put her hands on either side of the skull and drove in with her thumbs, pulling the two pieces apart. The viscous goo inside the ant's head spilled out onto the table. Grimacing, she picked through the mess. "Which one is it?" she asked.

"Check your diagram."

Maddie grumbled and glanced at her notes. The venom sack was located near the front of the skull, where the pincers met the head. She picked up her forceps and stuck them in.

"Not too fast," Maeve cautioned her. "You'll pierce it."

Maddie's stomach heaved. Witchcraft was disgusting. She forced herself to slow down and gently pressed her middle and index fingers into the space behind the ant's jaw. They brushed against a smooth, oval-shaped gland. Carefully, she slid the neck of the forceps down along her palm, guiding the tip of the scissors with her thumb. Snip.

She pulled the gland out and gagged as it jiggled in her hand. "Can't you do this?"

"Magic requires a personal connection," Maeve said. "Your participation is not optional. Now, put the venom in the pot."

Maddie complied, draining the contents of the sack into a bowl, which she carried over to the so-called pot. Maeve was the queen of understatement. It was a cauldron, pure and simple. Solid stone, it came up to Maddie's waist and probably weighed a thousand pounds.

Maddie tipped the bowl into the cauldron, picked up a long wooden spoon, and stirred. She'd already added more than a dozen ingredients: robin's egg yolk, ground locust antennae, live beetles the size of baseballs, vinegar, fermented apples, rat intestines, and what must have been 30 gallons of beef tallow. According to Maeve, fat was a better conduit for mingling the ingredients than water. The liquid smelled like death warmed over.

Nevertheless, a thrill had crept into the back of Maddie's mind, as though she were tip-toeing closer to something she'd been missing all her life. She was doing magic. Real magic. Fear and excitement hung in the air like electricity, and goosebumps raced across her skin.

A thin layer of luminescent slime coated the walls of Maeve's lair beneath the palace, filling the room with a sickly green light. Bare wood, dripping with sticky sap, formed the walls, split and broken by deep fissures that plunged into even deeper darkness. Three low tables, polished black with mineral oil, squatted around the cauldron in the center of the room.

Maeve leaned over the bubbling brew and drew in a long breath through her nose. She exhaled with satisfaction. "Mmm, almost done."

Maddie grimaced. "That's really messed up. You know that, right?"

Maeve chuckled as she reached her arm into one of the shadowy cracks along the wall. "You will have to do more than smell it before we are finished," she said, fetching out the next ingredient.

Maddie glanced back at the cauldron. "You've got to be kidding me."

"One preparation, one spell," Maeve replied, returning with a glass jar filled with yellow jelly. "The mixture will mingle with your humours and allow the magic to do its work, forming the connection between you and the world around you."

"And we're making this much because . . . ?"

Maeve upturned the jar into the cauldron. The jelly hissed and popped as it dissolved into the mixture.

"It is a very special spell," she said.

Maddie had to admit, she should have known this would be the way faerie magic worked. Wizards had spell books. Magicians had magic words. Witches had brews.

She began to wipe her fingers off on her dress, another hand-me-down from Theresa, when Maeve reached out and smacked her hand.

"Do not wash," she said. "It stifles the magic."

Maddie sneered down at the goop on her hands and then looked back at the cauldron. Steam rose from its oily surface and saturated her nostrils, coating her throat like spoiled milk. Her excitement about performing magic was dwindling rapidly.

"What next?" she asked.

Maeve glanced at the clock on the wall. It was 11:50.

"The spell is ready," she answered. "And it is almost time. Remove your clothing."

Maddie blinked. "I beg your pardon?"

"Trust," Maeve said, moving to the nearest table.

Maddie grumbled and got out of her clothes. She stood by the cauldron, nude. Maeve returned carrying the same long, stone knife Maddie had seen in the queen's apartment.

"This is for you," she said, holding it out. "Never let anyone borrow it. A witch's blood creates the final link between herself and the magic, but you must never mingle your own humours with those of another. What we take into ourselves, we take in forever. Do you understand?"

Maddie took the knife. The heavy, triangular blade was chipped to a razor edge along its entire length, and a purple braid wound around the handle. Her initials were carved into the pommel.

"You couldn't have made this just now," Maddie said. "How did you know I would need it?"

"I began to suspect the moment you arrived," Maeve answered. "No ordinary human could have survived your wound. Understand this: the practice of magic lies in the understanding of connection, but the true power of a practitioner is a matter of perspective. Our powers link us to the forces of nature: to the animals, to the trees, to the wind and the fire, to the past, and even to the future."

Maddie looked up. "The future?"

"It occurs rarely," Maeve said. "And we never know how our premonitions will manifest themselves when their time arrives. Did you ever wonder why Gwynedd was waiting for you in the woods? Or why our wardens happened to be near enough to save you?"

"I guess I just figured I was lucky," Maddie said.

Maeve took the knife and set the edge against Maddie's palm. "Luck had very little to do with it. There is a reason you came to the Veil, Madeline Foster, and there remains a chance that, from the moment you arrived, you were never destined to return to the world you knew."

Maddie's mouth fell open. "What does that mean?"

"Very soon, you will see."

The clock struck midnight.

"It is time," Maeve said. "Make a cut across your palm, deep."

Maddie felt a pressure building in her chest, as though something deep inside her was straining to get out. It pressed against her soul, eagerly tossing aside her fear and confusion. She struggled to slow her breath as hot anticipation flowed like liquid fire in her blood.

"I have to do this," she said.

"Yes," Maeve answered. "You do."

Maddie took a deep breath, counted to three in her head, and tugged.

The blade cut deep. Maddie let out a yelp and almost dropped the knife as her hand clamped into a fist against the pain. Blood filled her closed palm until it flowed over her fingers and dripped down into the cauldron.

The potion burst into flame.

Maddie gasped and jumped back. The fire flashed and swirled up, stirring into the air, a curl of green light mingled with black. The mixture in the cauldron churned, frothing as the blaze consumed it in a surge of thick, black smoke. The fumes smelled of disease and rancid fat, but there was a sweet, metallic thread running through them that tickled Maddie's nostrils. Somewhere, deep in the most primitive corners of her mind, a terrible instinct rumbled awake. Her mouth began to water even as her conscious mind recoiled from the sight.

The brew settled into a thick, black broth that stank like a swamp. A rainbow of colors played across its surface. It reminded Maddie of motor oil on pavement.

Maeve produced a tall clay cup from her robes and dipped it in the liquid, filling the vessel to the brim. "Drink," she said, holding it out.

For the briefest flicker of an instant, Maddie hesitated, remembering Maeve's warning. What we take in, we take in forever. If she was right, the magic would never leave her.

Maeve pulled the cup back. "You must be certain."

Maddie wiped the knife off against her thigh and set it aside. She took the cup and held it to her lips. They said she might not be human, and that was a hell of a thing to be unsure about.

"You're right," Maddie said. "I do."

She tipped the foul liquid into her mouth. The smell climbed into her nostrils and slithered down her throat like an over-sized, wriggling eel. Maddie forced down every last drop before, heaving for breath, she let the cup slip out of her hands. It broke on the floor.

Maddie shuddered as she stared at the shattered fragments. "God, that's awful," she said, resisting the urge to throw up. "What now?"

"You will feel it in a moment," Maeve answered, stepping back.

Maddie leaned against the cauldron. "Feel wha—?"

A sound like the beat of a huge drum exploded in her skull.

Allsight

Maddie doubled over, choking as the room went black. A burning pressure built up inside her eyes as the potion churned in her gut and pushed out into her body. She clutched her stomach with one hand; with the other she grasped the edge of the cauldron, struggling to stand. Her vision swam as the black ooze burned through her insides, and staring down at her hands, she looked on in horror as her veins turned black.

"Maeve!" she shouted, stumbling to the table.

Her mistress's voice sounded far away. "Do not fear. The magic is reaching out to you. Embrace it."

Maddie leaned over the table and wretched. Black smoke billowed up from her throat, spilling out like hot foam, carrying with it a strange mix of bittersweet odors. Maddie clawed at the stone surface, screaming as the fog spewed from her mouth. The taste of charcoal and raw meat coated her tongue.

Thoughts of bile and blood flooded her thoughts as she lurched to the cauldron and leaned over the edge, every nerve in her body tingling with desperation as sensation crawled down her stomach and tightened in her loins. Her knees buckled. She could feel the humours filling her legs and arms until even her fingertips felt alive. The magic wrapped around her body from the inside. Her pupils dilated as she sucked in a deep and willful breath.

Maeve's voice whispered in her ear. "Do you feel it?"

"Yes," Maddie gasped.

She felt her body lift up and fall. She plunged into the cauldron. The black liquid slithered into her head, and her thoughts dissolved. Maddie drank deep, and when she could drink no more, she breathed the potion in, allowing the dread power to fill her lungs as the thoughts and feelings of every stone and creature all across the world joined in harmony at the center of her mind.

And for an instant, Maddie Foster was gone.

The world snapped back into focus and she shrieked, lurching out of the cauldron, a mass of black sludge and beading sweat. She rolled onto the floor and lay on her back.

"What was that?" Maddie said, raking in a breath.

Her mistress answered, standing over her. "You."

Maddie sat up. Something was different. A dark curtain had fallen over her eyes. She could barely see through it, and yet what she perceived was clearer than ever before. Her whole perception shifted and wove around the room, flitting from object to object like a moth drawn to too many candles. She was the chair, then the fire, then the strange ingredients in their jars and boxes, stuffed in the cracks around the room. For a moment, she even felt like she was staring out of Maeve's eyes, looking back at herself, skin draped with a dense lace of blackened veins, eyes as hollow as beads of polished ebony.

I knew I was right. I wonder how much she has already understood.

Maddie blinked. The thoughts were not her own, but Maeve's consciousness was all around her as she tried to understand. How much had she understood about what?

She is the Foxglove. It has come back.

"Stop that, please," Maeve said, flinching. She put out a hand and touched Maddie's shoulder.

The sensation shocked her back into her own mind and body. She shook herself and pressed her eyes shut, but it didn't help. The room and everything in it drifted through her head, demanding her attention. The chair, and then the fire, and then Maeve. Her own mind was lost in a smear of thoughts, feelings, and sensations.

"I—I'm sorry," Maddie said, fighting to pull herself back together. "I didn't mean to. I don't know what's going on. What's happening?"

Maeve let go of her shoulder. "Try to focus on the room. Let yourself feel it, but do not dive too deep. Float on the surface. Allow your mind to drift."

Maddie tried to do as she was told, but the task was strange and difficult. The room no longer existed on its own. Maddie felt like a cloud of smoke, perceiving the world through the senses of everything she touched. She felt the strong legs of the chair, the solid stone of the cauldron, the crackling of the fire as it consumed the wood. She could feel the decay of the magical ingredients around the room, bathed in Maeve's preserving liquids. The bitter mixture clung to her like a second skin.

"This is the Earth Sight," Maeve said. "The space between things. The realm within and without. It is the highest form of magic, and the spell that connects us to all of nature: near, far, past, present, and future. We see though every eye, hear through every ear, taste with every tongue, and perceive the world with the understanding of every mind around us, no matter how vast or small. Every witch begins her training with this experience, to show her what it means to be truly joined with the world."

Her training. To show her. The meaning behind the thoughts caught in Maddie's mind like a bird in a snare.

"What about the male witches?" she asked, but she knew the answer before her mistress could respond. She said, "There are none."

"Very good," Maeve replied. "There are male practitioners among the Erlkin, but there are none among the Faerie. Their sense of self is too fragile. They become lost in the minds of the world."

The images and emotions of a thousand men, howling as they gripped their heads, flowed like black water into her mind.

"You've seen it happen," Maddie said. "How did I know?"

Again, her mistress didn't answer. She only tilted her head, and the understanding came to Maddie as clearly as if she had known the answer all her life.

Maddie whispered, "We can read minds?"

"Yes," Maeve said. "But you are unpracticed. Your conscious mind still fights to hold the line between yourself and the perception of the Earth Sight. You seek thoughts as answers to questions as if you were reading a book. In time, you will grow to understand that the magic grants far more than that. You will *be* the minds and objects you inhabit. Memory, understanding, bias, emotion, belief, and sensation will come to you as easily as your own breath. I told you before—"

"—the true power of the practitioner is a matter of perspective." Maddie lay back on the floor, flabbergasted. "How far does it go?"

"The masters among us have gazed across entire oceans, but most witches manage no more than a few miles. Why do you ask?"

"Earlier, when I drank the goo—"

"The spell."

Maddie said, "The spell, right. It was so intense. I felt like I was connected to everything, and I mean *everything*. I didn't even know who I was anymore. Is that normal?"

Maeve paused for a long moment and then shook her head. "No," she answered. "What you experienced, however briefly, is called the Allsight."

"And what is that?"

Maeve lifted her up off the floor. "A state of pure connection, without bounds or limits. In our history, no witch in the world has ever attained it."

"Until now," Maddie said.

Maeve helped her to a chair and set her down. "Indeed."

"But it was terrifying."

"Only because you do not understand it. In its natural state, the consciousness of the Foxglove encompasses all things. It does not think and feel as we do."

One creature, a single, global view of the world, as close to godhood as any mortal being could ever hope to come. The enormity of it fell onto Maddie like a lead blanket and her hands began to shake. She clamped them down onto her legs.

"If you'd never come along, I would have been just a normal girl," she said, her voice quaking.

"No, you don't understand," Maeve replied. "You do not possess the Foxglove, you *are* the Foxglove."

"But how can you be sure?"

"Humans have no magic. If you were not the Foxglove, you would have died in the woods when Gwynedd cut out your heart, and you certainly would not have been able to enter the Earth Sight."

Maddie rocked back and forth, forcing herself to breathe. "But how?"

"There is no way to know how this came to pass," Maeve said. "Nothing with a mind can pass through the barrier. I have always surmised that the old queen must have transformed it into something else, but whatever happened to it, you must realize that the Foxglove cannot die. Its life force is immortal. It would have lived, eternal, taking on one form of life after another. One can only imagine that it somehow passed into your mother shortly before she conceived you, and it took the form of her human child."

"Passed into her?"

"It might have been anything: a speck of dust, a mote of bacteria, or even a piece of fruit. Tell me, do you know if your parents had dinner before they mated?"

Maddie recoiled. "Ugh! Don't ask me that!" She got to her feet and paced across the floor and asked, "Can you take this thing out of me?"

Maeve pinched her eyes shut, massaging her forehead. "Madeline, the Foxglove is not inside you. It is what you are."

"Then how come I can't feel it? How come I'm not all . . . transcendent or something?"

"The power must be dormant."

Maddie spun around. "I don't suppose you know how to keep it that way."

There was a long pause.

"You are afraid," Maeve said, realization dawning on her face.

"You're damn right," Maddie answered. "I lost myself a moment ago, and it felt like dying. Maeve, I never want to feel that way again."

"It may not be avoidable."

"So then what am I supposed to do?"

Maeve came across the room and steered Maddie over to the cauldron. "We will tell Rose and Theresa. They will undoubtedly inform the captain of the wardens, the matron of the house, and the prince."

"Fantastic," Maddie said. "You just listed almost every person I know." She leaned down on the edge of the cauldron and sighed. "They're going to think I'm a freak."

"I'm sorry, but now that we know Gwynedd's suspicions about you were correct, we must do everything we can to keep you safe."

"And what about me? What about my life?"

"You will have to make a choice," Maeve said. "If you wish, you can remain in the palace and pursue your studies. Rose will protect you, and perhaps in time she will find a solution to Gwynedd. Alternatively, we could instruct Kidhe to take you far away, someplace where perhaps she will never find you."

"Neither of those sound particularly promising."

Maeve bent down and picked up Maddie's knife from the floor. Maddie didn't even remember dropping it.

"I do have another option," Maeve said.

"And that is?"

"You could become my apprentice. I will teach you to become a witch and to harness the power you carry. Achieve that, and even someone as powerful as Gwynedd will be beneath your concern."

Maddie took the knife. It wasn't exactly the career path she'd envisioned in high school. She turned the thought over in her head as she stared at the glossy surface of the potion.

Black veins and dark eyes stared back.

A Noble Pursuit

Maddie rested her chin on the desk as Finn sat across from her, staring.

"Will you stop looking at me like that?" she asked.

He leaned down and reached out a finger towards her face. "It's just incredible," he said.

She swatted his hand away.

"Back off! I feel weird enough already."

"But you're—"

"The Foxglove, I know. Don't remind me."

"So, have you decided yet?"

"Decided what?"

"About becoming a witch."

Maeve had given her two weeks to think it over. If Maddie became her apprentice, her other studies would have to be abandoned. There simply weren't enough hours in the day, and Maeve worked at night, which meant that

Maddie's sleep schedule would have to be reversed. Nine days had come and gone since then, and Maddie was no closer to a final decision. In fact, she was beginning to think that hiding out in the woods somewhere might not be such a bad idea.

At least Ebba had come through with the goods. It felt great to be back in jeans.

"I don't know," Maddie said. "I don't even know if I *want* to be a witch."

Finn leaned back in his chair and kicked his feet up onto his desk. "Well, it seems like it'd be right up your alley."

"And what makes you say that?"

"You're smart, driven, and you love to feel like the smartest person in the room." He reached into his pocket and pulled out a handful of candies wrapped in wax paper. Unwrapping one, he popped it into his mouth. "Plus, no need for people skills."

"You're an ass."

"What?! I'm just saying, you like to be the one to make the power play. A little egocentric, maybe, but it's actually kind of attractive."

"Gee, thanks," Maddie said, slumping onto her desk. "Jerk."

Finn paused. "I'm sorry," he said, pushing a candy towards her across the desk. "I didn't mean to upset you."

Maddie took it. "I've only ever done what was expected of me," she said. "And the worst part is, I've been doing it so long that now, even if I see something I like, I can't be sure if it's me who wants it or if I'm just rising to meet the same expectations I've been chasing my whole life."

"So, then you admit you liked it?"

Maddie peered up at him and ate the candy. "It *was* kinda cool."

"Truthfully, I'm jealous," Finn said, looking up at the ceiling. "I've only ever had my sister and mother to look up to."

"That's not such a problem," Maddie replied. "They're certainly good role models."

Finn drummed his fingers on his desk. "True, but no matter how much I learn from them: all the studying, and the tutors, and the fencing lessons. None of it really matters. I can make myself look like them, but I can never have the life they're leading me towards."

He got up and walked to the blackboard, idly reading Cedric's leftover notes. "We're a pretty antiquated society. Chalk it up to being a member of a species that lives hundreds of years. Old habits die pretty hard when the original habit-formers are all still around. I don't know if you've noticed, but I'm not exactly built for high office."

He let out a sigh. "It's going to be a long time before our culture changes, if it ever does."

"I'm sorry," Maddie said.

He spun around, came back to the desks, and flopped back into his chair. "Anyway, you see my point," he said, forcing himself back to a smile. "You're lucky."

"Except for the part where I'm basically a weapon of mass destruction."

Finn put his feet back up. "Yeah, except for that." He tossed her another candy.

"I guess it would be nice for you," Maddie said, catching it. "Me giving up my studies. You'd have the classroom to yourself again. No more arguments."

Finn let his head fall back and stared up at the ceiling. "Actually, I kind of like the arguments."

"You do not."

"At least they keep things interesting. It'll be awfully boring around here without you."

Maddie straightened up and cracked her back. "I don't even know what's involved with being a witch."

"Well, we're in a library," Finn replied, gesturing at the books. "Look it up."

Maddie looked around, scanning the stacks. "I just don't think that will help. I've already seen magic, and I've experienced it, but we're talking about a career that could last a lifetime. What if I want to go home someday?"

Finn sat quietly for a moment, arms folded, before springing out of his chair. He crossed the room to the door.

"What are you doing?" Maddie asked.

"I figured out what you need."

"Oh? What's that?"

"A field trip," he said.

"A field trip?"

"That's right," he said, whispering as he cracked the door open. "Get your stuff. We're going out."

Field Trip

Finn led Maddie to the front hall of the palace, where a circle cut from the outer bark of the tree served as the main door. The faeries had it propped open to let in the breeze.

"It's always so windy here," Maddie said. "Why is that?"

Finn took her outside. "They do call it the Windy City."

"But not because it's *actually* windy."

"I know," he said. "The weather is the way it is because of the Veil. Every layer has its own special quality. There are some where it never stops raining, others where it's always night, but here, it's windy. My mother built the city here because of that, actually. It's good for windmills."

"There were windmills when she built the city?"

"When she built the city, it was a bar," he said, smirking. "But she knew that someday it would grow. That's my mom. Always keeping an eye on the future."

They crossed a sweeping courtyard. A dozen guards stood in attendance, each one carrying a tall spear. Long red ribbons fluttered in the breeze, fixed to the weapons' thin, lethal points. Their bodies were clad in shining steel, engraved with the same stalk-like flowers that had adorned the princess's armor.

"And the flowers?" Maddie asked.

"Amaranth," Finn answered. "For my father. She took his death pretty hard, and I think seeing his namesake around really helped her."

"Does it help you?"

He stopped walking. For a moment, he turned his eyes to the ground and put a hand on his neck, fidgeting. "I was really young when my father died. I never knew him."

"I'm sorry," Maddie said.

Finn spun around. "It's alright. It was a long time ago, and we're out here for you. The cable cars are this way."

There was a carriage house at the far end of the courtyard. A gear set with a thick, metal cord rotated slowly over the roof. The lines went all the way down to the city, where they met in a matching structure at one end of an open plaza.

"I'm not supposed to leave the palace," Maddie said.

"Prince," Finn replied, pointing a finger towards himself. "Something tells me they won't stop us. Just don't freak out when we get inside."

"Why would I freak out?"

Finn took her into the carriage house and Maddie paused.

"Oh," she said.

The gears powering the lift were driven by team of ants, each one the size of a VW bug. A pair of handlers urged them on with globs of sugar on long wooden poles.

"Good afternoon, your highness," they said in unison.

Glistening black lacquer and gold filigree encased the cable car like a candy shell. Finn skipped over to the carriage as it swept around a shallow track in the floor.

"Your chariot awaits," he said, opening the door.

Polished wood and thick black cushions adorned the carriage's interior. As they took their seats, red cloth window shades thumped and billowed in the wind.

Maddie turned to Finn as the carriage bobbed out into the air. "Okay, seriously. What is it with the giant animals?"

"What about them?"

"They're the size of pick-up trucks!"

The prince laughed. "I'm not the one who flies through the air in a metal tube powered by exploding chemicals. We work with what we have. Not a lot of oil drilling in the Veil, and this way we don't have to worry about a carbon footprint."

Maddie shook her head. "But wouldn't it be easier to use an engine? It's not like you couldn't pull one into the Veil, right?"

"True," Finn said. "But then we'd have to steal gasoline to power it. Moral considerations aside, we prefer to be self-sufficient, and as far as the insects are concerned, this is just the way things are. The Veil is a reflection of the human world, but it's not the same. There's magic in the air. If you go deep enough, you can see it with the naked eye. It makes sense that things here would be a little different, including the wildlife."

Maddie look a long breath and mumbled, "Just when I think I'm getting used to this place." She glanced out the window and said, "What about other animals?"

"What do you mean?"

"I've seen birds, and ants, and beetles. Are there any hotel-sized pigs I should be aware of?"

Finn leaned back against the cushions and let his head rest against the windowsill. The sun cut across his face, lighting up his hair as he sighed in contentment.

"Not really," he said, eyes closed. "Maybe in the deep Veil. I've never seen anything larger than a cat, and it was massive. We caught a glimpse of him on a hunting trip. He turned to look at us and you could almost see him thinking. I half-expected him to open up his mouth and speak."

"Him?"

"We're pretty sure, but we weren't that close. Thank goodness he wasn't hungry. An animal that size would be practically unstoppable. As for the rest, we have mice and rats, and some large birds, but the higher orders of animal never seem to get through the barrier."

He paused to give her a sideways grin. "Which says a lot about you."

Maddie hit him on the shoulder as the carriage came around to hover along the edge off a short, wooden platform. Finn jumped out and helped Maddie down. Together, they descended a staircase to the street.

"Welcome to the Spiral Market," Finn said.

Maddie stifled a gasp. There had to be a thousand people in the plaza, wearing clothing from what looked like every conceivable era, from tailcoats to denim jeans. The aromas of a dozen cultures drifted through the air like clouds of fragrant dust.

They walked past an open-air rotisserie roasting insect legs on spits. Someone was selling peanut-sized larvae, batter-fried and served in paper cones like popcorn shrimp, and there was a sandwich-bar specializing in beetle. Across the square, an enormous dead caterpillar hung in a window like a side of beef. The butcher cut away steaks with a huge knife, some of which went onto a grill, while others got wrapped in paper and sold raw to the passing throng.

The street rose and fell, following the contours of the underlying branches, and with every step, the hollow thump of open air under the boardwalk thudded beneath their feet.

Finn led the way along the crowded street, pointing out a pair of huge ramps in the middle of the square. They descended from street level and wrapped around the trunk of the city tree: one with traffic going up, the other going down.

"This is the largest shopping center in the city," Finn said. "The shops run for almost half a mile, all the way around the trunk and out like a spider web. There are others, of course, but this one is the oldest and the busiest. When the centennial comes, most of the festivities will be organized here, and this whole place will be full of tents and stalls."

Maddie glanced around. "Sounds like the Taste."

"The what?"

"You really need to get out more," Maddie said. "The Taste of Chicago is a kind of food festival. It happens every year. Restaurants from all over the city set up tents in Grant Park."

"I haven't spent much time at the Veil surface," Finn said. "I only went once, with Cedric. I think we went to a museum, but I was pretty young, so I don't know for sure. All I remember is that everything smelled like car exhaust."

"Well, it's worth it. You haven't lived until you've tried a genuine Lou Malnati's pizza, or a *real* steak."

"I've had steak."

Maddie huffed. "Sure. Bug steak."

"It counts!"

"It does not."

They passed a cloth merchant. The storefront looked like a rainbow captured in a loom. Maddie's eyes lingered on a bolt of white fabric woven through with gold.

"How do they get the metal into it?" she asked.

The store owner pounced.

"You like this one?" she asked. "It's my best. Very beautiful. Perfect for a dress. How many yards do you need? Or I can measure you, if you're not sure."

Finn waved her off. "Thank you. We're fine for now. We might be back."

They left and split off the main street, following a twisting branch that dropped down before curving under the road. Here, wooden shingles advertised less glamorous wares. They passed an apothecary with dried herbs hanging in the windows, a woodcarver specializing in canes, a haberdasher, and a music studio before they finally arrived at their destination.

A tiny, round hut sat alone in the center of a square barely larger than the building itself. It had the feeling of a church or a mortuary — not avoiding society, but maintaining a discrete distance to escape the hustle and bustle of the city. The walls were made from brown clay, overgrown with tall grass and cream-colored mushrooms that covered the roof like a blanket. A single window faced the street, and there wasn't a soul in sight.

Darkened windows loomed in the buildings that surrounded the hut. Their drawn curtains allowed only a few faint glimmers of fungal glow and candle-light to escape.

"It's a little creepy," Maddie said.

Finn swept his eyes across the square. "Really? I never thought so."

"It's like the set of Jack the Ripper."

Finn chuckled as he approached the hut. "Do you see the signs on the doors?"

She looked and discovered that a read cross on every one.

"The apartments are for long-term care," Finn said. "The practitioner makes rounds twice a day. The hut is for aesthetics. Witches have to connect to the natural world, so they craft their environment extremely carefully. A cramped office simply wouldn't do."

Maddie turned a full circle in place. "You're saying that this is a hospital?"

"And this is an operating theater," Finn said, knocking softly on the door of the hut. "Come on. Let's see if they'll let us watch."

Higher Education

The door creaked open, revealing a woman in a long, off-white robe holding a butcher's cleaver.

"Your highness!" she yelped, dropping the knife on the ground.

Bloody smears in a variety of colors stained an apron that hung loose her shoulders. Finn bowed and extended a hand. She bent down and kissed it. As she straightened up, she brushed her hair away from her face, leaving a yellow-green smudge. Finn took a step aside and gestured to Maddie.

"This is my friend Maddie," he said. "She's considering becoming a practitioner. Is there any chance she might be able to speak with your mistress?"

The woman glanced back into the hut. "Um, she's working with a patient right now. Could you come back later? I could make you an appointment."

"Actually, we were hoping she might be busy. If we promise to stay out of the way, could we watch the procedure?"

The nurse glanced nervously into the room again.

"Please?" Finn asked. "It would mean a lot to her. You won't even notice we're there."

The woman wavered for a moment before she said, "I'll ask."

The door shut. Maddie could hear people talking inside. When it opened again, the woman leaned out and whispered, "She says it's alright. Just don't make a fuss."

Finn bowed again and thanked her as she led them in.

"Don't we have to scrub down or something?" Maddie asked, stopping at the threshold.

Finn took her by the shoulders and ushered her through the door. "It's not that kind of medicine," he said. "Just watch and try to stay quiet."

Glowing orange fungus blanketed the ceiling inside, filling the hut's single room with warm light that flowed into every corner. A broad fireplace burned on one side, set with swinging iron hooks to hold dangling pots, filled with bubbling liquid. Around the walls, piles of boxes and heavy jars rose almost to the ceiling. Maddie noted a little bed in the corner beside a dresser and a stout wardrobe.

A young woman in her thirties, wearing a deep green robe, stood over a long table in the center of the room. Dark brown braids fell over her shoulders nearly to the floor, while in front of her, a young boy no more than eight lay sleeping on the table.

Another witch, Maddie thought.

She didn't look at all like Maeve. An expression of quiet compassion lay across her face as she examined the boy. His right leg was missing below the knee, wrapped tightly in linen bandages stained green with blood. Two older faeries, a man and a woman, stood anxiously beside him.

"What happened?" the prince whispered to the nurse.

The nurse answered in a low voice. "He was caught in an Erlkin snare. By the time he was rescued, the poison had already traveled up his leg. He's been recovery from the amputation for five days. This is the second procedure."

The nurse returned to her mistress while Finn and Maddie retreated to the edge of the room. She whispered a few words to the witch, who glanced up at Maddie briefly before returning to her work. The nurse bent down and lifted a long, wooden case from under the table.

Maddie tugged at Finn's shirt. "What are they doing?"

He gave her a little smile. "Magic, of course."

The witch took up a small glass vial of cloudy green liquid. Removing the stopper, she consumed the potion in a single gulp, shutting her eyes as the magic invaded her veins and covered her face in a black web. When she spoke, her voice emerged in a hollow echo.

"The leg, please."

The nurse opened the case and produced a milky-colored piece of wood. The bark had been removed, revealing the still-wet surface underneath, newly cut and beading with fresh sap. She handed it to her mistress and stepped around the table, gently removing the bandages from boy's wound. Maddie's stomach lurched at the sight of the exposed leg. Fine thread held the flesh shut, and it reminded her of the scar she'd found on her chest the day she'd arrived in the Veil.

The nurse cut away the stitches, and green blood flowed out onto the table. Maddie's eyes went wide. Her mouth fell open, and she put a hand up to cover it.

"Watch," Finn hissed.

The witch's hands began to glow. A soft green light bloomed into the air, swirling gently like smoke blown by a draft under the door. It settled on the log and seeped into the wood, moving through the fibers like living water until it disappeared inside. The witch turned to the two older faeries.

"Hold his hand," she said.

The mother closed her hand around the boy's palm as the witch set the log down beside the stump of his leg. With one hand on his bleeding limb and the other on the cut wood, she pressed the pair together.

A rush of energy burst in the center of Maddie's chest, spreading out to her legs and arms. She gasped as light flashed from the length of wood, weaving through the air like threads of luminescent silk. It coiled around the bleeding stump of the leg and tightened. Maddie could hear the wood flexing and bending, cracking as the magic flowed between them. The log reformed, taking on the shape of a knee . . . a calf . . . a foot, until finally the light faded. The witch took her hands away, and the boy opened his eyes. The wooden toes wiggled.

His parents burst into tears, hauling him up from the table and into their arms. The witch gave a bow and stepped away, leaving her assistant to clean up. She came towards Finn and Maddie.

"I don't usually allow visitors," she said as the prince bowed. She kissed his hand. "These procedures can be very personal, and the people deserve their privacy."

Her voice had mellowed, but the dark vibration of the magic still drifted in the air.

Finn said, "Thank you for making an exception."

The woman looked Maddie over with a discerning eye. "You are the apprentice?" she asked.

"Soon, maybe," Maddie replied humbly.

"A human?"

Maddie nodded meekly. "Yes ma'am."

The woman reached out, put a hand to Maddie's chest, and shut her eyes. "I can feel your power," she said. "I think you would do well. And the heart is a fine graft. Expertly done, though I've never seen the spell performed on one of your kind. There must be something very special about you."

Maddie forced a smile. "That's what they tell me."

The witch opened her eyes and took her hand away. "I hope you found your visit worthwhile. Now, I have to attend to my other patients."

Finn bowed to her again. "Thank you," he said.

The witch kissed his hand and left with her nurse, escorting the Faerie parents and their child from the room. Finn took Maddie back out to the street and they headed for square.

"That was incredible!" Maddie said, barely able to contain her excitement.

"See?" Finn said. "It's not all dark rooms and scary stories. That could be you someday."

Maddie felt a tremble of excitement in her chest. She giggled as she ran in front of the prince and walked backwards. "Do you think so? I never thought about becoming a doctor."

A broad smile brightened his face as he replied, "There's nothing stopping you."

Maddie danced back around beside him. "Doctor Madeline Foster," she said, trying it on for size.

Finn put up a hand. "Madeline Foster, Practitioner."

"Practitioner?"

"It's the official title, unless you prefer 'witch.' They're both acceptable."

"But do you think I could really do it?"

He stuck his finger out and poked her in the middle of her forehead.

"You've got the head for it," he said.

Maddie grinned and felt her cheeks tingle. She put a hand on her face to hide the blush as they emerged onto the main road. Maddie practically skipped along the street.

"What will happen to that boy?" she asked. "When he grows up, I mean. Will he have to get his leg replaced?"

"No," Finn said. "They're joined by the spell. It's not just a piece of wood anymore, no more than your heart is."

Maddie bounced with anticipation. "That is so cool!" she said, stopping in the middle of the street and planting her hands on her hips to survey the market. "We should celebrate. This is the Spiral Market. Where's the Triple-C?"

"You mean the cafe?"

"Yeah," Maddie said, scanning the signs above the crowd. She pointed. "There it is. Come on!"

She dragged him over to the crowded storefront. The smell of hot beef, cheese, and ketchup hung in the air like smoke.

Finn wrinkled his nose. "What do they sell here?" he asked.

Maddie's stomach rumbled. "Chicago's finest."

Dramatis Persona

The sound of clattering trays rattled through the door, and Morrow looked up. More customers. He was in the back, updating inventory. The owner, Leoh, had absolutely no sense of organization. It was a miracle he was still in business. The only thing that kept the caravan profitable was the fact that the city of Amaranth possessed an inexhaustible craving for junk food.

Leoh popped his head through the door. "Moira? Could you take over on the counter for a minute? We're swamped."

"Yes, sir," Morrow said, suppressing the urge to glance behind him at the sound of his own voice. After three weeks, the higher pitch still caught him by surprise.

The name was part of his cover identity. He'd had selected it for its leading syllable, which made it easier to connect it with his own name in his head. Morrow set down his ledger and followed Leoh out into the dining room.

A line of hungry faeries extended all the way to the door, winding around the stainless steel tables. The caravan borrowed its styling from the diners of the 1950s, complete with black and white tile, polished bar stools, and bright red vinyl cushions on the chairs. Shining taps dispensed soda in every color of the rainbow opposite roaring deep fryers full of nachos. Vats of boiling water filled the air with steam, brimming with hot dogs ready to be served.

As the salt and fat coated his tongue, Morrow suppressed a gag. He preferred his people's native dishes of root vegetables, insects, and mushrooms, though the Erlkin seldom prepared them anymore. It was far to easy to steal from the humans.

Morrow took his place behind the register and began calling out orders. Money flew across the counter, and the bell over the door jingled as each new patron pushed through the door, until the crowd suddenly parted and the room fell silent.

"Welcome to the Triple-C," Morrow said, on autopilot as he looked up. "What can I get" — The human girl stood across from him, reading the menu over his head — "you?"

The prince of Amaranth was right behind her. Morrow wiped his hands on his uniform and brushed his hair out of his face. The moment had come. There wasn't much to go on, but he was going to have to find a way to make a lasting impression.

"Let me guess," he said. "Two nachos, a hot dog, and a . . . Mountain Dew?"

She tilted her head quizzically. "How'd you know?"

"It's a gift," Morrow said with a grin. "I'm guessing you're from out of town."

The girl tapped a finger beside her round, human eyes and said, "How'd you guess?"

Morrow put the order in. "You do stand out," he said. "But also, word gets around. I've never met a human before. Allow me to be the first to welcome you to the Triple-C. I'm Moira." He stuck out a hand, and she shook it.

"Maddie."

"Can I get you a table?"

Maddie glanced back at the crowd. "That would be great."

"Hey, boss!" Morrow said, turning to Leoh. "We have some special guests."

Leoh spun around. "Hey! It's you!"

"Nice place!" Maddie said, waving.

"Want me to charge them?" Morrow asked.

"No way," Leoh answered. "It's on the house."

Morrow grabbed their food and took them to a table, his heart thumping the whole way. "Bon appetit," he said, laying down their trays.

Maddie breathed in over the food and shuddered as she slid into her seat. "Are these *real* nachos?" she asked.

"As real as nachos can be," Morrow answered.

She grabbed a cheese-coated chip and popped it in her mouth.

"Oh. My. God," she said, nearly drooling.

Morrow grinned. "I'm glad you like them. Do you want anything for your hot dog? Ketchup?"

Maddie looked up with sudden disdain, but Morrow was ready. Hot dogs in Chicago were served in a very particular way, topped with an assortment of fresh vegetables, pickles, and celery-seasoned salt. The Triple-C served them in the same fashion, and while for some, additional toppings were a preference; for others, they were a sin against nature.

"Just like this is perfect," she said.

"A purist, eh?"

Maddie fixed him with an assertive stare. "There is no other way to eat a hot dog."

"I couldn't agree more."

Maddie lifted the dog and took an enormous bite. Morrow chuckled, quietly charmed by her brazen gluttony.

"It has been *so* long," she said.

Morrow did his best to put on a bashful smile. "I know the feeling."

Maddie wolfed down a second bite. "But you work here," she said. "Don't you eat the food?"

"It's pretty expensive," Morrow replied, "and I just moved into town. I'm trying to save up to get a place."

Maddie set down her hot dog. "Well, it's nice to finally meet someone who's newer in town than me. Are you here for the festival?"

"Something like that. I used to live downtown. Now I'm just trying to get on my feet. The Triple-C looked as good a place as any to find some work."

"Well, we'll be sure to leave you a big tip."

"Maddie . . ." the prince said.

She caught herself. "Right. I'm broke. *He'll* leave you a big tip. Moira, this is Prince Finn. He's not cultured enough to have a hot dog preference."

"Maddie!" Finn yelped.

Morrow bowed. "Your highness."

He took Morrow's hand and kissed it. "It's a pleasure to meet you, and I assure you, my level of culture is just fine."

"Hah!" Maddie scoffed. "He's never even had pizza. Do you guys sell pizza?"

"In the evenings," Morrow answered.

"Man, it's been forever since I had pizza," said Maddie.

A server blew by with their drinks and Morrow popped open the caps. "Was it your favorite?" he asked, setting them back down.

Maddie nodded. "I haven't had a good slice in forever."

"Then you should come back."

Maddie snatched up her soda and guzzled it down. "Maybe I will." Then she slumped. "No. Nevermind. I'm not supposed to leave the palace."

"But you're here now, aren't you?"

Maddie glanced at the prince. "Today is a special circumstance," she said. "I don't suppose you deliver?"

"Not normally," Morrow said, putting a hand on her shoulder. "But for a fellow Chicagoan, I'll see what I can do."

He left them alone to eat, pleased to have engineered a reason to get back in touch. It wasn't much, but it was a start.

His stomach churned. The fading daylight reminded him that it was the end of his shift, and he was nearly overdue for his next dose of Gwynedd's potion. Throwing his apron in the laundry bin, he clocked off and returned to his apartment.

The flat lay in a cheaper area of the city, part of his cover as a poor new arrival. Morrow had the money for a better place, but the idea of getting comfortable set him on edge. While he was growing accustomed to the noise and the sunshine that saturated the Faerie city, he longed to return home, though he confessed that it hardly felt like home anymore. It was merely the swamp in which he lived. Part of him couldn't wait to take his next dose, and let Gwynedd's essence to force his doubts away.

He had already discovered that, while they might be loud and unrefined, the Faeries were not the greedy oppressors his mistress had made them out to be. He could only speculate about what drove her to hate them so much.

Shutting the door behind him, he crossed the one-room space, reached under the bed, and pulled out the box of vials. The potion felt like poison in his mouth, but as it ran down his throat, its acid sting turned to a burning satisfaction that reminded him of alcohol and smoke. His misgivings slowly disbursed, and he remembered once again the lingering hatred that sat in his soul: a hatred for the Faerie, for their history, and for their way of life. A dark resolution to bring it all to crashing down slithered into his thoughts.

Moving to the mirror, his image ambushed him as he got undressed. It had taken some time to grow accustomed to the sight of his new form, which he found to be decidedly inconvenient in terms of both body and mind. Faerie impulses invaded his thoughts. Just the other day, he caught himself staring at one of the cook's rear ends.

He grumbled, pushing away the chaos in his head. As he shut his eyes, he hoped that he would dream of caves, moonlight, and the forests of the deep Veil.

Soon, he prayed, it would all be over.

Witchcraft 101

"Again," Maeve said.

Maddie groaned and rolled over on the floor. Classes took place at night, to take advantage of the witching hour: midnight to 1am. According to Maeve, now officially Maddie's mistress, the connections of magic were at their strongest during the transition from one day into the next. It was a kind of universal rhythm. The magic of the witching hour was surpassed only by the power that came during the transition of the year: the summer solstice, which was only a few short weeks away.

Maddie pulled herself up and went back to the table, where the spell's mixture filled a shallow bowl.

"Aren't potions supposed to come in bottles?"

Maeve loomed over her. "Bottles are for witches, not apprentices. Until you possess the skill to work your spells, there is no point to keeping them ready to hand."

Maddie lifted her head up heavily and let it fall, her best impression of a nod. Her muscles throbbed and sent a flash of pain racing up her spine.

"We've been at this for hours," she said. "What's wrong? Why isn't it working?"

"Did you suppose the practice would be easy?" Maeve replied. She pointed to the bowl of potion on the table. "Again."

Maddie picked up a wooden ladle and dipped it into the potion. She grimaced as she drank it down. The spell they were working with was meant to give her the ability to throw stones. It wasn't nearly as awful as the potion that brought on the Earth Sight, but it still tasted like mud. She'd spent the first hour of class leaned over a mortar and pestle, grinding away at a mixture of granite, maple seeds, and blood.

Maddie's chest lurched, and a familiar pressure built up behind her eyes as the magic took hold. Her body froze and her mind went numb as a rock.

Shit, she thought.

It was the fifth time she had paralyzed herself. Maeve waited patiently for the spell to abate before she ordered Maddie into the "apprentice's position" on the floor. Maddie knelt down and sat on her ankles in front of her mistress.

"The problem is you," Maeve said.

"Me?"

Maeve glided over to the table. "You are not strong enough."

"But how can that be?" Maddie asked, twisting to face her. "Aren't I supposed to be some kind of . . . I don't know, infinite thing? Maybe I didn't make the spell correctly."

Maeve leaned over the bowl and sniffed. "The preparation is accurate."

"So, what's the problem?"

Maeve ladled out a bit of the potion and sipped. As her eyes went black, she brought up her hands and a dozen stones floated into the air. She snapped her fingers and they shot around the room like panicked sparrows.

"You are losing yourself to the magic," she said, "because you have no sense of yourself. Until you do, the essence of nature will overpower you, just as it did when you entered the Allsight."

"You're saying a rock has more willpower than I do?"

"I am."

"That doesn't make any sense."

Maeve let the stones drift back to the ground, catching one out of the air as it fell. "Doesn't it?" she asked. "This stone has been a stone since the beginning of the earth. You have not even been a woman for 20 years. Do you presume to know your existence better than the pebble understands its own?"

"But mistress, it isn't even alive."

"And that makes a difference?"

"You're saying I have to be a million years old to control a rock?"

Maeve came towards her and dropped the stone into her hands. "No," she said. "But you do have to control yourself. You must know what you want and understand the will that drives you to it."

Maddie started to get to her feet. Maeve's head snapped around, and she returned to her knees.

"But I do know what I want," Maddie said, tightening her jaw in frustration. "I want to be a witch."

"Do you?"

"Yes!"

Maeve sat down in her chair. "Why? Only a few short weeks ago, you did not even know the profession existed. Why do you care so much about it now?"

"Because I . . . I . . . " Maddie faltered. Maeve lifted an eyebrow, waiting. Maddie planted her fists on the floor and glared. "I could be good at this."

"True," Maeve answered, leaning back in her chair. "But that is not the first step. You are a fledgling, Madeline Foster, a bird in the nest, unable to fly on its own, and even the bird knows that it yearns to touch the sky. You have no such commitment, only curiosity and a vague sense that you must pursue whatever course seems most difficult. Perhaps you were an able student as a girl, but you are a poor example of a grown woman, and I cannot each someone who does not know the nature of their own ambition."

The witch's words cut deep, and Maddie winced.

"But I can learn this," she insisted.

"No, you cannot," Maeve said, her words falling on Maddie's shoulders like an anvil. "Witchcraft is not about learning, apprentice. It is about doing."

"But I can! Finn took me to see another witch in the city. I saw the work, and I want to do it!"

"Why?"

Maddie fumed. "Because!"

Maeve stood up, eying her with disdain as she turned sharply and walked to the door. "That is not good enough," she said. "The study of magic is a journey. The path is difficult, and it will not tolerate the footsteps of idle interest. You must *choose* to follow it, and until you can understand the urge that moves you, your efforts will inevitably fail. The Foxglove has gifted you with power, but the gates of magic do not open for children." She pulled the curtain aside. "You are dismissed."

Heart to Heart

"It isn't fair," Maddie said, pacing across the old kitchen while Rain cooked, tinkering with a new recipe for corn chowder.

"What isn't?" said Rain.

"This stupid training! There hasn't been a single class I've ever taken in my life where I haven't been able to manage at least a B."

"A what?"

"It's a grade. A good grade." Maddie threw herself onto a stool. "Why can't I handle this?"

Rain stirred the pot. "I wish I could help you," she said, "but I don't know much about witchcraft."

Maddie threw her arms up. "And Maeve is no help at all! All she tells me is that I'm not good enough."

"Really?"

Maddie paused, catching herself. "Okay, so she said more than that, but it wasn't very useful."

"What did she say?"

Maddie sat up straight and adopted an imperial pose. "'The gates of magic do not open for children,'" she said, feigning her mistress's voice. She furrowed her brow. "What the hell am I supposed to do with that?"

"Is that all she said?" Rain asked.

"No, she said other stuff," Maddie answered, kneading her tired eyes with her fists. "A bunch of crap about how I don't know why I want what I want. I mean, does it even matter? Isn't it enough that I agreed to become her apprentice?"

"Apparently not."

"So, you agree with me?"

Rain took her eyes off the pot and glanced over her shoulder. "Actually, no."

Maddie's face fell. "What do you mean, 'no'? Why not?"

Rain took the pot off the heat and sidled over to the table. "If you ask me, you sound a little entitled."

Maddie paused, stunned.

"I can't believe you just said that," she replied. "You think I feel like I deserve this?"

"No," Rain said. "I think you feel like you deserve everything."

Maddie stood up and backed away. "Rain! That's a horrible thing to say!"

"I'm just telling you the truth. You said it yourself: you don't know why you want to be a witch. So, why should you get to be one?" She came around the table. "Let me put it to you like this: When I spoke with Rose about becoming her matron, do you think she didn't ask me why I wanted the job?"

"I suppose she would have."

"And do you think I didn't need to have a good answer?"

"Sure."

"Well, this is the same, except instead of a person making the decision, it's the job itself. You say that you can learn to do anything, but that's not the same as *wanting* to do it. You're going to have to demonstrate that you're worthy of what you're asking for. I may not know much about witchcraft, but I know enough to tell you that magic is about what's in your heart, not your head. Do you see what I mean?"

Maddie grumbled. "I guess so, but I still don't know what to do."

Rain went back to the stove and ladled out a bowl of soup. "Go with your gut," she said. "Speaking of which, you look like you just clawed your way out of a graveyard. Eat this, and tell me what you think."

The first bite of the hearty cream stew brought on a wave of hunger. Maddie's spoon became a blur as she ate it up.

"How did you know you wanted to be a matron?" she asked between mouthfuls.

Rain grabbed another bowl and spoon and set them on a tray with the pot. "I guess I always knew," she said. "Growing up here, the palace was more than just a place to me. I owe everything I have to Rose and her home. When the time came, I wanted to be a part of taking care of it."

Maddie set down her spoon. She'd never felt that way about anywhere. Her home was just a house. "That's very sweet," she said.

Rain reached across the table and pressed a finger against the middle of Maddie's chest. "You see what I mean?" she said. "Heart."

Maddie stared down at her bowl. It was empty. "I don't have a heart anymore."

Rain wrapped her up in a hug. "That's not true of anyone." She said, letting go to gather up the tray. "Actually, you know who you should talk to?"

"Who?"

"Kidhe."

Maddie crossed the room to the window and peered out. The aviary was just barely visible through the branches.

"Why?" she asked.

"Because," Rain said, joining her. "He's the only person I know who's always known exactly what he wants."

Away from It All

"So," Maddie said, "will you help me?"

Kidhe leaned up from the railing, lifted a sack of birdseed, and tipped it over into a trough. A donkey-sized finch began pecking away at the kernels. Maddie stood across from the two of them, trying to forget the fact that she'd been up all night.

"I don't know. It's tough," he said.

"Well, apparently you're the man for the job."

His eyes twinkled. "Is that so?"

"Don't let it go to your head. I still think your beard looks stupid."

Kidhe tossed the empty sack aside. "Strange thing to say to someone you're asking for help."

"Hey, you were the one that started all this."

"How do you figure that?!"

"You introduced me to the princess. If it weren't for you, no one ever would have figured out that I'm some kind of ancient . . . whatever."

Kidhe picked up a rag and cleaned off his hands. "Well, that *definitely* makes sense."

"It does!"

"And far be it from me to argue with the most powerful being in the universe."

Maddie clenched her fists. "I am not the most powerful being in the universe."

"You might be."

"I am not!"

He backed off, putting up his hands. "Okay, okay!"

Maddie took a deep breath, glaring at him as he stood in front of her. "Are you going to help me or not?"

"Get in touch with your heart? Yeah, I'll help you, although right from the start, I can tell you you're going about this the wrong way." He flopped down at a little table covered in tools and strips of leather.

Maddie sat across from him. "Oh?"

He picked up a couple of the strips and started braiding them together, fingers working deftly while he spoke. "You're too good a student. That's your problem."

Maddie scoffed.

"I'm serious! You approach everything so analytically. I joined the wardens because I wanted to fly, not because I thought it would be a great career opportunity. If you want to understand your heart, you're going to have to learn to let go."

"And you can teach me to do that?"

He glanced up with a wily grin. "I have a few ideas."

Maddie crossed her arms. "I swear to God, Kidhe—"

"Relax! Relax, it's not a pick-up line." He paused. "Okay, it would be a pretty good pick up line."

"Kidhe!"

He sat back and tossed the braided leather onto the table. "Alright," he said. "What makes you happy?"

Maddie thought it over. "I don't know."

"It's a simple question."

"I don't know!" Maddie insisted. "Video games, jogging . . . What do you want me to say?"

"A-ha!" he said, jumping up and pointing a finger at her face. "See? You're looking for the right answer!"

Maddie pushed his finger away. "Well, what the hell else am I supposed to do?!"

"Think for yourself," he said. "*Feel* for yourself. You're too close. You've got to find a way to step back. Maeve said she wanted to know why you wanted to be a witch, but why does anybody want to do anything? You have to think about the things that bring you joy, and make your heart beat faster. One of them is bound to be the reason becoming a witch feels right."

He pulled her towards the stairs. "Come with me."

"Where are we going?" Maddie asked as they emerged onto the flight deck.

Kidhe put his fingers to his lips and blew a shrill whistle out into the forest. "Anywhere," he answered. "I've got my own ride."

A black shape emerged from the trees, and Maddie gaped as a 30-foot crow banked around the flight deck, swooping in to perch on the edge. The boards creaked under its weight as it hunkered down like a chicken and Kidhe took her over.

"Oh my God," she said. "You're *that* guy."

Kidhe climbed up onto the crow's back, gripping the feathers like he was climbing a ladder. "I'm who?"

"The guy!" Maddie said. "The guy in high school who already has a car and thinks it makes him look cool."

Kidhe threw down a rope. "Does it?"

Maddie paused. "A little," she said, fighting the words as they came out of her mouth. "Maybe."

"His name is Earnest," Kidhe said, brushing the bird's feathers with his palm. "Want to go for a spin?"

Maddie craned her head back. "How? I don't see any saddle."

The bird cawed. The sound was like a stick of dynamite going off in her ears.

"Hey!" Kidhe shouted, calling to the bird. "Calm down!"

He slid down the rope, leaned in, and whispered, "Earnest doesn't like the 's' word. I can barely get him to wear the harness, so we'll be flying au naturel."

"Is that safe?"

Kidhe cackled. "Not in the least."

Maddie followed Kidhe up the rope, grabbing onto the complex weave of hempen cords that made up the bird's harness, which wrapped around the animal's neck and shoulders like a vest. She sat down in front of him.

"There are loops by your legs," he said. "Put your feet in."

Maddie slipped her toes into the ropes and pressed down with her heels. She felt the ropes stretch under her boots.

Kidhe reached forward to tie a rope around her waist. "It's going to feel choppy when we take off, so try to stay loose. If you want to grab onto something, hold this piece here . . ."

He pointed to a thick, round knot twisted into the harness where a saddle-horn would be. Maddie latched onto it as Kidhe took up the reins. The bird's shoulders shifted as it got to its feet, flapping its wings for balance.

Maddie's hands tightened as a trickle of adrenaline threaded its way into her chest.

"Ready?" Kidhe asked.

"I think I need a minute," Maddie answered, tightening her grip.

Kidhe whipped the reins and whistled. "Here we go!"

"No, I said wai—*whoa*!"

Maddie screamed for a solid minute as the crow's voice shattered the air in a flurry of beating wings. Wind rushed past her as she clung to the ropes and did her best to "stay loose," but her muscles seized up so tight they might as well have been turned to stone.

The bird thundered into the air, its huge limbs pumping up and down as it climbed into the sky. The air thumped past Maddie in waves, and she clenched her teeth, pressing her eyes shut until the sound and motion gradually leveled out, leaving only the quiet whisper of the breeze.

"You can relax now," Kidhe said.

Maddie opened one eye and then snapped it shut. "You expect me to relax after that?!"

"We're in the air now," Kidhe said, thumping her on the back. "It's alright. Try to balance in the stirrups and let the ropes do the work."

Maddie let her muscles ease as she maintained her grip on the harness. The ropes yawned and stretched, and she flinched, eyes still clamped shut.

Kidhe pulled her up into a sitting position. "Take it easy. You can't fall, remember? You're tied on. Have a look around."

Maddie opened her eyes and drew in a breath. The forest rolled out beneath them like a patchwork quilt, teeming with color and life. In the distance, the outline of the skyscrapers stood in silhouette, towering over a horizon of trees.

It was easy to forget that the Veil was more than just a city in a tree. It was here in Chicago alongside everything else. Kidhe pulled gently on the reins and Earnest banked around, swooping through the air like a kite on a wire. Maddie tightened her grip on the saddle knot.

"Lean into the turns," Kidhe said, "and loosen up. The stirrups will hold you."

He banked around again. Maddie did her best to lean a few inches.

Kidhe shoved her. Maddie felt the ropes go taut as her foot pressed down in the stirrup and she found herself staring down at the ground with nothing to hold her but a few inches of weathered rope. She screamed and thrashed, grabbing Kidhe by the arm as he held her shirt.

"I'm going to kill you!" she roared.

Earnest leveled out. Kidhe kept his hand gripped tight around a clump of her shirt as he steered the bird through the air in lazy swings, and gradually, heartbeat by heartbeat, Maddie felt her pulse slow down and the muscles in her neck and shoulders loosen, until the air rushing over her face and the subtle pull of gravity no longer felt like death. They carried on for half an hour before Kidhe pulled on the reins and Earnest settled down on a branch.

"Better?" Kidhe asked.

"A little," Maddie admitted. "I'm still going to kill you. That was awful." She could just barely see the rising crown of the city tree in the distance. "We're really far," she said, chewing on her cheek. "Rose asked me to stay in the city."

"I know."

"You do?"

"Captain of the wardens, remember?" he said, pointing to his badge. "Don't worry, we'll head back soon. You've still got the ward Maeve gave you, right?"

Maddie pulled it up out of her collar. "All present and accounted for."

"Then we should be fine," Kidhe said. "And if anything does come up, I'll protect you." He thumped a proud fist against his chest.

"Uh huh," Maddie said.

"Hey! I'm very qualified!"

"Sure, you've even got a beard."

"Will you stop making fun of my beard?!" His hand moved protectively to the thin line of fuzz on his chin.

Maddie stuck her tongue out at him and leaned back, hanging onto the saddle knot as she surveyed the landscape. "Do you fly like this often?" she asked.

Kidhe picked his feet up out of the stirrups and perched cross-legged on the bird's back. "Pretty regularly, though I usually go deeper in the Veil. It's kind of my escape. I like to get away for a few days every month or so."

"Like camping?"

"More or less, but the deep Veil isn't like a regular forest. It has layers and moods. The place where I go, it's always warm, the weather is calm, and there isn't a sound in the world."

Maddie closed her eyes and tried to picture it. "You make it sound like paradise."

"I guess it is, for me."

Maddie envied him. She never seemed to be able to get away from her problems for long, or maybe she just didn't have the head for letting them go. It was like she preferred to be haunted, as though anything less would be somehow irresponsible. She'd spent too much of her life under pressure. Another honors course, another AP class, another after-school tutor . . . Now, anything less than the most she could give felt like a cop out. And for what? Another call from her mother? A few, brief words of congratulation?

She grumbled and pulled herself forward to lie down on Earnest's feathers. She'd lived for those calls.

Thanks, mom, she thought. *I can't even get away from you in fairy land.*

Her daydream was cut short by a roll of thunder, and both their eyes shot up. A smattering of thick raindrops began to fall as a line of black clouds darkened the sky overhead, flashing with hidden bursts of lightning.

"We should go back," Maddie said.

Kidhe's eyes scanned the clouds, and he shook his head. "We'd never make it in time," he said, flicking the reins. Earnest took to the sky. "We'll have to try to get under it."

"Under it? You mean on the ground?"

The crow dipped down into the trees and began threading through the trunks.

"No," Kidhe answered. "Deeper."

He shut his eyes. A crack of thunder shattered the sky, and all around them, the forest began to change.

Concerning Flight

Maddie did her best not to develop a fear of flying that day, but even under the shelter of the trees, the wind, rain, and thunder introduced her to a whole new variety of terror. She couldn't even keep her eyes closed as she clung to Earnest's harness. When she did, flashes of lightning and the roar of thunder came through all the more clearly, and the swirling wind made her feel like she was falling. So she hung on, eyes open to the stinging rain, staring in wide-eyed horror at the storm.

Kidhe still had his eyes shut as they streaked through the trees. Earnest was steering himself. The forest rose higher into the angry green clouds as they plunged through the layers of the Veil. Smaller trees vanished, disbursing like fog as their huge cousins replaced them. Below, the underbrush crept up, scaling the trunks, a jungle of emergent growth.

AARON MCQUEEN

An oak tree the size of a water tower sprang into view directly in front of them. Earnest squawked, turning sharply, and Maddie held on to the harness with all her strength, shoving her arm under the ropes in a desperate attempt to steady herself. Her foot slipped out of its stirrup and swung into the air.

"Shit!" she shouted.

Kidhe's hand shot out and grabbed her ankle, pulling her back down as Earnest dove, sweeping into the undergrowth to get out of the rain.

Maddie's skin crawled as a familiar feeling of magic began to fill the air. It raced across her skin like electrified water, prickling in her hair and behind her eyes. She could taste it, bittersweet, like a battery on her tongue. The sensations were so intense, she didn't even notice the storm beginning to die down as they tucked and turned through the brush.

"It's over," Kidhe finally said.

It was still raining, but the thunder and lightning were gone, replaced by the low white noise of a soft and heavy wind.

"What happened?" she asked.

Kidhe loosened his grip on the reins. "We got under it. The storm is above us in the Veil."

Maddie allowed herself to breathe as her eyes took in shimmering wet leaves and sparse light seeping down from the canopy. Waterfalls of emerald vines hung from the branches, shifting gently in the breeze, while boulders the size of houses littered the ground. Between them, huge wildflowers burst in flashes of vibrant color like splats of neon paint.

Earnest swooped down into a narrow ravine. The wind whistled along the passage, and Maddie shivered.

"I'm sorry about this," Kidhe said. "I should have checked the weather report before we left."

"It's alright," Maddie said through chattering teeth. "I'm sure I'll forgive you eventually."

Kidhe steered Earnest to the bottom of the ravine, and they came to rest on a sheltered ledge at the mouth of a cave. Storm runoff broke over smooth stone a few feet below, casting white foam up into the air to wet their shoes.

"We're here," Kidhe said, undoing Maddie's safety rope.

He threw the rope down, and Earnest settled onto the stone floor of the ledge. Maddie kicked her foot over the harness. Her muscles stretched like old rubber bands as she made her way to the ground.

"Where is here?" she asked.

Kidhe jumped down. "My place." He undid a few knots and pulled the harness off Earnest, who fluffed out his feathers and shook, spritzing them with water. Kidhe stroked the bird's neck.

"Thanks for getting us through that, buddy," he said. Earnest chortled.

Maddie wrapped her arms around her shoulders. "You live in a cave?"

Kidhe hung up the harness on a row of pegs driven into the cave wall. "Not exactly," he said. "Come on. It's this way."

He led her towards the back of the cave. The smell of musty pine needles and dirt followed them as they passed into a low tunnel, and behind them, the forest slipped away into darkness.

A warm wind emerged from the shadows ahead, where a tiny spec of light came into view. Maddie kept her eyes it as she followed Kidhe forward. They left the damp tunnel behind and emerged onto a gentle slope at the edge of an open field.

Tall grass carpeted the ground, reaching her knees, broken only by patches of red and white mushrooms and prairie flowers the color of polished silver. The moon shone bright above their heads, filling the sky with sheets of white light that fell like blankets in the wind. Specks of multicolored pollen drifted on the breeze.

"This is impossible," Maddie said.

Kidhe glanced back over his shoulder. "Not bad, eh?"

"But we were underground," Maddie said, reaching out to catch a mote of pollen in her palm. "And it was daytime. How can this be?"

"Magic, of course," Kidhe replied as he took her hand and led her down the slope and across the field. "Practitioners call places like these 'delves.'"

"Delves?"

They came to stand on a hump of earth overlooking the landscape.

"Think of it like a pocket," Kidhe said. "Moving deeper into the Veil is all about your state of mind. Most people these days can't get very far. We've gotten too used to the ordinary world, but a delve is connected to the shallow parts of the Veil. If you know where the entrance is, you can walk right in."

"The cave," Maddie said.

He nodded. "No one knows how they form, but they're very rare and filled with powerful magic." He pointed to a cluster of trees at the bottom of the slope. "That's where we're going."

Maddie pulled back. "What about the curtain? Won't we lose our memories?"

"Don't worry. Delves are protected from the mist by a layer of magic. It usually manifests as some kind of physical barrier. See those mountains?" He pointed back up the slope. In the distance, it rose up into a barrier of steep, gray peaks. "We're safe," he said, reaching out to her.

Maddie took his hand and followed him into the trees. Their path wound back and forth until it finally broke free into a clearing, where she found herself suddenly staring up at an enormous tree stump. Moss grew up the sides in thick patches around little wooden windows set deep into the wood. Clear glass made up the front entrance, which looked like a cross between a greenhouse and a street lamp, glued to the stump with hard-packed clay.

"Home sweet home?" Maddie asked.

The glass door creaked as Kidhe swung it open.

"It's where the heart is," he said. "Good a place as any to get in touch with yours."

Delve

Maddie stepped into the room, and her footsteps echoed with a hollow thump against the floorboards. Moonlight streamed through the windows, washing the furniture with tomb-like calm. A clay fireplace sat in the corner, fixed with an iron rack and spit, with a low, ramshackle couch in front of it. In the kitchen, a manual water pump protruded from the floor, dripping into a steel washtub.

Half-finished projects lay out on every surface: a torn harness here, a broken buckle there . . . There were dirty clothes on the floor and a week's worth of dishes piled in the sink. A smile crept onto Maddie's face as Kidhe buzzed around the room, hastily tidying up.

"Sorry about the mess," he said, heaping the clothes up into his arms. "I'm not actually ready for company." He tossed the pile into the next room.

"It's alright," Maddie said, peeking through the door. It was a bedroom. "It's nice. Very homey."

He blushed and hustled to the fireplace. "You're the first person I've ever brought here," he said, lighting it with a long match. "I've got some dry clothes in the closet, and we can hang the rest up on the mantle. They'll smell like smoke, but at least they'll be dry. I'll make us some tea while you get changed."

The fire crackled, hissing as the flames took hold. Kidhe took her through to the bedroom and went to a wardrobe against the wall, returning with a fur poncho and some trousers.

"Here you go," he said, showing himself out.

Maddie thanked him and shut the door before surveying the room: dresser, wastebasket, wardrobe. Her eyes settled on the bed, a heap of mismatched cushions and furs arranged in a fuzzy mound. She shivered as she peeled off her clothes, slipped out of her shoes, and got changed. She tied her hair up, headed back to the couch, and all but stuffed her feet into the fire.

Kidhe was in the kitchen. He'd ditched his shirt, which was now hanging from the mantle. Maddie watched him work, pumping water into an iron kettle. There was something pleasing about the image. Maddie found herself staring for just a moment. It was a childish reaction, she knew, but she was in a tree trunk in the deep Veil with the Faerie version of Davy Crockett, so she gave herself a pass. Besides, she didn't even know she *liked* tattoos.

Ink flowed down from his shoulders and across his chest in a pattern of tangled vines and thin red flowers. Maybe it was the twilight outside or the glow from the hearth, but Maddie's eyes locked on for a full 30 seconds as he hung the kettle over the fire and went to change. He didn't seem to notice.

The water was boiling when he came back. He fetched a pair of wooden cups from the kitchen, poured out the tea, and sat beside Maddie.

She looked down into the cup. The liquid was cloudy and had a musty smell.

"What is it?" she asked.

"Pine needles and herbs," Kidhe answered.

Maddie took a drink. The tea tasted like summertime and sage, with a hint of citrus that was bitter and refreshing. It soothed her throat and warmed her from the inside out as she laid her head against the couch and sighed. They sat in silence as they drank the tea and let the fire slowly bake them dry.

"What do I do now?" Maddie asked.

Kidhe lifted his head off the couch and opened his eyes. "Hmm?"

"You're supposed to be my guide, right? What's next?"

"That's up to you," he said, groaning as he sat up and refilled his tea. "I'm not a witch. I don't know how it works."

"You're not very helpful."

"Hey, I made the tea."

Maddie glanced at the kettle. "The tea was great," she said, "but I'm supposed to be figuring out why I can't do magic, remember?"

He stood up with a grunt. "Maybe it's good that we ended up here," he said, taking her hand to pull her off the couch. "It's probably the most magical place for hundreds of miles. Why don't you go outside and poke around? Get in touch with your roots."

"Just . . . poke around?" Maddie said, looking out the window. "By myself?"

"It's completely safe. No one but me even knows this place exists."

AARON MCQUEEN

"What if there are wild animals or something? What if I get lost?"

"Maybe getting lost is the point. You're trying to discover something new inside yourself. It makes sense you'd have to get away from what you know to find it."

"And how will I get back?"

Kidhe went to a workbench and rooted around in the clutter before returning with a wooden object. "Take this," he said, dropping it in her hands. It was a whistle, hand-carved from an old, worn branch. "The sound carries for miles. Just blow on it when you're ready, and I'll come get you."

Maddie ran her fingers across its pitted surface. "Are you sure this is going to work?"

He grinned and walked her to the door. The moonlight poured in through the glass as he opened it and said, "Have a little faith."

Natural Inclination

It's not the worst idea in the world, Maddie thought as she marched into the woods. There was a kind of straightforward logic to Kidhe's plan that she could appreciate. If you think too much, find a place where there's nothing to do but feel.

She was no good at feeling. Years of public education had trained it out of her.

The branches parted on their own as she walked, revealing thick, velvety grass, stained by the moonlight. Maddie wished she'd brought her running shoes. She'd never been in a forest so cooperative.

Think about what makes you happy. One of them is bound to be why becoming a witch feels right. She recalled Kidhe's words pointedly and knelt down to brush the earth. The grass was soft, and the stones were smooth beneath her fingers.

Why not? she thought.

She stretched for a minute and ran, dashing barefoot through the trees. The brush rolled back like a retreating tide, leaving only cushioned earth bathed in silver light. The air flowed into her lungs like cool water, washing away her fears until the only feeling that remained was the burn of exertion growing in her legs and the wind pushing against her back. She forgot about time and school and how she still needed to figure out the answer to Maeve's question. It was just her and the trail, like it was back in high school, when her father was alive, and life was simple and sure.

She emerged on the other side of the woods and ran out into the field, feeling the grass brush against her skin. The ground yielded to the pounding of her feet, and for a moment it was as though she could feel the beating of her own steps against her chest. The sense of the ground bled into her thoughts as she shut her eyes and carried on, losing herself in the sensation. Grass. Chest. Ground. Light.

It wasn't until her foot splashed into cold water that she opened her eyes and looked around. The woods lay far behind her, a smudge against the landscape. At her feet, a clear, narrow brook wound its way slowly downhill. The sound of the stream played in her ears like music, joined in harmony by the soothing breath of the wind.

Maddie followed the water, drawn along the dreamlike path, strange and yet familiar. Sometime, somehow, she was sure that she had been this way before. Her eyes flicked out ahead, pursuing an elusive impulse around each new corner. Down and down, away from the woods and the hill she tracked the current, quickening her pace until the grass fell away and she came upon a pool. The sight of it stunned her in her tracks.

It can't be, she thought, turning in a circle as she examined her surroundings. It was the pool from the forest preserve. Her body suddenly rippled with tingling sensation as the magic in the air gathered around her and beaded on her skin like morning dew.

It was impossible, but it was true. This was the Veil, after all, a reflection of the so-called real world. As she stood beside the crisp, clear water, staring down at the silver slice of the moon on its surface, she knew that not two months earlier, on the other side of the looking glass, she'd been standing on this very spot. She knelt down, dipping her hand into the crystal surface to bring the water to her mouth.

It tasted like perfectly ordinary water, and nothing happened.

Maddie flopped down and let her head fall back, staring up at the sky as she laughed. She wasn't sure what she'd been expecting. A vision? Another trance? Or perhaps some magical creature that would tell her what to do next? But there was no answer; only a pool at the bottom of a hill. Lesson learned.

"This is stupid," she said aloud. "I give up. Maeve can find someone else to be her apprentice."

But even as she spoke the words, she knew she didn't believe them. She would never let herself do something like that. Finn said she liked to feel like the smartest person in the room, and maybe he was right. She'd spent her entire life trying to live up to her potential, and now here she was, standing on the threshold of infinite possibility. All she had to do was reach out and take it.

And she did want to take it.

Maddie got on all fours and crawled back to the pool to look at her reflection. She had her father's eyes, but the rest came from her mother. Maddie could see her genes in the lines of her cheekbones and the way her hair fell around her shoulders.

Her mother liked knowing she could look after people. Maddie wondered, how much of the world could she look after as the Foxglove? The whole thing, probably. The truth was that she didn't want to live out her life in a library, or leave the world behind and hide in the woods, or even heal one poor kid's leg. She wanted to be responsible for more. She knew she could be, and if not her, who?

Okay, maybe I am a little egocentric, she thought, swishing her hand through the water as she got to her feet. *I guess it runs in the family.*

Kidhe's whistle trilled across the landscape. There wouldn't be a phone call this time around, but somehow, Maddie believed her mother would know that she was doing the most she could.

Big people needed big dreams, after all.

Resolve

It was late by the time they got back to the city. Maddie left Kidhe at the aviary and went straight to Maeve's. She found the witch sitting in a chair by the fireplace, perusing the pages of Rose's old, weathered book. Maddie looked at the woman with newfound respect as she stepped forward, summoning as much confidence as she could muster.

"You're back," Maeve said, not looking up.

Maddie stood in front of her. "I am."

Maeve set the book aside. "And have you found your purpose?"

What do you want to be when you grow up? Maddie thought, recalling the old thoughts with a hidden smile. Crossing over into the Veil hadn't given her the answer; it had supplied the beginning of the real question. Who did she want to be? Turns out, she knew the answer all along. She just couldn't bring herself to say it.

"I have," she said.

Maeve folded her hands in her lap and fixed her with an impassive stare. "So, why do you want to be a witch, Madeline Foster?"

Maddie took a long breath.

"I am my mother's daughter," she said. "I used to think I loved my father more. He was always there for me. He helped me do my homework, and took me to the beach. He gave me my childhood, but he never really taught me about growing up.

"My mother showed me what it would be like to be strong. It's lonely, and . . . thankless." Maddie choked back a pang of guilt. "I didn't want to be anything like her, but the truth is, there's more of her in me than anything else."

She took out her stone knife. "I want to be a witch," she said, "because I have what it takes to use that power. If I don't, all the good I might have accomplished with it goes undone." She cut her hand, and held her bleeding palm out in front of her. "And I wasn't raised to accept that kind of failure."

There was a long silence while Maddie held her breath.

Maeve crossed the floor to a cabinet in the corner and opened it. "You will find your tools and supplies in here. Ensure that they are clean whenever you put them away."

Maddie's wooden heart skipped a beat. The folds of a long, black robe hung inside, embroidered with a nearly invisible pattern of dark thread. Maddie tiptoed over to it and felt the thick cloth between her fingertips.

"You knew I would be back," she said.

"I suspected," Maeve replied.

Maddie put the robe on. A heavy mortar and pestle, a hand-cranked grinder, and a dizzying array of silver tools and glass containers shimmered in the dark. Maddie paused when her eyes fell upon a familiar steel cleaver hanging on a hook. There was a leather butcher's apron beside it.

"Prepare yourself, apprentice," Maeve said. "We have work do."

The Matter at Hand

"A dinner party?" Maddie asked. "Isn't it a little late? I thought I was going to get another chance to do magic."

Maeve carried on up the stairs in front of her, heading to the royal apartment. "Being a member of a royal house often entails compromise, and it is not a 'dinner party.' Rose is meeting with several ambassadors from the other faerie realms. Our presence is required as a matter of protocol."

"But why?"

"They are influential members of very old cities, and their votes will determine the fate of Amaranth. Rose has been the leader of this realm for more than a hundred years. She is not about to let it slip through her fingers by failing to observe the social graces."

"So, she wants to impress them?"

"Indeed. Rose must demonstrate that Amaranth is capable of standing on its own, against social disorder, natural disaster, political pressure, and if necessary, war."

"Kidhe told me about that," Maddie said. "Do you think it will happen?"

Maeve stopped, pausing for a moment as she considered her response. "It does not appear likely," she said, "but there are powerful parties at work, and it would be foolish to take risks."

"So, what do I do?" Maddie asked.

"Speak when you are spoken to. You are an apprentice, and your role is to assist me. Do you understand?"

"Roger that."

Maeve's head snapped around, and she gave Maddie a sharp look.

"Yes, mistress," Maddie corrected herself. She was still getting used to the terminology.

They stopped in front of the door. "And the introduction I taught you?" Maeve said, cracking it open.

"I remember, mistress."

"We're down here," Rose called as they walked in. "Come join us!"

Maeve gestured for Maddie to go ahead of her, and she obeyed, standing up straight as she preceded the witch down the stairs.

"Good evening," she said, stopping at the bottom to recite her lines. "May I present my mistress, Maeve fer Carline."

Rose stood up along with her guests and bowed. "Welcome."

There were two guests in attendance, gathered around what Maddie was fairly certain was an elaborate tray of raw bug slices and roasted fruit. Maddie eyed the dish warily. She'd been in the Veil long enough to know that the faeries rarely ate "normal" food, but insect sushi was over the line.

One of the guests set down her drink and came to stand in front of Maddie. A cascade of hair the color of roasted coffee fell to her waist. Woven bands of tartan plaid lay in folds across her dress.

"The human," she said with an accent that rolled like wind off the hills. "And I hear you're a witch as well."

Maddie looked down at the floor and curtsied. "Yes, ma'am."

"A pleasure to meet you," she said, extending a hand. Maddie held it briefly.

"Maddie, this is Brynna fer Dynna," Rose said. "The ambassador from Thistle."

"Or Glasgow," Brynna said. "Whichever. And it's okay if you think it's a funny name."

"Funny name?" Maddie asked.

Brynna set her hands against her broad hips and gave her shoulders a roll. "Brynna for Dynna? For dinner? Get it?"

Maddie's cheeks went red. "I didn't!" she said. "I mean, I don't!"

"That's sweet of you, my dear," Brynna said, returning to her seat on the couch as the queen's second guest approached. A flash of white hair, trimmed almost to the point of baldness, ran back along the center of her head, all but disappearing against her pale complexion. A sleeveless dress of pearl silk embraced her slender arms and legs.

"This is Ida fer Egrette," Rose said. "Her city is Mullein, outside Stockholm."

Ida put out a hand. "Lovely to finally meet you," she said. "I've been looking forward to speaking with a human. How's your civilization coming along?"

"We're getting by," Maddie said, taking her hand and smiling to suppress a laugh. "What do you mean, 'finally'?"

Rose ushered them all back to the table. "News travels fast. Word of your arrival in the Veil has brought on quite an interest."

"Aye," Brynna added. "I can think of quite a few ambassadors who will be coming just to see you." She handed Maddie a glass of cloudy liquid. "You're quite the celebrity. Come, sit. Have some wine with us."

Maddie looked between the drink, Maeve, and Rose. "But I'm only an apprentice," she said. "And I'm not 21."

"21?" Brynna asked, furrowing her brow. "What does that have to do w —"

"You'll have to forgive her," Ida interrupted. "Brynna, in this country, children aren't allowed alcohol."

"Children? She's a grown woman!"

"I'm sure one glass wouldn't hurt," Rose said.

"Thistle was one of the first faerie cities," Ida said as they all sat down. "It's deeper in the Veil than most. Brynna probably hasn't seen a human in 50 years."

The sharp flavors of lemon and grass cut bitterly across Maddie's tongue as she sipped her wine. "What is this?" she asked.

"Honeydew wine," Rose answered.

"As in the melon?"

Ida drained her glass. "As in the aphid."

Brynna gave a hearty laugh. "Thank mother nature for sap-suckers," she said. "Just don't ask how the farmers collect it. I saw the process once, and it almost put me off it for good."

"Is this everybody?" Maeve asked.

All eyes turned to Rose. "I'm afraid not," she answered. "We're still waiting for someone."

Brynna sneered. "Don't tell me you invited *her*. When did she even get here?"

"This morning," Rose answered. "As I understand it, she has orders from Aster to do everything she can to vote us down. I'm hoping the three of us can convince her to change her mind."

"Impossible," Ida responded, shaking her head.

"Well, we should at least try."

"Hell of a reason to muck up a good evening," Brynna commented.

Someone coughed. They turned as a tall older woman descended the stairs. Iron gray hair, bound in a painfully tight bun behind her head, swept back from her face. The silk of her dress flowed over her feet in a wash of dusky silver.

"Delilah," Rose said, opening her arms and moving to greet her as everyone got to their feet.

"Rose," Delilah said tersely. She turned to Ida. "Madam Egrette."

Ida bowed. "Ma'am."

Delilah did not address the Scottish ambassador. Instead, she directed her eyes to Maddie. "You are the human witch," she said.

Maddie bowed low and extended a hand and said, "Yes, ambassador."

The woman turned up her nose. "Disgusting."

Maddie straightened up and took a step back, anger flaring in her chest. She glanced at Maeve, who shook her head to keep her silent.

"You needn't worry about your evening," Delilah went on. "I won't be joining you. My instructions are clear, and there is nothing you can say that will change Aster's opinion. Amaranth must be dissolved. There can be no other outcome."

"Not if I have anything to say about it," said Brynna.

Delilah stared down her nose at her. "Where is your matron?" she asked Rose. "My party will require quarters."

Rain materialized on cue and Maddie practically jumped. She hadn't even noticed her in the room.

"Rain will see to your needs," Rose said.

Maddie shivered when the door swung shut.

"What the hell is her problem?" she asked.

"An old argument," Rose answered as Brynna brought her a fresh glass of wine. "Amaranth used to be a part of Aster. If the vote fails, we will be rolled back into their kingdom. Obviously, her motivations are clear. As for her personality, I'm fairly certain she was born with a stone in her shoe."

Brynna barked out a laugh. "Or a stick up her a—"

"Brynna!" said Rose.

Brynna sat back down. "Fine, fine. I'll be polite, but only to make things easier on you. It doesn't matter, anyway. Aster gets one vote like everybody else, and my people are telling me that diplomatic opinion is heavily in your favor."

"No one wants to see Aster get any stronger," Ida added.

Rose returned to her chair. "Let's just hope nothing changes now that she's here. Aster has a healthy treasury."

"She's going to try to buy the vote?" Maddie said.

"Undoubtedly," Ida replied. "Rose, you can count on our support. Brynna?"

The Scottish ambassador tipped the last of the wine into her glass. "Oh, absolutely. I'd sooner see that bitch in the grave than sitting on your throne."

"We should reach out to everyone who's already here," Rose said, massaging her forehead. "Let them know they'll be getting a visit from Aster. Hopefully we can keep them from becoming intimidated."

The meal ended with tea and coffee, and the ambassadors retired to their rooms, leaving Maddie and Maeve to sit alone with Rose by the fire. The queen finished her wine. "That could have gone better," she said, staring forlornly at the empty bottle.

"Indeed," Maeve said. "I doubt Brynna's impression helped matters."

Rose sighed. "She was right, though. Aster was never going to vote our way."

"She called me disgusting," Maddie said. "I wanted to punch her in the face."

Maeve went to a table in the corner to fetch another bottle of wine. "Delilah is part of an old family," she said, refilling the queen's glass. "They have very . . . traditional opinions on the subject of humanity. She believes that faeries and humans should remain separate, while Rose has always taken a more modern approach, allowing human food and goods to be brought into the city, for example."

"Human food is illegal in Aster?" Maddie asked.

"No," Rose answered. "But that doesn't stop the aristocrats wishing it were. I've known Delilah for over 500 years, and she and I have never gotten along. I suppose it's just her upbringing."

"Or the stick Brynna mentioned," Maddie said.

Rose chuckled and sat back against the cushions. "Or that," she said. "Either way, your presence here is a problem for her. Brynna wasn't joking when she said you've caused a stir. I suspect she's worried that your celebrity will somehow tip the scales in our favor."

Maddie glared at the door. "I'll do everything I can to help."

"Thank you," Rose said. "How are your studies going?"

"Better soon, I hope. It took me a little while to get my mojo working."

"Speaking of which," said Maeve, "we should return to the laboratory."

"Now?" Maddie asked. "I haven't slept in over a day!"

The clock chimed 11.

"Come along, apprentice," Maeve said, starting up the stairs.

Rose stood up as Maddie got out of her seat. The queen swept her into a hug. "I'm so proud of you," she said. "Now go on. Back to work."

The words echoed in the halls of Maddie's memory. Her mother used to say the same thing. A day ago, the sentence would have stung; now, it made her feel at home.

She hurried up the stairs after Maeve. The witching hour was approaching, and this time, she was ready.

Tricks of the Trade

Morrow swept the mop across the floor, spreading gray water and suds over oil and spilled soda. It was late, the restaurant was closed, and Leoh had left early, leaving Morrow behind to clean up.

It was funny. Morrow couldn't think of a single person back home that he could trust, yet here he was, alone and unsupervised. Leoh hadn't even locked up the day's earnings. They were a genial people, these surface-dwelling Faeries. Morrow was reminded of the years he'd spent with his mother in his youth, before Gwynedd's rise to power and the slow decline that followed.

The mop slid across the tiles rhythmically. It was honest work, and he felt good doing it.

The bell over the front door rang.

"We're closed," Morrow said. "Sorry, I forgot to lock up."

A cool voice answered him. "I'm here for a private party."

Morrow stopped and took a breath before turning to face the person he already knew was there. "I suppose it was only a matter of time before you came around," he said.

Gwynedd swept across the room to the counter. "Not happy to see me? You certainly seem to be settling in. What have you been doing all this time besides cleaning floors?"

"Following your instructions," Morrow said. "The girl hasn't come around much. What are you doing here?"

His mistress waved an idle hand back out at the city. "I came to meet some friends."

"Friends?" Morrow asked, crossing his arms.

"Of sorts. Then I thought I would come visit you, since I was in the area." She put out a hand to his cheek. His skin practically froze over at her touch. "My humble ward," she said. "The time has come to move our little plan forward."

Morrow pulled away and retreated behind the counter. "I'm doing everything I can. I've built a relationship here, just like you said, but you have to be patient. These things take time."

His mistress tutted. "Have you forgotten everything I taught you?" she asked. "And so quickly? Opportunities don't come knocking, little prince. The solstice is approaching, and you and I have no time left to waste."

Morrow took a deep breath. He had not missed her pet name for him. "What would you have me do? Go to the palace and knock on her door?"

Gwynedd reached into her robes. "You will invent a reason to visit her," she said. "And when you do, you will leave her with this." She held out a pendant the size of a large coin, fixed with a copper wedge molded to look like a slice of pizza.

"A necklace," Morrow said as he took it. "Cute."

"You've been living among these Faeries too long," his mistress said. "Look closer."

Morrow turned it over. His eyes picked out a tiny hole drilled into the edge of the pendant's design. "A microphone?" he asked.

His mistress nodded. "The girl is warded," she said. "Ordinarily, I deplore human technology, but in this case their ingenuity will work to our advantage. The battery has enough charge to last three days. Be sure to get it to her before then. There must be time once she has it to obtain the evidence I need."

"Evidence of what?"

"That she is the Foxglove, of course, and that Rose has been concealing her true nature from the representatives of the realms."

"But why go to all the trouble?"

"Because I require their outrage. Do not ask questions, little prince. You need only do as you are told."

Morrow rubbed his thumb across the pendant. The copper glinted in the moonlight coming through the windows. Morrow's heart sank as he realized that it was exactly the sort of trinket that Maddie would love. She would probably be thrilled.

"I don't know if I can do this," he said, his voice barely audible.

Gwynedd hissed, "What?"

Morrow stared her down. Now was as good a time as any. "This is wrong," he said, letting the necklace slip through his fingers. "This woman has done nothing to you, and neither have these people."

Gwynedd slithered across the room, gathering shadows as she approached. "What did you say to me?" she asked.

Morrow opened his mouth to answer, but his voice died in his throat, emerging in a choked cough as his knees buckled and he crumpled to the floor. Gritting his teeth, he strained against his paralyzed bones and clawed for breath.

Gwynedd stood over him, her eyes leaking darkness as she reached into her robes and drew out her knife. "Poor thing," she said. "I should have known you would develop an attachment, but these people are not your friends. They are your oppressors."

Morrow shook his head. "No, they aren't."

"They are. You have only forgotten." She drew the knife across the skin of her forearm. "Don't worry," she said. "I will remind you."

A familiar hunger boiled in Morrow's chest. "Stop . . . " he gasped.

Gwynedd held out her arm. The blood ran black and thick down her wrist, and across her palm, before dripping to the floor. Morrow felt his legs moving on their own. He forced himself to look away as he pulled himself to his knees in front of her. His nostrils sought the iron smell of her blood. With shaking hands, he opened his mouth and moved to grasp her arm.

"No, little prince," she said, pulling it away. She pointing to the floor. "From there."

Morrow held out as long as he could, but the pool on the floor dragged him down. His back sagged, and he dove onto his stomach, lapping up the blood to the shrill accompaniment of his mistress's laughter. He felt his mind go blank. His conscience fell away into shadow, overpowered by the cold, gripping certainty of anger and revenge. When it was over, he got to his feet, wiping the blood off his chin with his sleeve.

"Better?" Gwynedd asked.

"Yes," he answered, picking up the pendant from the floor. "But you'll need to make a small change to this."

Learning Curve

Maddie staggered up the stairs to her room. As far as jobs went, she could imagine worse. Regular hours. Saturdays off. She even got a stipend. Her hand drifted to the wallet on her hip. It was made from shiny purple silk. In her usual tactful style, Maeve had refrained from giving it to her until after her first successful spell casting. No sense paying an apprentice that couldn't perform.

Finally, she had. The magic buzzed in her veins, leftover energy from the evening's activities. She reached into her pocket and drew out a stone, a souvenir. She could still sense it: the hardness, the weight, the eons of pressure and time that brought about its form. It danced in her palm like a top, and she sent it whizzing around her head and back into her pocket.

Magic is, by far, the coolest thing ever, she thought.

They'd worked all the way through the night with only a brief pause for lunch, which they took in the lair. Now that the sun was coming up, Maddie was looking forward to crashing for a few hours.

Finn was waiting outside her door with his book bag.

"Busy night?" he asked.

Maddie led him inside, fully aware that she looked like a plague victim.

"You could say that," she said. "Sorry about the mess."

Finn glanced around the room. "What mess?"

Maddie swept her hands over her body.

Finn gave her a quick look up and down. "Don't sweat it. Magic looks good on you."

"Yeah, right," Maddie said, cackling. "I heard the typhoid motif is in Vogue."

"What's 'Vogue'?"

Maddie flopped down onto her bed. "Nevermind."

Finn sat at her dresser and produced a cloth satchel from his bag, which he unwrapped to reveal his breakfast. "Want a sandwich?" he asked. "You must be starving."

Maddie lifted her head up. "What kind?"

"Grasshopper on rye."

"Pickles?"

"Mhm."

"Gimme."

Finn handed it over, and Maddie chowed down. She didn't even blink at the food anymore.

"I don't understand how you can get up this early," she said. "Cedric won't start class for hours."

He got out a second sandwich and took a bite. "What can I say? I'm a morning person."

"Bull."

"And I thought you might be lonely. You've been training with Maeve non stop. How long has it been? Four days? You know what they say about all work and no play."

"It's not so bad," Maddie said. "And you're one to talk. Besides, I still see Rain in the evening when I have breakfast, and Kidhe got transferred to the night shift. We chat before he goes to work."

Finn finished his sandwich and leaned back against the dresser. "I guess that's fair enough. In any case, I don't have much of a choice. The solstice festival is in three days, and there are a thousand preparations to make. The high-profile guests are driving my sister nuts."

Maddie finished her sandwich and poured herself a glass of water from a jug beside the bed. She poured another for Finn. "Why are they so unruly?" she asked, handing it to him.

"Just a lot political pressure. You met Delilah?"

"The ambassador from Aster?"

"That's the one. She's been leaning on everybody, doing her best to muck things up. We're doing everything we can to keep her away from the others, but she goes out almost every night. Theresa wanted to put a tail on her, but Mom decided it would be impolite, so it's anybody's guess who she's meeting with."

"Sounds like trouble."

Finn yawned and rubbed his eyes. "It'll pass. The representatives are still on our side. How are your studies going?"

"It's amazing," Maddie said, fighting the urge to gush. "I've only been at it for a few days, but I've never been so excited about anything in my life. Watch."

She pulled the stone back out and sent it spinning into the air. It buzzed around like a fly before coming to rest on the nightstand.

"It's coming so naturally now," she said. "Ever since I got back from the deep Veil. I don't think I've ever felt this way before. Thanks for convincing me to give it a try."

"My pleasure."

He gathered his things and stood up with a tired groan. "I should get going. Theresa wanted to meet before class. Something about decorations."

"Decorations?" Maddie asked.

Finn put up his hands. "I don't know. But she seemed to think it was important. I guess royalty's not all fanfare and fancy parties."

Maddie stood up and gave him a hug. "Thanks again, and thank you for coming to visit."

The door opened suddenly to reveal Ebba standing outside. "Miss Maddie," she said, "I'm here to pick up your laundr—" Her eyes blew up to the size of dinner plates. "Y-y-your highness!" she stammered, bowing.

Finn let go of Maddie and headed for the door, patting Ebba on the head as he left. "See you later," he said.

Maddie waved. "Later."

Ebba shut the door behind him, turned, pressed her back against it, and said, "Oh. My. God."

"What?" Maddie asked as she changed into her pajamas.

Ebba cracked the door open and glanced into the hall before shutting it again. "Maddie. The prince likes you!"

Maddie gave her a doubting look. "No way," she said. "Ebba, we're just friends. He was just coming to visit. We hardly see each other anymore."

Ebba stomped over and grabbed her hands. "Maddie, you're not a Faerie, so I get it if you don't understand, but do you really think that the *prince* is getting up every day at sunrise to swing by for breakfast for no reason at all?"

Maddie shook her hands loose and went to her dresser to brush her hair. It had grown significantly since she'd come to the Veil, and was becoming more and more difficult to contend with. "You're reading too much into it," she said. "Finn and I have been friends for more than a month. If he had feelings for me, he would have asked me out, or at least said something."

Ebba rolled her eyes. "Oh my God, you are so clueless! Maddie!"

"What?!"

The girl took a breath. "Alright," she said. "As your official professor of Faerie studies, I've decided that it's time you got the talk."

Maddie furrowed her brow. "The talk?"

Ebba jumped up to grab the brush out of Maddie's hands and set it aside. "Come on," she said. "We're going to find Rain."

The Birds and the Bees

Maddie stood with her arms crossed. "It's not funny," she said. Rain was practically rolling on the floor.

Ebba sat on a stool with her elbows propped up on the table, smiling triumphantly. "Told you."

They'd found Rain in the old kitchen, planning out the schedule for her staff. Tears streamed down her cheeks as she fought to catch her breath. She looked at Maddie, steadying herself . . . and started laughing again.

"Would you stop that!?" Maddie said.

Rain put up a hand and took another moment to recover herself. "I'm sorry," she said. "I guess it was inevitable. I mean, you're the same age, and new, and exotic, and the fact that you're training to become a witch doesn't hurt. They probably can't help themselves."

Maddie leveled her voice. "What do you mean, 'they?'"

"Finn and Kidhe, of course."

"What about Kidhe?"

Rain clapped a hand over her mouth to suppress another laugh, pausing to go to the sink, where she filled a glass of water. "Kidhe is the captain of the wardens," she said, taking a sip. "No one can transfer him anywhere. He moved *himself* to the night shift."

Maddie stared, dumbfounded.

"Maybe you should sit down," Ebba said, pulling her onto a stool.

"I don't believe it," Maddie said. "They're just my friends. That's all."

Rain brought her a glass of water. "You just have to understand our culture. Faeries are just as varied as humans are, but you've got to remember that deep down we *aren't* humans. We're not driven by the same instincts."

"And what do you mean by that?"

"It's hard to explain," Rain said, taking a seat. "Let me try this. If you met a guy you liked and you got the feeling he liked you, would you go up to him and ask him out?"

Maddie pondered the question for a moment. "I don't know," she said. "Are we friends already, me and this theoretical guy?"

Rain shrugged and said, "Sure."

Maddie massaged her forehead. She was so tired. Why did she let Ebba drag her down here? "I guess. Maybe. I don't know. I've never felt that way about anyone."

"Why not?"

Maddie gave an exasperated shrug. "Look, I really don't know. I guess I always expected that the right man would be charming or something."

"Waiting for someone to sweep you off your feet?" Rain asked.

Maddie gave her an impatient stare.

"Okay, maybe that's a little old fashioned," said Rain, "but the point is, you imagined he would to come to *you*, right?"

"Not necessarily."

Rain waved her hands. "Don't get me wrong. It's a modern world, but the expectation in human culture is for the guy to make the first move. Here in the Veil, it's the opposite. Faerie men don't just walk up to women and ask them out. They expect *us* to approach *them*. They flirt, give signals, and make themselves available, but what they're trying to say is, 'If you asked, I would say yes'."

Maddie groaned and put her head down on the table. Her forehead thumped gently against the wood. "So, what do I do?"

"Well, are you interested?"

Maddie tilted her head up. "I don't know," she said, resting on her chin.

Ebba practically flipped the table. "You don't *know*?! We're talking about the prince here!"

Maddie turned to her with a frustrated look. "That's enough!"

"But come on! It's not fair!"

Rain walked around the table and gave Ebba a hug. "Don't worry. I'm sure someday you'll have your own royal bachelor to run down," she said. "Maddie, you're just going to have to decide what you want. Just remember that the festival is coming up, and if you don't ask the two of them out, some other girl will come along and steal them out from under you. Understand?"

"I guess," Maddie mumbled. She paused, squinted, and looked up at Rain. "What do you mean, 'the two of them?'"

Rain had an ear-to-ear grin plastered across her face, and Ebba giggled.

Maddie's eyes went wide. "You're kidding."

"Nope," Rain replied.

"I can date them both?"

"Duh!" Ebba said. "How else are you supposed to decide which one you like better?"

"But that's crazy!"

"No, that's our culture," Rain said, correcting her gently. "Matriarchal society has its perks. Look, there's no pressure. It's not like they're going to hate you if you decide not to date them. They're not jerks; they're grown men. I'm sure they'd be happy to stay friends. You just have to decide if *you* want more."

Pots and pans began to clatter in the next room. "That'll be my staff," she said. "I've got to get to work. Will you be okay?"

Maddie hopped off the stool. "I'll muddle through. Have a good day."

"You too."

Ebba took Maddie back to her room, and Maddie collapsed into bed.

"Hey, Maddie?" Ebba said, pausing in the door before she left.

Maddie pulled up her blankets and shut her eyes. "Yes?"

"The prince!" she whispered, giving a little squeal before dashing out the door.

Maddie rolled her eyes and buried her face in her pillow. The last thing she needed right now, on top of her new job and the whole business with the Foxglove, was two suitors waiting with bated breath for her to make some kind of romantic overture.

Two days, she thought. *That's all I want. Two days in a row without any complications. Is that so much to ask?*

It was an interesting idea, though. Two boyfriends. The faeries sure had their quirks. And it wasn't as though the notion didn't have an appeal. Breakfast with Kidhe, dinner with Finn, flying lessons on Tuesdays, royal excursions on alternating Thursdays. She would need a day planner, or possibly a secretary.

Frankly, she wasn't sure if she wanted to act on any of it. Her life was full.

And yet she couldn't help but wonder how many times her mother had come to the same conclusion. Ten times? A hundred? Until one day, she ran off and married her father on . . . what, a whim? Maddie had never asked about the beginning of their relationship. All she knew was how it ended, with her mother far, far away and her father raising a child alone.

It wouldn't be fair, she thought, as her fatigue pulled her gently down to sleep. *The men would have to wait.* If there was one thing she still had control over, it was that.

Matriarch

"You want me to do what?" Maddie asked, storming across the room. She picked up her brush and tugged it through her hair.

Rose gave her a pleading look. It was strange to see it on her otherwise dignified features. "Please don't be mad."

"Mad? Why would I be mad?"

"You have to understand the position I'm in," Rose said. "There was nothing I could do."

Maddie glanced over her shoulder. "So, you offered me up?"

Rose slid in between Maddie and her wardrobe. "I didn't offer you up," she said. "Think of it as a royal invitation. You know how important this review is, and I'm not asking for much. Just come to dinner and talk about your experiences. I wouldn't ask you if it weren't important." She went to the edge of the bed and sat down, fidgeting.

"Rose, what's happening?" Maddie asked.

The queen took a quick breath and stilled her hands. "Politics, of course."

"You mean Delilah?"

"She's gaining ground," Rose said. "It's not much, but little by little, she's chipping away at my support. These sorts of things have tipping points. If she can get enough people to come around, the others will change their minds just to avoid ending up on Aster's bad side. I've been arguing with Delilah all day." She put her hands up, flapping her fingers as she spoke in a snooty voice. "A palace and a few guards do not a country make."

"How is she doing it?" Maddie asked.

"Taxes, mostly," Rose replied.

"Taxes?"

Rose massaged the back of her neck. "It's just as boring as it sounds. As an independent nation, we don't have to pay taxes or tributes, not to a parent government or anyone else. If the other kingdoms don't certify our independence, Amaranth and all its territories would be folded back into Aster. We would have to start paying taxes to them again, and they can promise a portion of them to other nations in exchange for their votes."

"Sounds like a bribe to me," Maddie said.

Rose sighed out a weak laugh. "Well, they call it tribute, and that's why I need your help. You're a symbol."

"Of power?"

Rose shook her head. "No. We haven't told anyone about what you are, and we don't intend to, but you are a symbol of the fact that this kingdom can stand on its own, that we can protect not only our own subjects but also . . ." She trailed off as she searched for the word.

"Foreigners?" Maddie suggested.

Rose flicked her hand towards her in agreement. "Exactly. None of them believe we'll actually go to war over recognition. They're focused on the numbers, like it's nothing more than a business transaction. But Amaranth can't win in a bidding war. I need something that speaks to their hearts."

Maddie walked to the wardrobe and pulled out her witching robe. The sun would be going down soon, and she still had to find some breakfast before heading over to Maeve's.

"Would you?" Maddie asked. "Go to war over recognition?"

Rose stood up and opened to the balcony door, staring out at the city. "Truthfully, I don't know. I sometimes wonder if this was always their plan. You never know with Faeries. When monarchies last for hundreds of years, the game can get pretty long. It might have been a ploy from the start, to let us go off on our own, avoid the expense of establishing a new territory, and then yank it all back a century later. I guess I always figured that when the time came, I would have more allies to call on. I love leading this city, but I'm not sure it's worth my citizens' lives."

"I thought you did have allies," Maddie said.

"A few," Rose replied. "Brynna and Ida are old friends, and there are a few others who are on the fence, waiting to see how far Aster will take the contest. Some of them might come onto our side in exchange for tribute. And of course, I could probably get a freebie by letting someone marry a son off to Theresa."

Maddie gave her a doubting look.

"Don't worry," Rose said. "I'm not planning on it. Theresa would probably give up her crown on the spot. But now do you see why I need your help? You could really put it over the top."

Maddie cringed as she gathered the last of her tools. "Oh, alright," she said. "I'll help. What's one excruciating state dinner among friends?"

Rose let out a sigh of relief. "Thank you. I'll have Rain and Cedric bring you everything you need to know about our guests. We're going to have to get you up to speed on traditional etiquette and protocol, but don't worry. We'll make sure you're prepared, and Rain can teach you the dances."

Maddie's head snapped around. "Dances?"

"It'll be fine," Rose said. "They're easy, and there are only five or six."

"Six?!"

Rose wrapped her up in a hug. "I'm so proud of you. Thank you for doing this." She headed for the door, stopping as she was about to exit. "Oh, and I almost forgot," she said, "you'll need to bring a date."

Maddie dropped her tools, and they clattered to the floor. "A date?"

"Absolutely," Rose said. "I don't want them thinking of you like you're just a refugee."

"I *am* a refugee."

Rose took Maddie by the shoulders and gave her a little shake. "But you're so much more than that! You're an apprentice witch and a brilliant young woman. We want them to see that. You know, healthy! Vibrant! Full of drive and ambition!"

"And so I need a date," Maddie said, unamused.

Rose grinned. "No. This is the Veil, remember? You don't need a date; you *wanted* a date."

"Uh huh."

Rose knelt down and gathered Maddie's tools. When she straightened up, she dusted off Maddie's shoulders as though she could brush her skepticism away. "I know it sounds weird, but it will give the people in the room something familiar to connect with: a human girl with a Faerie in tow. They'll eat it up. It doesn't need to be a big deal. Ask anyone."

"Rose . . . " Maddie groaned.

The queen put her hands together, begging. "Please? Just for one night."

Maddie grumbled, squirming before she finally gave in. "Fine, I'll find a date," she said, "but only because you begged."

Rose leaned in and planted a kiss on her cheek. "You're the best." Her steps were light as she left.

Well, I'm glad she's feeling better, Maddie thought, flopping back down onto her bed with a sigh. This was going to be awkward.

Matchmaker

Green, red, and yellow ribbons covered the front hall of the palace when Maddie walked in. Rain's staff raced around the room, hauling out tall wooden tables and stools for the party. Maddie found Rain directing traffic in the middle of the fray.

"Hi, Maddie!" she said, before turning to shout at a pair of faeries setting down a table. "No, not there! There!" She pointed. "By the window!"

Maddie jumped back when someone tossed a pair of scissors across the room.

"Hey!" Rain snapped. "Safety!"

"Is this a bad time?" Maddie asked.

"No, don't be silly," Rain answered, hurrying to the edge of the room, where she picked up a hammer and started pounding hooks into the wall. "What's up?" she said, holding the nails in her teeth.

Maddie sidled up to her. "So . . . are there any special rules for asking someone out? Any weird Faerie traditions I should be aware of?"

"Not really," Rain said. "Wait, I thought you were putting this off?"

Maddie squirmed in place. "I was, but Rose asked me to come to the solstice banquet to put on a show for the ambassadors, and she thinks it will look better if I bring a date."

"The things we do for politics," Rain said, giving Maddie a wink. "I've never heard of anyone starting a relationship based on a royal request." She grabbed a big painting off a rack in the middle of the floor.

Maddie grabbed the other side and helped her hang it. "Me either, and I'm not even sure I want it to be the start of a relationship. Rose said that it would be fine if it was just for show, but the only guys I know to ask are . . . well, you know."

"Interested?"

"Right. You see what I mean? It would be complicated. Am I making any sense?"

"You are. It would almost be easier if they weren't into you, and it probably doesn't help matters that you're obviously into them."

"I am not!" Maddie said.

Rain gave her a sideways glance. "Please."

"It's the truth!"

"You're telling me that if one of them asked you out, human-style, right now, you'd say no?"

"Absolutely, I would."

"You're sure?" Rain asked.

"I am."

"Because you're busy, right?"

"Yes."

"But not because you don't like them."

"No. Wait, hang on, I mean yes. What was the question again?"

Rain cackled evilly and poked her in the shoulder. "Got you."

Maddie found a chair. "That was a cheap shot," she said, falling into it.

"Just keeping you honest."

A member of Rain's staff approached from across the room with a question about flower arrangements. Rain pulled a sheet of paper out of her dress and explained the placements to her while Maddie went back over her thoughts from the night before.

Rain was right. She did feel something. It wasn't much, and maybe she wasn't in the mood to act on it, but she had to admit that finding someone special in this new home of hers wasn't the worst idea in the world. After all, unless something changed drastically, she was going to be living in the Veil for a very long time.

Rain finished with her staff. "Where were we?" she asked. "Oh, right. You were admitting that you've got the hots for the prince, or the captain of the wardens, or both."

Maddie glared at her. "I do not have 'the hots.' But even if I were willing to entertain the possibility that *maybe* there might be something there, that doesn't mean it's a good idea. I mean, what am I supposed to do, walk up to Finn and say, 'Hey, your highness. I kind of like you, but my life is totally upside-down right now, and I'm not ready for a relationship, but I need you to go to a royal banquet with me as my date and promise not to read anything into it'?"

Rain giggled. "Well, I would come up with something more charming than that."

"Thanks. Great advice," Maddie said, collapsing in her seat.

A trio of faeries set a table down beside them, and Rain threw a tablecloth over it. "You're settled on the prince then?" she asked. "Ebba will be thrilled."

Maddie chewed on her lip. "I don't know. It's weird. Finn is great. He's charming and intellectual and—"

"— very you."

"But Kidhe likes the outdoors and animals and appreciates hard work. And he's got such a carefree attitude."

"Also you, except for that last part." Rain leaned in and whispered. "You stayed at his house, right? Did you see his tattoos? Not to mention the *rest* of him."

"Rain," Maddie said, eyes flicking up to her, "you are not helping."

"Hey, I've already told you how to handle this problem."

"Date them both, I know, but that would be even more messed up." Maddie stood up with a huff and leaned against the wall. "This isn't fair," she said, crossing her arms.

Rain slid in beside her. "You want some real advice?" she asked.

Maddie thumped her head against the wall and looked up at the ceiling. "Yes, please."

"Tell them how you feel. They'll understand. And if all else fails, just show them who's boss. It worked for me."

"And the banquet?"

"Don't stress over the banquet. It's a diplomatic function, and around here, those happen all the time. Treat it like a, I don't know, friend's wedding or something. Beautiful venue, nice dinner, a couple of speeches, some drinks . . ."

"And a date."

Rain gave her a little bump with her hips. "Or two."

Maddie pushed away from the wall. "Well," she said, "I guess I'll let you know how it goes. Thanks, Rain."

She was about to leave when an armload of pizza walked in the door and a woman's voice said, "Could someone tell me where to find Maddie Foster?"

Maddie jogged across the room. "Moira?"

Moira set the pizzas down on the table and said, "In the flesh."

"What are you doing here?"

"Well, I heard you'd been working hard, so I decided to make good on my offer."

"Your offer?"

"Pizza delivery, remember?" She thumped the boxes. "One cheese. One pepperoni. One sausage."

"That's way too much food."

"Well, then you'll just have to share the wealth."

Maddie eyed the faeries in the room, who met her gaze with hungry glances. "Looks like the wolves are already circling," she said. "What do I owe you?"

Moira said, "Nothing. These are on me. Leoh will be happy enough to know his food's getting served in the palace. Oh, speaking of which…" She fished a necklace out of her pocket. "How about a little branded marketing?"

Maddie held the necklace up. It was a metal disk with a piece of copper in the shape of a slice of pizza. The words "Cook Country Caravan" were etched along the bottom.

"Nice, eh?" Moira said.

Maddie put it on. "It's cute. I like it."

"Keep it. We've got more."

"Do you have time to eat?" Maddie asked.

Moira glanced back at the door. "Actually, no. I have to get back to the restaurant. The dinner rush will be coming in soon."

Maddie's face fell. "Well, thank you for bringing these. Will I see you at the festival?"

"Maybe," Moira said. "I'll be working. Are you going?"

"I am." Maddie grabbed the box of cheese pizza. "And on that note, I've got to make some arrangements."

Rain snorted.

Maddie glanced up at the ceiling in frustration for a moment, propping the pizza box against her hip. She leaned in and gave Moira a half hug. "I'll see you later," she said.

Moira answered, "I'm sure you will."

Friends with Benefits

Maddie stood on her balcony, fiddling with the hem of her witching robes as she stared down at the city. Despite the hour, the markets were bustling with activity as every Faerie for a hundred miles packed the streets, scrambling to finish preparing for the biggest event of the year, the solstice festival. And with the centennial vote looming, it promised to be a blowout.

Someone knocked on the door. Maddie straightened her robes, turned around, and said, "Come in!"

The door opened a crack and Ebba poked her head through. "Miss Maddie?" she said. "They're here."

Maddie braced herself. "Alright, send them in, and then wait outside."

"But I want to watch!" said Ebba, whining.

Maddie shot her an impatient look. "Please, Ebba. This is awkward enough."

"Fine." Pouting, she shut the door, and Maddie heard whispering in the corridor.

A moment later Kidhe and Finn walked in, side-by-side. Maddie had never seen Kidhe so tidy, and Finn was wearing the same red outfit he'd had on when they first met. His sword hung from his belt, shining with fresh polish. Neither one of them said a word.

"Relax," Maddie said. "This isn't a job interview."

They both returned a nervous laugh. Maddie had been told about the role of the Faerie men, but she'd never really believed that it was true. Seeing them like this made Rain's meaning perfectly clear. They weren't human, and they behaved, thought, and felt in different ways. It would be up to her to reach out, though exactly what she was reaching for, she had no idea.

"I'm glad the two of you came," she said. "I hope this isn't too awkward."

Kidhe answered first. "Of course we would come."

"And it's not awkward," Finn added.

"I'm going to start with the bad news," Maddie said, wringing her hands. "I'm not sure I'm ready for a relationship. With everything that's going on in my life, I wasn't sure that it would be fair to you . . . to either of you."

"But . . . ?" Finn said, perking up.

Maddie shot him an annoyed look. "How do you know there's a but?"

He flashed a grin. "I couldn't help but notice that you used the past tense just then."

"God, you are so annoying," Maddie said, covering her eyes.

"And?"

"Will you stop that!"

Laughing, Kidhe put a hand on Finn's shoulder. "Just let her finish, highness."

Maddie took a moment to frame her thoughts. "So, you've heard about the review," she said.

They answered, "Of course."

"Well, Rose thinks it will help swing the vote if I'm there to give a speech about my time here, and she . . . " Maddie looked down at the floor. "She suggested that it might help the ambassadors accept me if I bring a date."

"You're doing this for my mom?" Finn asked, his face falling.

"No!" Maddie said, snapping her head back up. "That's . . . no. That's not it at all. The truth is, I've been thinking a lot lately about what I want for myself—here in the Veil, I mean—and I've decided that . . . " She trailed off, abandoning the thought. "I'm not good at this."

"It's alright," Kidhe replied. "You're doing fine."

Maddie pressed her hands together and said, "Listen, I'm the Foxglove. Being with me isn't going to be easy. My life is going to be complicated, but the truth is, I like spending time with you . . . with both of you, and I guess around here, that's allowed."

They nodded in unison and said, "It is."

This is so weird, Maddie thought. She fixed them both with an assertive look. "I don't know how far this will go, but if you're interested, I would like you both to attend the solstice festival with me," she said, and waited anxiously as a moment passed in silence. Kidhe and Finn glanced at each other briefly.

"I accept," Finn answered.

Kidhe said, "I'm in."

They stepped forward and bumped into each other. Kidhe took a step back and gestured for Finn to go first. Finn did the same.

Maddie threw up her arms. "Will the two of you just get over here?"

Finn approached and leaned up, and Maddie gave him a kiss on the cheek. Kidhe leaned down and she did the same for him, chuckling inwardly as she took a step back. Something told her that, for the foreseeable future, a great many things in her life were going to start arriving in pairs.

"Now, no fighting," she said, pointing a finger at each of them in turn. "Or posturing. Or silly competitions. I may be in Faerie land, but I'm still a human girl, and we don't tolerate that kind of nonsense. Got it?"

"Okay," they said.

Maddie turned to Finn. "And no banishing Kidhe to Alaska."

"Dang," Finn said, snapping his fingers. "There goes plan A."

Maddie walked them both to the door. "Now, I have to get to work," she said. "Maeve's expecting me. I'll be working right up to the morning of the festival, so I'll see you both in a couple of days. Sound good?"

"Sounds great," Kidhe said. "It'll give me time to get all dolled up."

They each leaned in to offer another kiss before they left. Maddie obliged and watched them go. When the door shut, she lay down and stared up at the ceiling, counting the rings as she'd done on the evening of her first day in the Veil.

Bloom

"Maddie, wake up! Look!" Ebba jumped up onto the bed and Maddie rolled, shielding her eyes against the sun streaming in through the window. Ebba stood over her, two wrapped boxes tucked under her arms. "Presents!" she squealed.

Maddie sat up. "Presents?"

"Actually, they're called 'enticements'," Ebba said with an evil grin. "Did you ever read that book Rose gave you?"

Maddie shuffled back against her pillows and sighed. "I glanced at it. Is this is how they're going to compete?"

Ebba dumped the boxes in her lap. "It is when you tell them they can't fight each other. I swear, Maddie. You have no respect for tradition at all."

There was a note of disappointment in her voice that Maddie found very disturbing. Ebba sat down and pushed the gifts towards her. "Do the big one first!" she said.

Maddie gave her an amused look. "You think it's from the prince, don't you?" she asked as she unwrapped the gift. Yellow wood polished to a mirror shine met her eyes as the paper peeled away and revealed a box inside.

"Definitely from the prince," Ebba said.

Maddie opened the box and gasped. "Woah," she said, gazing at the contents.

Ebba giggled and squirmed. "It's gorgeous!"

Cream silk spilled over Maddie's fingers as she examined the dress. Gold embroidery swept up across the chest and shoulder in a pattern of oak leaves caught in the wind. The sunlight coming in through the balcony door lit the fabric up like shining fire.

"It must have cost a fortune," Maddie said. She stood up. The dress fell to her ankles, splitting on one side just below the thigh. It was the same fabric she'd seen in the market. "He must have been planning this for weeks."

"It comes with shoes!" Ebba reached back into the box to pull out a pair of pale, willowy sandals with long leather laces that reminded Maddie of ancient Greece.

Ebba thrust them into her arms and said, "Put it on."

Maddie laid the dress down. "Now?"

"Well, you're going to wear it, aren't you?"

"I'm not sure. It's a little formal for a day out, don't you think? I was going to wear my robes."

"But Maddie, look at it!"

"I know!" Maddie said. "It looks like it cost about a gazillion dollars. What if something happens to it?"

"But he'll love it!"

"I swear, Ebba," Maddie said. "You're like a weird, man-eater version of Jiminy Cricket."

Maddie folded the dress carefully back into the box. Her mother would certainly approve of Ebba's angle, and Maddie was grudgingly willing to admit these days that her mother was, perhaps, not so crazy in the way she managed her affairs.

"I'll think about it," she said. "Now, give me the other one."

Ebba was still staring at the prince's gift. "What other one?" she said absently.

Maddie smacked her on the shoulder. "The other present, you dork. Come on."

"I still think you're crazy for not just picking the prince," Ebba said, handing the other gift over reluctantly.

Maddie tore open the paper and discovered a round reed pouch tied shut with a bit of string, which she undid. "Sometimes," she said, "status isn't the most important thi—" Her words trailed off as she reached into the bag and drew out the contents. A long braid of soft, leather cord hung from her fingertips, studded with turquoise and smooth, white quartz. The braid secured speckled feather and a thick disk of glassy, black stone.

Ebba was not impressed. "It's a rock," she said.

Maddie ran her thumb over the pendant as her mind conjured up images of the deep woods. "No," she said. "It's more."

The music outside grew louder as the city stirred awake, announcing that the festival would be starting soon. Maddie put the necklace back into its box and popped over to the bathroom to wash up. When she returned, her pint-sized companion had laid out the dress again.

"Fine," Maddie said. "I'll wear it. Happy?"

Ebba helped her get into it, lacing up the back. Maddie turned in front of the mirror, brushing her hands down the smooth material. It breathed so easily that it felt like she was barely wearing anything at all. Chalk it up to Faerie craftsmanship. That, and the lack of underpants.

"You're beautiful," Ebba said.

Maddie blushed. "You think so?"

Ebba nodded rapidly. "Come on," she said, climbing onto the bed. "Sit over here. I'll braid your hair."

Maddie turned from the mirror and put her foot down. "No," she said. "No way. I am not doing my hair."

"But he'll like it! They'll both like it."

"Isn't the whole idea that they have to convince *me* to like *them*? Why do I have to get all fancied up?" Maddie grabbed her brush from the dresser and brushed her hair straight. "These guys fell for me in a pony-tail," she said, securing it with a white ribbon and a basic knot. "They can certainly date me in one."

Ebba groaned as Maddie put on the necklace she'd received from Kidhe, donned her lacy sandals, and took one last look in the mirror. Her eyes were back to normal, but she could see in the mirror that there was still a little black in her veins from her last night with Maeve. She decided not to sweat it. The menfolk were probably down for that sort of thing anyway.

"How do I look?" she asked.

Ebba gave her a hard stare. "Like you're *almost* taking this seriously."

Maddie spun around and squared her shoulders. "Perfect."

The Man from the Woods

Every inch of the city fluttered with streamers and string. Flowers covered every wall and rooftop, musicians played in every hall, and a thousand lanterns hung over the streets, waiting for the sun to set. Maddie grinned as the cable car descended into the sprawling arms of the city tree.

Kidhe met her on the platform, bowed, and put out a hand. Maddie gave a little curtsy and kissed it.

Still weird, she thought.

He wore a deep, green doublet with matching pants. His boots were a dark and woody brown, new and polished. While he didn't own a sword, a hatchet and dagger hung against his hip, the first tucked away in a hand-embossed sheath, the second polished to a mirror shine and tied securely in a leather thong.

"You look very nice," Maddie said, folding her arms in front of her. "I especially like the sharp objects."

Kidhe gave a nervous laugh. "It's tradition, is all," he said, turning green.

Rain and Ebba had filled her in on this. Couples went out armed, a holdover from the chaos after the Faeries arrived in the Veil, before their civilization had formed itself.

"Isn't that supposed to be my job, though?" she asked, tapping her hand against her leg. Her witching knife hung on her hip in a purple scabbard.

Kidhe answered with a twinkle in his eye. "Nice."

"Shall we?" Maddie said, putting out her arm.

They walked out into the city. Maddie was in the driver's seat when it came to goodies. It was her date, after all. She'd had 24 hours to plan, her stipend had come in, and the human equivalent of over 600 dollars jingled in her wallet in the form of limbs, branches, and leaves.

"I'm going to need your help making change," she said. "I've never used Veil money before."

"No problem," Kidhe said. "What do you want to do first?"

Maddie looked out over the street. Every merchant in the Chicago Veil had set up shop in Amaranth. Canvas tents, wooden stalls, and every shelf in every store window sparkled with the region's finest. The smell of roasting meat blew through the air, cups of fresh fruit sat in bowls of cream, and all around the wind was heavy with the aroma of fragrant spice.

Maddie took Kidhe up to a long table where half a dozen faeries worked over glowing coals and a marble slab. A slurry of shining chocolate flowed like a mudslide over the warm stone.

"You like chocolate?" she asked.

He gazed down at the table. "I don't actually know."

Maddie turned to him in shock. "You've never had chocolate?!"

He looked away sheepishly.

Maddie cackled like a diabolical mastermind. "Well, Mister Faerie," she said, "allow me to introduce you to the rest of your life."

She bought two slabs: one with nuts and one without. The look on Kidhe's face when he took his first bite was almost enough to make her cry as they moved on, snaking through the crowd.

Two couples in leather halter-tops strolled past them, chatting as they chowed down on smoked grasshopper, the meat still steaming in the shell. Another couple took a carriage ride on a coach pulled by a team of mice, while off the street, a group of women hurled knives at wooden targets to win prizes for their dates. Children and teenagers frolicked through the streets, chasing each other as they fought over trinkets and melting bags of sweets.

The Cook County Caravan rose like a monolith in the middle of the square, slinging enough hot dogs, cheese fries, and nachos to choke the whole city. Maddie breathed it in like sweet perfume.

"What is it?" Kidhe asked.

Maddie took his hand. "Nothing," she said. "This is just . . . great, that's all. Let's go see Leoh and Moira."

The cafe was in a frenzy. Leoh appeared to have drafted a brigade of local teenagers to help him serve, handing out combo boxes for 10 branches a piece. It was over-priced, but Maddie was willing to give him a pass. The festival was on, summer was in bloom, the review was on the horizon, and it was best to strike while the iron was hot.

There were two options for food: hot dog and a soda, or pizza and a soda. Maddie bought one of each and waved to

Leoh, who waved back over the roaring crowd. Moira was nowhere to be seen.

"Is Moira in the back?" Maddie asked, shouldering through the crowd.

"She didn't show up," Leoh answered.

"Is she okay?"

"No idea. I sent a runner, but no one answered at her apartment. She probably blew me off for the festival."

"That doesn't sound like her."

"I know," Leoh said. "But I don't have time to think about it. You guys got everything you need?"

Maddie held up her food. "We did, and it looks delicious." She followed him as he ran to wipe down a table. "Maybe I'll come back later," she said. "Just in case she comes in. Tell her I said hi, okay?"

"Will do." He said as he zoomed off. Maddie took their food, collected Kidhe, and went back outside. As they walked down the street, she stared at her sandals and kicked the cobbles

"Everything alright?" Kidhe asked.

"I don't know," Maddie answered. "It's probably fine. I'm just worried about Moira. It doesn't seem like she'd be the type to skip out on work. Do you think something's wrong?"

Kidhe put an arm around her shoulders. "Don't worry. It's a crazy day. I'm sure she's fine."

"I guess so," Maddie said. "Sorry for spoiling the mood."

"It's alright. I'm having a great time. Where do you want to eat? Should we find someplace to sit down?"

"Ah, I have a plan for that," Maddie said, perking up. "Follow me. We're having our lunch in style."

She led him to a wooden platform at the other end of the street, where a long rope rose up from a huge, man-powered crank. A woman stood beside it wearing a floppy jester's hat and a brightly colored red and blue uniform.

"Reservation for 10:30?" Maddie said, approaching.

The woman checked her papers and looked up. "Foster?"

"That's me," Maddie said. "Plus one."

The woman stuck out her hand. "That'll be $172.50."

"What is this place?" Kidhe asked, gasping at the price.

Maddie got out her wallet and started doing math in her head. "Hang on," she answered, counting out loud. "A limb is 50, branches are like fives, and leaves . . . crap."

"50 cents," Kidhe supplied. "What are we doing here?"

Maddie paid the woman and pointed up as the crank began to turn. "See for yourself."

The rope descended. Above their heads, an enormous hot air balloon made from red and yellow canvas emerged through the branches. Kidhe's jaw dropped.

"Come on. It's our turn," Maddie said as the balloon touched down and its occupants got out. A few minutes later, they floated over the city, drifting on the breeze while they enjoyed their meal in airy peace.

"You live on this stuff?" Kidhe asked, sipping his soda.

"Oh, no," Maddie replied. "You definitely can't live on it, but it's perfect for a day like this." She leaned on the edge of the basket and stared. The broad, blue field of Lake Michigan shimmered in the distance beyond the city. Maddie had been to the beach a hundred times, but the lake's reflection in the Veil was like an ocean. She could even see whitecaps cresting on the waves.

"It's so different," she said, gazing in wonder. "Have you ever been out there?"

Kidhe leaned out, one arm gripping the rope securing the balloon. "Sure," he said. "Before I joined the wardens, I worked for an air messenger service. We went all over."

"What's it like?"

"Incredible. Get away from the Veil-cities, and it's nothing but untamed wilderness for hundreds of miles. If you go to the deep Veil in those places, you find a jungle. Go far enough north, and it turns to alpine slopes that reach up and up and up until the mountains brush the clouds." His eyes were locked on the horizon.

"Do you miss it?" Maddie asked.

"Sometimes," he answered. "I go out every once in a while on vacation, but it's been a long time since I really traveled. Maybe the two of us could take a trip sometime and see some real sights."

"That's awfully presumptuous," Maddie said, allowing a smirk to grow across her face. "This is a provisional, first-date-type scenario, remember?"

"Of course," he said, blinking innocently.

Maddie sipped her soda, smirking as she turned her eyes back to the landscape. "You guys crack me up," she said.

"Why is that?"

"You're so focused on relationships. Where I come from that's pretty unusual, at least for a man your age."

"I could say the same thing about you."

"How's that?"

"Well, it's pretty uncommon for a woman under 25 to be in the mood for a real relationship."

"A Faerie woman, you mean," Maddie said. "You know, our species complement each other pretty well. Shame about the Veil barrier. Though I can only imagine what would happen if your girls met our guys."

"A second baby boom?" Kidhe replied.

Maddie almost spit out her soda. "Okay, no thanks. I take it back. The Veil barrier stays."

"Probably for the best."

They spent the rest of their balloon ride with Kidhe playing aerial guide, pointing out locations of settlements and landmarks in the forest around the city. By the time they came down, they had a 6-month flying tour of the Veil all planned out, in a provisional, first-date-type context.

They spent the remainder of the day visiting every shop on the strip. Maddie bought herself a pair of carved wooden bracelets and a matching set for Kidhe. He bought a pair of leather raincoats for them to wear on their next outing, just in case. Maddie commented that the gift was very 'him.'

In the evening, the city watch circulated up and down the street, lighting the hanging paper lanterns as the crowds filtered into the city's restaurants and pubs for dinner. An orchestra of a thousand instruments fluttered into the air, and Maddie let her eyes half close as they made their way back to the cable cars.

"I guess it's about that time," Kidhe said, stopping at the bottom of the steps leading up to the platform. "Your other date will be waiting."

Maddie smiled in spite of herself. "It's still so bizarre. Are you *sure* you're okay with all this?"

"I always expected to have to prove myself," Kidhe replied.

Maddie squirmed. "Does it ever feel . . . I don't know, lopsided?"

"You mean unfair?"

"Yes, frankly," Maddie said.

"No," said Kidhe. "Truthfully, I kind of enjoy it. Gives me an excuse to show off."

The car touched down, and Maddie stepped aboard. "I guess I can live with that," she said. There was a long pause.

AARON MCQUEEN

He's not going to kiss you, Maddie thought. She turned the idea over and over in her head, wondering whether or not he would be disappointed. Did Faeries kiss on the first date? Did she even want to kiss him?

The pause slowly drew on into an awkward silence. Kidhe ended the standoff and bowed, extending his hand, which Maddie took in her palm and kissed. His eyes flashed green, tracing up her arm as her lips touched his fingers, whispering a thousand silent invitations that trembled in her chest. Ideas that she had never considered fluttered in the corners of her thoughts and lit a fire across her cheeks.

The floor swayed as the cable car rose up into the night.

A Formal Affair

Glowing mushrooms covered the upper branches as they rose, artfully placed to create a shining portrait against the palace walls. Maddie stared up in awe. It was like looking at a bonfire, frozen solid in the midst of its motion. A hundred subtle shapes met her gaze: flowers, butterflies, ants, and millipedes. They danced, confounding her eyes, while a delicate chorus of stringed instruments and woodwinds played from the shadows, lifting the heart and thrilling the waiting ear.

She found Finn at the front gate, ensnared in a greeting line for the guests. Maddie approached from the side of the queue. He was shaking hands with Brynna.

"It looks like your date is here," the ambassador said, nudging Finn's shoulder. "Go on. Get out of this mess while you can."

Finn bowed and thanked her before he turned around. He and Maddie walked surreptitiously away.

"Thank you for rescuing me," he said.

Maddie gave him a mock salute. "Anytime. Having fun so far?"

"Let's just say I'm glad that I'm not in charge around here."

"We just have to make it through dinner," Maddie said.

"I hope so. Have you got your speech?"

"I do, and Rain gave me a quick run down on royal etiquette. I just wish I'd had more time to study."

"Well, I'll try to cover you if I can," Finn said as they approached the door. "Are you ready?"

"As ready as I'll ever be."

Finn held out his arm to escort her inside, but Maddie pulled back.

"You're supposed to hold my arm," she said.

"I'm reaching across the cultural divide," Finn replied. "What do you think?"

Maddie peeked in through the door at the party goers as they mingled and snacked on hors d'oeuvres. There were so many people, and not one of the women inside was being led around by their date. Finn's gesture was cute, but as much as she hated to disappoint him, Rose needed her to make an impression.

"It's not a bad start," she said. "But if you recall, I've been giving a lot of thought to letting myself settle in a little." She took his hand and placed it into the crook of her arm. "So just for tonight, let's see how this feels."

Finn was stunned into silence as they stepped into the hall. The entry corridor wound around in a snakelike pattern, interspersed with tall tables for people to gather around and chat. Faeries in black doublets and dresses circulated among them, passing out glasses of wine and morsels of food on little wooden plates.

Maddie snagged a cracker layered with cream cheese and spiced cricket, but she hadn't eaten since lunch, and the canapes were not going to cut it.

"Is there more food inside?" she whispered to Finn.

"Plenty," he answered with a soft chuckle. "Just don't eat the plate. Remember, the diplomats are watching." He stopped outside the dining room, where a short line of people had formed outside the door.

"What's going on?" Maddie asked.

"They're going to announce us," Finn answered.

"What?"

A woman standing just inside the door belted their names across the room.

"Madeline Foster and Prince Finn ap Rose!"

They entered to applause. Maddie bowed, and Finn followed suit. When she straightened up, she couldn't help but notice the stares and furtive glances pouring in. Suspicious eyes joined warm smiles as she and Finn made their way to the royal table, and Maddie couldn't began to wonder if it was possible that she had underestimated the significance of asking the prince out on a date.

"What is 'ap Rose?" Maddie whispered as they took their seats and a server poured them each a glass of wine.

"It means 'Son of Rose,'" Finn answered. "The given name gets passed down from the mother's side."

"You don't have last names?"

Finn sipped his wine. "Not traditionally, but it's not unusual for Faeries to take on human-style surnames, especially craftsmen. Smith, Baker, you get the idea."

"So, my children would be 'ap Madeline?'"

"Unless they're girls. Then they would be 'fer' Madeline."

A bell rang, and the crowd began to rise. The lively conversation fell to a low murmur as the usher led Rose into the hall.

"Honored guests!" the usher shouted. "May I present your host, Rose, Queen of Amaranth!"

The crowd broke into applause as the queen glided across the room, a dress whose color matched her name trailing behind her. The guests bowed low as she approached the royal table and stood in front of her seat.

"Thank you for coming," she said. "This evening marks the end of the first chapter of this city, a hundred years in the making. It is my hope that, as allies and as friends, we will all join together in writing the next."

"May it be long and glorious!" Theresa said, raising her glass.

Rose took up her wine. "To the Veil, Amaranth, and the peoples of the fair folk far and wide." The guests clapped again, sharing in the toast as Rose took her seat. She whispered to Finn and Maddie, seated beside her. "How was it? Too short?"

She sat at the head of the table with Theresa on her right alongside Maeve. Maddie sat on the queen's left with Finn, feeling very much on display.

"It was perfect," Maddie said as the servers brought out the food.

Roasted grasshopper, pill bug in the shell, blood pudding soup, and steaming, fragrant vegetables circled the table. Maddie took generously from every plate as they were passed around, an effort to follow a rather peculiar Faerie tradition Rain had outlined during her crash course on formal etiquette. It was bad form to pick and choose, and even worse to take sparingly from what was on offer. The first meant that you weren't grateful; the second implied that you were worried that the host couldn't afford to feed everybody.

"How do you like the food, Maddie?" Theresa asked, passing her a huge bowl of fried cricket legs covered in bright orange sauce.

Maddie smiled, picked up a leg, and took a bite. It was juicy, and the spicy sauce was off the charts. She grabbed her water and slugged it down. "Fantastic!" she said, gasping.

Theresa grinned and picked up her bowl of soup. "Glad to hear it. Right, Mom?" She drained the vessel dry.

Rose put a hand on Maddie's arm. "I'm glad to see you so happy settling in," she said. "Normally we don't put on such a show, but we're aiming to impress."

Maddie asked, "The diplomats?"

"And you," Rose said with a coy smile. "I want to get you hooked on the lifestyle."

"The lifestyle? You mean—"

"Can't blame a mother for trying, can you?"

Finn coughed as his face turned bright green. Maddie smiled in spite of herself and sipped her water to stop her cheeks blushing. Theresa cackled with glee.

They spent the next hour talking politics, but Maddie mostly just ate and listened. There were more than a dozen representatives seated at the table and she only knew two of them: Brynna and Ida. According to Finn, the queen's supporters had been strategically seated among the swing votes, and the voices in those areas were low.

"How do you think the vote is going to go?" Maddie whispered to Rose.

The queen leaned back in her chair, glancing down the table at Delilah. "I'm not sure. It's going to be very close. Our friend from Aster has been working overtime. She's capable of offering far more in exchange for votes than I am, and I've promised more in trade concessions and tribute in the last week than I ever thought I would in my entire life. It's like an auction. The only difference is we're bidding for our freedom, and no one knows what the other side's offering. At this point, it's so muddled . . . " She trailed off and sipped her wine. "I just hope it's enough. If we're lucky, your personal appeal will help them understand that there's more to this than money and sacks of grain."

The dinner bell chimed, and Maddie glanced over at Finn. As the queen stood up, the whole room got to their feet. Maddie's shoulders sagged. The time had come for the part of the evening she had been looking forward to the least.

"Do I have to do this?" she asked Finn. "What if I mess up?"

"Relax," he replied. "You'll be fine, and you look gorgeous."

Maddie took his hand and gave it a playful squeeze. "I suppose I should thank you for the dress. It's very beautiful."

"It was my pleasure."

The servers cleared away the dishes and tables with mystical precision. In minutes, the floor was empty, and a soft tremble of music grew in the air. Rose put out a hand to Brynna.

Maddie raised an eyebrow. "They're going to dance?"

"Brynna doesn't have any family here to dance with," Finn said. "Her husband is back in Thistle watching their kids. Theresa is going to dance with Hale, the son of the envoy from Hawthorne."

"Hawthorne?"

"It's in England. The ambassador is one of the undecideds, and she's hoping to set them up." Finn pointed with a nod and Maddie looked over. Hale stood in the corner in a white doublet and tall, leather riding boots accented with gray, an outfit to match his lean frame and pale blue eyes.

"He seems nice," Maddie said.

Finn took her to the edge of the dance floor. "My sister doesn't like him very much. Apparently, he's too brash. There's no way it's going to happen, but my mother's hoping it will be enough if we make it look like he had a chance."

The couples began to dance, first Rose and Brynna, then Theresa and Hale. Maddie watched them as they waltzed across the floor in daintily rotating squares. Maddie wrung her hands nervously as the first selection came to an end and the dancers left the floor.

When faeries dance, the woman leads, Maddie thought. It was an old saying that Rain had been careful to impress upon her. The first dances were the prerogative of the hosts. Theresa and Hale selected the next, and Maddie cringed as she watched the princess twirl rigidly around the room.

"She does not look happy," Maddie said.

Finn chuckled. "The things we do for politics," he replied, leaning in to whisper in her ear. "You may be the Foxglove, but I should tell you, dating royalty probably isn't going to be a bed of roses either."

"Then I guess I should wish us luck," said Maddie.

Finn squeezed her arm gently as Theresa and Hale left the floor. "Our turn."

Maddie took a deep breath. She'd been hoping to pick the waltz. It was the easiest, and while it wasn't technically a faux pas to repeat a previous selection, she suspected that the guests would be expecting more from the prince's consort. Luckily, she'd insisted that Rain teach her a backup. The courante.

As far as humanity was concerned, the dance hadn't survived the test of time, but the steps were easy to remember. Bend . . . step, step, step. She took Finn by the hand and stepped onto the floor. The musicians recognized the form and began to play.

Bend . . . step, step, step.

Bend . . . step, step, step.

Maddie did her best to smile as she and Finn went through the motions. Her heart pounded as she fought with every fiber of her being to avoid breaking out in a cold sweat.

"You okay?" Finn asked.

"Just fine," she answered rapidly.

His hands shifted down to rest on her hips. The supple silk of her dress revealed every detail of his touch.

"Hey . . . " he whispered. "It's alright. Look around. They love you."

The music slowed to give the other guests a chance to join them on the floor. Here and there around the room, Maddie caught a subtle nod or a little bow. When the music ended, she led Finn off the floor into the corner, where they headed down a twisting corridor and out onto a balcony. Maddie walked to the railing, and Finn came up behind her and put a hand gently on her back.

"Are you sure you're alright?" he asked.

Maddie turned around and laughed. She honestly didn't know what to say. Giddy energy bubbled in her chest.

"I just led a dance at a royal banquet," she said.

He gave a beaming smile, and his eyes glittered as he held her waist. "You did."

Maddie giggled.

"What is it?" he asked.

I could end up royalty, she thought. She wondered what her mother would think, knowing where she'd arrived and the strange path she'd taken. She would probably be proud. And it felt good.

"Nothing," she answered. "It's just funny how things turn out."

Finn let her go and leaned on the balcony railing. "Not bad though, right?"

Maddie turned and gave him a peck on the cheek. "Not too bad." He practically turned to stone.

The door behind them opened, and Theresa poked her head out. "Maddie? Are you out here?"

Maddie blushed as she turned around. "Yes."

Theresa looked between Maddie and the prince and grinned. "Sorry to spoil the mood," she said, "but—"

Maddie cut her off. "It's time."

A Century in Review

"I fail to see a problem," Rose said.

Delilah scoffed, standing opposite her. Two dozen other ambassadors sat around the table, which extended away from the throne and deep into the shadows beyond the light.

"Really?" she said. "That's odd, because from where I'm sitting, it looks like you can't even control your own territory. The Erlkin inhabit the Veil less than a hundred miles from this very spot, and not only do they pay neither taxes nor tribute, but they raid your settlements with impunity."

Maddie stood behind the throne beside Maeve and Theresa. Finn stood against the wall behind them. Only the representatives were permitted to sit.

"Is this everybody?" Maddie whispered. "Where's Ida?"

"Absent on instructions," Maeve whispered back. "Her city ordered her to abstain from the vote and stay in her quarters. They don't want to be involved in what happens here."

"But I thought they were on our side?"

"At least they're not voting against us," she said. "Now, be quiet."

Rose slid a ledger across the table. "Not with impunity. My jails are full of Erlkin brigands and thieves, but their common ancestry does not make them a nation. They have not been one people since the dissolution of the monarchy."

"You are naive," Delilah said. "Gwynedd is the oldest Erlkin alive, and she is their queen, whether the fact serves you or not."

"It is wrong to extract tribute from a broken society."

Brynna leaned forward into the conversation. "Besides which, competing claims on territory are hardly disqualifying. Even Thistle has its share of insurgents and border disagreements, and our kingdom is one of the oldest in the world. I would say that having to manage internal disputes is a prerequisite of politics. If anything, it strengthens Amaranth's claim."

"And have you managed them?" Delilah said to Rose. "Or have you left them, bleeding like a dagger in your side?"

"Not everyone is as eager as Aster to stamp out their malcontents," said Brynna. "Would you have her burn their city to the ground? Put its citizens to death? Those would hardly be the actions of a leader." Half a dozen others thumped their hands on the table in agreement.

Delilah was unmoved. "A kingdom that cannot assert its own sovereignty is not a kingdom."

"I am asserting it," Rose said, rising to her feet. "Right now. Amaranth has no need for Aster. We are capable of caring for our own, along with any person who passes through our territory, and we will continue to do so, just as we have done for the past hundred years." The queen shifted her gaze from the table and gestured for Maddie to come forward. "This young woman was attacked in the woods, a human girl, who crossed into the Veil by chance. We rescued her, healed her wounds, and she has made this place her home. I invited her here to recount her experiences so that you all might understand the care and comfort afforded by our city, its protectors, and its citizens. What better measure of our claim could there be?"

The ambassadors gave a rumble of support. Delilah sat down, grumbling.

Rose put her hand behind Maddie and ushered her gently to the table. "Go ahead, Maddie," she said.

Maddie pressed her hands to her sides to stop them shaking as the ambassadors stared her down. Their luminous eyes winked in the dim light. Rose was counting on her. Freedom. War. Political upheaval. It could all be riding on her next few words.

And I thought I was under pressure when I took the SATs, she thought.

"Thank you for hearing me," she began, bowing. "It's an honor to address this assembly." There was no reply. The ambassadors sat quietly, attentive as Maddie went on. "It's impossible for me to express my gratitude. I would have been killed if it hadn't been for Rose and her wardens, but the truth is that my rescue was only the beginning of a part of my life that . . . transformed me.

"I was an ordinary girl, with a family and friends. I went to school and worked hard, but I never really knew where my life was going to take me, and if you had asked me to guess or imagine or even to dream, I still wouldn't have come up with anything as strange and wonderful as the Veil. Thanks to Rose, I've come to know its people and their culture, continued my education, and earned an apprenticeship with her royal practitioner."

Brynna clapped, joined by a few others at the table.

"I look forward to the future," Maddie said. "A future that would not have been possible without Rose and the people of Amaranth, some of whom have become my close friends, and others . . . " She took a moment to look back at Finn. "More than friends."

She turned back to the table. "Rose told me that a life is something you build. She didn't have to help me, but she did, and she did it because she believes in protecting and enriching the lives of the people around her. I would have withered away if I had never come to this city, and any place that is capable of that kind of healing, and any woman that is capable of that kind of love and leadership, deserves the recognition you are all about to vote on."

The table applauded. Maddie felt her heart lift as Rose got out of her chair and wrapped her up in a tight embrace.

"Thank you," Rose whispered in her ear.

Maddie whispered back, "I hope it was enough."

As the applause faded, a single pair of hands continued to clap.

"A fine speech," Delilah said. "But it's a fraud."

Brynna's fist hit the table. "That's uncalled for," she said. "There is no basis for calling these women liars."

Delilah rose out of her seat like an approaching storm cloud. "Isn't there?" she said, addressing the table. "Friends and colleagues, it is my sad duty to inform you of an infamous and terrible truth. There is a conspiracy in this kingdom, to seize power. If we do not give the Queen of Amaranth what she wants, she has positioned herself to take it from us. This vote is a sham. Rose has seen to it."

Brynna laughed. "Ridiculous," she said. "We're all sitting right here! The armies of our nations stand ready to uphold the result of this assembly, and with the deepest respect to Rose, in the face of that, what could she possibly do to override our decision?"

Delilah fixed her eyes on Rose, and Maddie shuddered, tracing the lines of her gaze up the table to meet the queen's hard expression.

"Would you like to tell them?" Delilah asked.

Rose kept silent.

Delilah swept her hand around the table. "This assembly has gathered in good faith. Would you like to explain why this so-called nation of love and leadership has brought a weapon of mass destruction into their midst?"

The ambassadors sat up, heads pivoting as they scanned the room. The guards stood against the wall, swords still in their sheaths.

"Not the soldiers," Delilah said. "The danger cannot seen with the naked eye." She lifted her arm and pointed straight at Maddie. "It's the girl."

"What are you talking about?" Brynna said with a scoff.

"This woman is not human," Delilah answered. "She is an ancient weapon, recovered from the human side of the Veil barrier, disguised as a girl to keep us from discerning her true purpose: to provide a lever for Rose to exert political control beyond her borders, and perhaps to embark on a conquest of the Veil itself."

"An ancient weapon . . . from the human world?" Brynna said. "You're talking about the Foxglove."

"I am."

"Foolishness. The Foxglove is a myth."

"Is it?" Delilah replied. "I have brought a guest with me who knows the truth. Queen Rose does indeed possess the

Foxglove, and with the assembly's permission, my witness is prepared to prove it."

Maddie's heart caught in her throat as she watched the conversation unfold. It was like watching the room catch fire, and the blaze grew brighter and more terrifying with each passing moment. Her chest tightened as the door opened and the assembly began to murmur.

This isn't possible, she thought. *Rose, Maeve, Theresa, Finn, and Rain. They were the only ones who knew.*

A woman in a long, dark robe walked into the room. Maddie shook her head as she neared the table and drew back her hood. Pale skin and coal-black eyes glistened in the firelight. Rose fixed her gaze on the intruder.

Gwynedd.

"Seize her," Rose said. The guards began to move.

"This woman is under the protection of Aster!" Delilah snapped.

Brynna stood up. "Outrage!" she shouted. "This woman is the leader of a rogue state. She cannot speak here!"

Gwynedd laughed. "I'm glad you have so high an opinion of my people," she said. "But you will be thankful for my rogue state in a moment. Had I not been in the area, Rose's deception might have gone unnoticed."

"She has relevant information," Delilah said. "Is the Queen of Amaranth so afraid that she would suppress her testimony?"

The assembly began to nod, and one by one, the representatives broke their silence in support of Gwynedd. Maddie watched as Rose's shoulders began to sag.

"Let her speak," she said.

Gwynedd seemed to grow taller as she drew herself up to the table. "I'll do better than that," she said. "You will hear the evidence in the Foxglove's own words."

From the folds of her robes emerged a flat, metallic object. Maddie squinted through the low light. So much time had passed since the last time she saw a piece of technology, she almost failed to recognize it.

"This is a digital voice recorder," Gwynedd said. "A human device with which I'm sure you are all familiar. It has been listening to this young woman's conversations, and two days ago, it recorded this . . ."

The recording began to play, and Maddie listened in horror as her conversation with Finn and Kidhe trickled out into the room.

"I am the Foxglove. Being with me isn't going to be easy," she heard her voice say.

"A touching moment," Gwynedd said when the recording finished. "But sentiments notwithstanding, she admitted to the fact herself. Rose and her highest lieutenants have been concealing her true nature from the moment she appeared."

The ambassadors turned on Rose, raising their fists and voices as they shouted accusations of betrayal. Hatred burned across their faces. Only Brynna kept her seat.

Maddie threw herself onto Rose's armrest. "Oh my god, Rose," she said. "I am so sorry. I had no idea . . ."

Rose put a hand on Maddie's arm. Her touch was soft, but her fingers were trembling. "It's alright," she said.

Maddie felt her throat close, and she bit back tears. Gwynedd stepped back from the table and Delilah took her place.

"Rose," Delilah said. "On the authority of this assembly, I must ask that you submit yourself for arrest, turn over the Foxglove, and relinquish your throne."

Rose sat back in her chair. "I will not."

Delilah smiled. "The people of the Veil will not tolerate a tyrant. You leave us no choice but to take this nation from you."

Toil and Trouble

Maeve stood over her. "Don't reach. Invite."

Maddie propped herself up on all fours, shuddering with fatigue on the laboratory floor as she watched her blackened veins pulse with magic.

The spell was a difficult one. For the Purging of Poison. Maddie was having trouble wrapping her head around it. How could a person be expected to open their mind to poison? It was perfectly safe, of course. The poison never actually entered the witch's body, but feeling it . . . experiencing the vicious death of it . . .

Maddie shivered, recalling the insects they'd gone through during practice, the latest of which lay writhing on the table in front of her. The grub was about the size of a softball. Maddie could feel the relentless assault of the toxin as it attacked the creature's systems, severing the basic threads of life. Bringing the sensation in was like injecting her chest with cyanide.

"This spell sucks," Maddie said.

Maeve gave her a stern look. "This spell has saved more lives than I can count. The sensation will become familiar over time. As your body adjusts, the discomfort will fade."

"Isn't that a bit like developing a drug tolerance?"

"Of a sort," Maeve said.

"And that's good?"

"It is a matter of perspective. Witches are creatures of nature. To become more accustomed to its parts is to grow in your craft. You must cultivate a personal relationship with the world around you. Now, try again."

Maddie hunkered down. Maeve was right about one thing. Having walked a mile in the shoes of the rocks, the dirt, the water, and the trees, very little remained that did not feel personal. This was the first time that the magic had connected her to an animal, and already she was thinking about becoming a vegetarian.

It was all about opening up. You didn't just have to believe that you were connected; you had to feel it. You had to let the magic in and allow it to weave the world into your soul. It sounded easy. It sounded like the magic was doing most of the work, but in reality it was damned hard to let your mind allow the outside to exist inside. Every natural instinct went against it.

The grub began to still. Maddie's heart raced with fear and confusion as its consciousness spilled into her mind. There wasn't much time left.

"Stay calm," Maeve said. "You can do it."

Maddie forced a breath. "I'm *trying*. "

"Try harder. The fight-or-flight response will only make it harder for you to accept the spell. Clear your mind, and focus on your senses. Listen. Touch. Feel."

"I feel like my skin is about to crawl off."

Maeve didn't answer. Maddie shut her eyes and tried again. As she opened her mind, the poison lurched into her chest, and her skin broke out into a cold sweat. The venom spread into her arms and legs, creeping out until it was practically welling up in the back of her throat.

"There. You have it," Maeve whispered. "Now, complete the spell."

Maddie choked, waiting until the last possible moment to make sure she got it all.

"Now!" Maeve said.

Maddie bent over and vomited. Black bile spilled out onto the floor as she heaved for breath. The grub uncurled and began to crawl away.

"Oh, no you don't," Maddie said, scrambling on her knees to catch it. "We've been through too much together." She staggered to the shelves and took down a cage, placing the bug inside.

Maeve lifted an eyebrow. "Sentiment?"

"Call it a souvenir," Maddie said. "Unless you've got a black cat lying around."

Maeve fetched a mop from the corner. She handed it to Maddie. "We do not keep cats."

Maddie staggered over to the sludge and cleaned it up as Rose and Theresa came down into the room.

"Well, we found it," the princess said.

Maddie answered, "Where?"

Theresa held out the pendant from the Triple-C. There was a nail punched through it.

"A clever design. Who gave it to you?"

"A friend of mine from the city," Maddie said, approaching to cup the pendant in her hands. "She didn't show up for work yesterday."

Maeve called an end to the practice session, and they gathered on the couches by the fire.

Rose gave Maddie a once-over. "Working hard?" she asked.

"Yes, your majesty."

"That's a little formal," Rose said with a smirk. "I thought we agreed that you could call me Rose."

Maddie lowered her eyes. "It's part of my training. Maeve wants me to adopt a more professional sense of decorum."

Rose gave Maeve a critical look. "Seriously?"

"Yes, your majesty," Maeve replied. "She may work for another house someday, and it is never too early to develop good habits."

"Shall we get started?" Theresa asked. "I'll have my people search the city for your friend, but my guess is that she was an Erlkin spy."

"But she looked like a Faerie," Maddie said.

"No doubt thanks to Gwynedd's magic."

Maddie slouched in her seat. "I'm so sorry," she said. "I should have been more careful."

"There was no way you could have known," said Rose.

"Gwynedd is going to try to parlay this into a political takeover," Theresa said. "Once you're off the throne, she'll swear fealty to Aster in exchange for it."

"Will they give it to her?" Rose asked.

Theresa leaned back in her chair and shrugged. "It's 50/50. They might choose to install someone of their own. Either way, we can't leave. A government in exile is not an option. We'd never accumulate enough strength to get the city back."

"So, what do we do next?" Maddie asked.

"Prepare to fight," Theresa replied. "Raise an army, and pray that Delilah is bluffing."

"Could she be?" said Maddie.

"Maybe. Wars are costly and seldom popular. If we put up a tough enough front and make a few deals, we might be able to convince her to come to an arrangement. Provisional control. Maybe leave some people here to watch over you instead of hauling you off to Aster in a cage."

Maddie's eyes flicked over to Rose as apprehension gripped her chest. "Would they do that? Would they lock me up?"

"Undoubtedly," Maeve answered.

Rose added, "But we're not going to let that happen."

Maeve opened a cabinet and produced a huge, woolen bag. It gave a glassy clink when she held it out to Maddie. "Take this," she said.

Maddie looked inside. The wool sagged with the weight of heavy bottles, each bearing a tiny paper label, the results of countless hours of hard work and brutal practice. Maeve had collected every gram of excess potion she had not consumed.

"You saved them?" Maddie asked. "I thought you said bottles weren't for apprentices."

"Waste not, want not," Maeve replied. "And your studies have been coming along nicely."

Maddie reached into the bag and drew out a huge, black bottle. "And what's this?"

"The Earth Sight potion," said Maeve. "Do not use it unless it is absolutely necessary. A witch's task is to safeguard others. Pace yourself. You will be no good to anyone if you lose control."

Maddie put it back inside the bag and shut the flap. "Got it."

"How long will we have?" Rose asked Theresa.

"Two days," Theresa said. "Three at the most. However long it takes them to get here."

The sound of pounding footsteps came thundering down the stairs as Kidhe burst through the curtain covering the door. "Rose!" he shouted, leaning over to catch his breath.

She answered, "What is it?"

"We've got a problem."

A few minutes later, Maddie and the others stood on the edge of the aviary roof, the highest vantage point in Amaranth. A thousand campfires surrounded the city.

"So much for days," Theresa said, staring down. "They must have already been en route, ever since Gwynedd first got her hands on that recording, or even before."

"You mean they've been planning this all along?" Maddie said.

Rose clenched her fists. "It would seem so."

"I'm sorry, Rose," Kidhe said, falling to his knees. "I should have seen them coming."

Theresa looked down at him with a scowl. "Not to be too hard-nosed, but why didn't you? An army can't march through the forest without a trace."

"Gwynedd," Maeve said, cutting in. "And the Erlkin. They made their homes in the deep Veil only a few decades ago. Despite the loss of their society, there are certain to be many among them who remember its hidden paths. The wardens are not at fault."

"Call out the volunteers and distribute weapons," Rose said. "And muster the city watch. Our only chance is to hold them at the ramps. Kidhe, gather your wardens and prepare to repel an assault from the air."

"Yes, majesty," Theresa and Kidhe said in unison.

Maddie gazed down alongside Maeve and the queen, quiet for a long moment.

"This is really happening, isn't it?" she said. "Why don't you just hand me over?"

"That is not an option," Rose said. "We do not trade lives in this city."

"But people are going to die! I can't let that happen if there's something I can do about it. I'm not worth it."

"That is not the point," said Maeve. "Gwynedd serves only one purpose: obtaining the Foxglove. There is no way to predict what could happen if we delivered you into their hands. Above all else, she must be kept from your power."

"And giving you up wouldn't matter," Theresa said. "Now that the politicians are on her side, Delilah won't settle for anything less than the city and the throne."

"I thought you said that she might make a deal."

"That was before there was an army on our doorstep. The diplomatic process only works if there's time to let cooler heads prevail. Something tells me they aren't going to give it to us. We just have to hope we can hold them off until they lose interest."

"Can we?" Maddie asked.

Theresa glared down at the multitude and said, "Maybe."

"We'll need a backup plan," Rose said. "Brynna and Ida. They can take Maddie out of the country."

Theresa said, "I'll let them know."

The sound of drums rose up from the forest floor, and in the darkness, the footsteps of 10,000 soldiers beat into motion.

"Let's go," Rose said. "There isn't much time."

Battle Lines

Maddie adjusted the strap on her witching bag against her robes, and glanced over her shoulder. A formation of volunteers and city watchmen waited patiently for the battle to begin, lined up behind a deep thicket of spears and shields. Theresa's call to action summoned over 5,000 faeries to the square. Only half of them were ready. The city watch was still distributing weapons and armor in the rear, where Rain and the palace staff were evacuating as many people as they could to the safety of the palace. The birds of the aviary brooded in the upper branches, ready to take to take flight with the wardens and repel an assault from the air. Earnest sat among them on a thick limb, a giant among his smaller kin.

The armies of Aster surrounded the city-tree's trunk. Rose stood at the head of the formation with Finn, a full suit of armor hanging from her shoulders. The long blade of a sword as tall as Maddie hung strapped to her back.

Maeve stood beside her with a witching bag of her own, and Maddie found her place behind her mistress. Together, they watched Theresa come up the ramp to rejoin the group.

"What did they say?" Rose asked.

Theresa scoffed. "Surrender the city and the Foxglove. We've been given 24 hours to leave. I told them to shove it."

Rose took a long breath and unslung the blade from her back. "I guess it was inevitable," she said.

Her daughter blew a shrill whistle through her teeth, and a pair of birds dropped down from the canopy. Kidhe was sitting on the first, guiding the other with a long rope. Theresa climbed up into the empty seat as Kidhe slid down to the ground.

"Remember," Theresa said. "Hold here as long as you can. If you have to give ground, fall back all the way back to the palace. There'll be no way to hold the city once they're inside."

A trumpet blew across the sky as Aster's army formed ranks and trudged up the winding ramp, coiling around the truck like a steel-gray vine. A field of spears glinted in torchlight, casting back the light of their torches like a prairie on fire.

"I wonder where the Erlkin are," Maddie said.

Theresa adjusted the straps on her saddle. "Oh, they'll be along, just in time to mop up after the hard fighting. Gwynedd will want to keep them fresh."

"Why?"

"So that she can generously offer to provide security and restore order. What a crock."

"I'd hoped it wouldn't come to this," Rose said.

"We can't always pick our battles," the princess said. "Sometimes our destiny comes to us. Right, Maddie?"

Maddie managed a weak smile and said, "I suppose so."

The ground began to tremble, quaking under the weight of Aster's booted feet.

"Delilah was right about one thing," Rose said. "I should have taken care of Gwynedd long ago."

Theresa cracked the reins of her mount. "It is what it is."

Rose brought Maddie into a tight hug. "I'm sorry for all this," she said. "You don't deserve any of it."

Maddie felt her chest go tight. "I'm not ready."

"No one is ready for times like these. Just do your best. It will be enough." She kissed her on the cheek. "I'm so proud of you."

"I don't know why. If it weren't for me, you wouldn't have to fight."

Rose clasped her hands around Maddie's. "If it weren't you, it would have been something else. Just concentrate on staying safe." Rose let her go and turned to Finn. "Both of you look after each other," she said.

Maddie looked up at Theresa. "And you look after Kidhe."

"Speaking of which," the princess said, "we should be going."

Kidhe glanced at Maddie nervously. "You be careful, okay?"

"I will," Maddie said, giving him a kiss on the cheek. "You know, I feel like I should have something more important to say, but we only just got started."

Kidhe said, "There's still time."

"There better be," Maddie replied. "I've still got a mountain of junk food to introduce you to. Take care of yourself, okay?"

Theresa coughed.

Maddie let him go, and he vaulted up into his saddle. He and the princess flew up into the canopy. A moment later, the entire flock took flight. Maddie reached into her bag, took out a vial of her stone throwing potion, and popped the lid off with her thumb. She drank it and shut her eyes, feeling the magic seep into her body as the cobblestones in the street began to tremble.

"You know, it's really attractive when you do that," said Finn.

"And you're not intimidated by the fact that I'm a super weapon?"

Finn nodded, wrinkling his chin in deep thought. "I could date a super weapon," he said.

Maddie rolled her blackened eyes and said, "Faerie men are weird." The magic in her voice boomed and echoed as she spoke. Maddie felt her dignity crumble as the soldiers around her chuckled. One of the men behind Finn gave him a light thump on the shoulder.

"What's it going to be like?" Maddie asked. "Fighting, I mean."

Finn drew his sword and shook his head. "I don't know. I've never done it. At least not like this."

They stared down the ramp. A short while later, the enemy marched into view. The bright white Aster uniforms caught the firelight from the square. Heavy armor and spear points glistened while white banners fluttered over the approaching mass like a swarm of ghosts.

Maddie heard a thump. A javelin embedded itself into the shield of a man not six feet away.

The queen bellowed, "Shields!"

The crowd stepped forward and formed a wall six layers deep, shields held high to guard the line. Rose lifted her sword up over her head and brought it down.

"Loose!"

All around them, hundreds of archers emerged from their hiding places in the branches above, and a thousand arrows rained down onto the steps. Pain burst in Maddie's chest, followed by the sharp sting of metal and wood in her shoulder and cheek. She grasped at her robes, gasping as the first screams rose from the throats of their stricken enemies. Her pulse jumped, and her heart clenched. Maddie covered her ears and closed her eyes to shut them out, but the images and feelings continued to pour in. Her knees buckled, and she collapsed onto the ground.

Finn knelt down and held her. "Maddie?" he shouted. "What's wrong?"

Maeve knelt down beside him. "Did you take the Earth Sight?" she asked urgently.

Maddie shook her head, flinching. "No, but I . . . I can't keep them out! What's happening?"

Maeve gripped Maddie's shoulders and leaned in close. "It is the Foxglove," she whispered. "Your true self must sense the danger. Its power is bleeding out, but you must keep it under control. Focus on your spells, and concentrate."

"I can't!" Maddie said, gripped the sides of her head as tears forced their way onto her cheeks.

Maeve slapped her. The blow stunned Maddie back into her own senses.

"You must," Maeve said. "There is no time."

Maddie gritted her teeth, straining as she pushed the sensations out and the feelings down, and Finn helped her back to her feet. She brought up her hands. As she did, cobblestones the size of manhole covers rose into the air.

Maeve stepped back. The enemy continued to press forward through the hail of arrows only a dozen yards away, grim determination on their faces. Maddie's eyes reached across the shrinking distance. There was only one thing left to do.

In storybooks, there was always time for reflection, time to resolve the conflicting emotions of war and become inspired by the people and the cause. But this was no story. There was no time to learn to become a warrior. There was only the sound of drums, the thunder of her heartbeat in her ears, and the bitter taste of adrenaline at the back of her throat. For the next few hours of darkness, Maddie Foster, human girl and witch in training, would have to be enough.

The enemy charged, and Maddie thrust her arms forward. The stones flew as a hundred spears and shields smashed together in a roar of battle and blood.

Rising Tide

The deadly point of a leaf-shaped spearhead flashed out from the darkness, its cold edge glimmering in the torchlight. Maddie twisted away, sweeping a hand in front of her body as a huge flagstone flew around from her side, smashing into her attacker's ribs. The woman tumbled away and the spear wavered, falling to the ground as her lungs heaved against the blow to her chest. Maddie felt her choking, and she gasped.

The impressions of the Foxglove continued to pour in. To her left, Finn ducked a deadly strike and drove into a soldier with the point of his sword. The faerie's green blood flowed over the blade as she grunted and crumpled onto the ground. Cold fear broke into Maddie's thoughts for an instant before the press of the battle lines trampled the woman underfoot, and the feeling disappeared.

A storm of blood and metal swirled on the city's doorstep. Maddie clenched her teeth and hissed across blackened gums as the soldiers of Aster continued to push. After more than an hour of rage and combat, the strength of the volunteers faltered, wavering as the soldiers succumbed to fatigue.

But Maddie had never felt so alive. Her heart surged in her chest. Adrenaline and magic rippled through her body. Her muscles pulled against their joints and her skin was hot with sweat. Electricity crackled in her throat, and every one of her expanding senses tingled with unearthly power.

"Are you alright?" Finn shouted.

Maddie answered with a voice like a demolition blast. "I'm fine."

Finn ran over to her and grabbed her by the shoulder. "You don't sound fine," he said, examining her eyes.

"I'm fine!" Maddie said, shaking him off to stare at the frothing battle.

Aster was closing in. With each passing moment, the enemy pushed further and further up the steps, while above, the air was so full of birds that Maddie could hardly see the branches.

"There are too many of them," she said.

Finn stared up at the shrieking flock and answered, "I know."

Steel crashed, the line fractured, and a dozen enemy soldiers burst through the gap. Maddie threw her hands up and pressed them forward, shouting as a barrage of stones barreled into the advancing pack. Their bodies were hurled back into the swell of their comrades, and the city's volunteers jammed themselves into the breach.

Maddie's chest rumbled with exhilaration as blood, pain, and magic mingled in her mind. She stuffed her hand down into her bag and grabbed another potion. Maeve had instructed her to pace herself, but in the middle of the battle those instructions were impossible to follow. She'd been pounding vials of her stone-throwing potion like shots of liquor. Hunger swelled in her belly, and the rising temptation to drink greater amounts of the magic's sweet, sickly perfume was growing impossible to resist.

"Look out!"

Maddie cursed, snapping her eyes around. A tall faerie woman leapt over the shield wall and dove towards her. There was a glint of steel. A long blade flashed, and Maddie fell back, arms spinning. Her stones scattered as her focus broke. The back of her head smacked against the street, driving the breath from her lungs as the woman brought her blade down.

Steel rang against steel. Maddie looked up as Rose leapt in front of her, parrying the blow with her giant sword. She shifted her weight and rammed into Maddie's attacker with her shoulder, knocking the woman back as she brought the weapon around to strike. The woman lunged away as a tangle of woody vines burst from the ground, catching her arms and legs.

Maddie rolled her head to see Maeve, whose black eyes and firm jaw revealed nothing but iron resolve. Rose's sword slashed across the soldier's stomach and she fell, bleeding as her body went limp.

"That was too close," Rose said, pulling Maddie up off the ground. "Are you alright?"

Maddie fought to catch her breath. "I could have died," she said.

"You were reckless," Maeve said, approaching. "I told you to be careful."

The enemy began to fall back. Rose eyed the shrinking lines as they retreated around the trunk and out of sight. The weary volunteers leaned on each other and sat on the ground, stealing a moment to catch their breath.

"Are they leaving?" Finn said.

Rose answered, "Impossible."

Maddie felt a strange sensation overtake her legs. They twitched, rapidly tensing and flexing as though eager to dance across the ground. Her toes curled in her shoes like talons.

"Rose . . . " Maddie said. "What's going on?"

Rose stood beyond the line, eyes probing the darkness as the sounds of combat began to fade. A rattling, clicking sound grew into the air.

"What is that?" Maddie asked.

The queen retreated, sheathing her sword. She picked up a spear from the ground. "Cavalry," she said. "You have to get out of here."

Maddie stared at her in confusion. "What?"

Rose pushed Maddie into Finn. "You must go. Find Brynna and Ida. They will get you to safety."

"But what about you?" Maddie said.

"We'll be fine, but we cannot allow you to be captured."

"But what's happening? It's going to be okay, right?"

The queen turned away and hustled back to the front of the line. She shouted to the volunteers. "Reform! Quickly! Maeve, cover the ramp!"

Maddie grabbed her arm. "Rose?!"

Maeve reached into her bag and hauled out a large, green jug. She gulped it down and turned to the broad stairway as she brought up her arms. All around her, vines and branches sprang from the ground, snatching up crates, stones, and barrels to barricade the gap.

Finn began to pull Maddie away as a high-pitched squeal rose up from the steps. A shot of fear clamped around Maddie's throat as a black mass of legs, jaws, and glistening shell came around the corner. Beetles the size of elephants rumbled forward forward, their riders wielding long spears and bows. Six-foot pincers, sharpened and plated with metal, framed hungry jaws dripping with saliva. They smashed into Maeve's makeshift barricade, and the wood shuddered.

"Go!" Rose shouted.

Finn yanked Maddie away, racing up the street towards the lifts. Maddie looked over her shoulder as they ran. The defenders were shuffling backwards, tired and terrified, but each unwilling to be the first to turn and run.

Maddie stopped running.

"Maddie!" Finn said. "What are you doing? We have to go!"

"Running won't help," Maddie said. "We'll never make it."

She reached into her bag and drew out the bottle of Earth Sight unguent. The top was sealed with a wire frame. Maddie chuckled in spite of herself. In case of emergency, break glass.

She grabbed Finn's sword.

He barked. "Hey! What are—"

Maddie slashed the blade down the neck of the bottle, and the top snapped off with a rigid crack. With one hand, she emptied the potion down her throat.

"Maddie..." Finn said.

Her voice rumbled as the mixture burst in her gut and a black shroud fell across her vision. "Stay close to me," she said, returning his sword. *A witch's task is to safeguard others,* she thought.

Finn stared at her in wonder. "Maddie? What are you doing?"

Maddie's vision flew out into the night, and the war poured in. "My job."

As the battle line exploded, the black horde came pouring through the gap.

Fight or Flight

Maddie threw a building at them. Ten tons of rubble broke over the steps, crushing shell and armor as the insects and their riders howled in fear. Pain flashed across Maddie's skin like hot steam. Her bones cracked and her heart stopped beating as the deaths of a hundred soldiers lashed like burning whips across her mind.

"Shit!" she hissed, doubling over as she cried out.

Finn grabbed her as her knees hit the street with a crack.

"Maddie!"

The next wave of the enemy crested over the pile of stone, descending like an avalanche as the city defenders readied their spears in futile hope.

The vision of a thousand insects, soldiers, and civilians poured into Maddie's head. She searched through them wildly, looking for any sign of Maeve and Rose as the scything jaws of the beetles cut through the volunteers like blades of grass. Maddie's stomach wrenched as the power of the Earth Sight brought her the full weight of every sickening sensation. A thousand brutal deaths, a thousand howls of agony, and a thousand anguished cries and final breaths. Maddie experienced them all, lost in the horror, as Finn dragged her away.

The market was in pandemonium. Thousands of faeries flooded the street, desperate to escape to the safety of the palace. The cable cars creaked, ropes straining, as the people heaped themselves aboard and clung desperately to the sides. Finn elbowed their way to the front and climbed the platform, where a thin ring of soldiers fought to organize the chaos. Brynna and Ida were among them.

"Where is the queen?" Brynna shouted.

"Still at the front," Finn said. "We have to get Maddie out of here!"

Ida reached forward. "I'll take her," she said, gesturing to the soldiers. "These are our personal guards. They'll hold the platform until we're safely away."

Maddie lifted her head, a swirl of chaos playing inside her eyes. "Finn? Come with me?"

Finn leaned in and held her head. "I have to find my mother," he said. "You go. Ida will take care of you."

Maddie felt her feet leave the ground as Ida threw her over her shoulders.

"Can you get her out of the city?" Finn asked.

Ida stepped onto the cable car with a grunt. "My birds are standing by. I promise, I'll do everything I can. Any word on the Erlkin?"

"Still no sign," Finn said.

Ida paused, grabbing the shoulder of the nearest soldier. "You," she said. "With us."

They climbed aboard with Brynna as the carriage lurched into motion. Maddie's shoulders relaxed as the fear and desperation of the city grew distant and the sounds of the battle faded to a dull roar.

"All those people," Maddie whispered. "They're going to die. They're going to die, and it's all my fault."

Brynna took her down from Ida's shoulders. There were no empty seats on the crowded car, so she laid her on the floor. "They won't all die," she said. "There are rules in war. Once you're safe, Rose will order her soldiers to lay down their arms. Aster will have to accept a peaceful surrender."

Small comfort, Maddie thought. *She will have lost everything because of me.*

Citizens of the city packed the palace courtyard when the carriage arrived at the top. Rain stood in the middle of the panic, directing traffic.

"Where are your birds?" Brynna asked Ida.

"The roof," she answered. "We'll go to the throne room and have them meet us on the balcony."

Rain came running over. "What's happening?"

"Rose called a retreat," Brynna said.

Rain's face fell. "No . . ."

"We knew it was a possibility. We're getting Maddie out of the city. Rose will hold the ground as long as she can."

Fear and regret splashed into Maddie's head, tightening in her chest as Rain turned and embraced her. Her friend's sorrow was like boiling water.

"I'm sorry," Maddie said, spilling tears as she held her. "I'm so sorry for all of this."

Rain sniffed and squeezed her tight. "It's alright. Everything will be alright."

"We have to go," Ida said. "There's not much time."

They raced through the packed corridors and up to the throne room. Ida shut the door behind them as Brynna made her way to the balcony. It was locked.

"I'll take care of this," Brynna said, picking up a chair.

"That won't be necessary," Ida replied. "We won't be leaving."

Maddie felt Ida's arm tighten around her.

Brynna slowly turned around, fingers tightening around the legs of the chair. "What?"

Greasy smoke rose from Ida's body, hissing as it twisted into the air. A black surge of eagerness and triumph caught fire in Maddie's head as the image of a dread, familiar face flashed into view.

Maddie struggled, pressing her arms to pull away from her. "Let me go!" she shouted.

Ida held firm as the trickle of smoke became a river, filling the air with a sickening fog as the woman's clothing and armor disappeared and her skin peeled away, revealing ivory-white flesh, dark robes, and hollow, impenetrable eyes.

"Gwynedd," Brynna murmured.

The pale witch tilted her head with an icy grin.

Brynna lifted the chair. "Where is Ida?"

"Dead in the woods, where she has been for many weeks," Gwynedd replied. "By now, her corpse will be food for the insects, along with the bodies of her guards."

Maddie's eyes flicked to the guard from the square. She was gone. Moira stood in her place. "You're monsters," she said.

Gwynedd pursed her lips. "Tut tut, Foxglove. Or have you forgotten? I am the queen of the Erlkin. *You* are the Foxglove, and nearer a monster than I."

"I am not!" Maddie said, yanking at her arms to get away.

Gwynedd's grip tightened around her wrist. "But you are. I built you to be a monster — *my* monster — but you betrayed me and destroyed the civilization you were created to protect. You owe my people a debt, and I will have it from you."

Rage boiled in Maddie's chest. Her body tensed as every piece of furniture in the room rose off the floor and broke into splinters. The shards trembled in the air and Maddie set her mouth in a thin, determined line. She'd experienced so many deaths already. Their cries of pain still echoed in her ears. She could suffer through one more.

"If I *am* the Foxglove," she said, "then I am more than enough to rid the world of you."

Moira took a step back as the wooden stakes hurtled through the air.

"You forget," Gwynedd said, reaching into her robes. The missiles halted, inches from their goal. "Your power belongs to me."

Maddie felt her body go stiff. Gwynedd drew her hand out of her robes, fingers clutched around a leather cord affixed to a heavy glass jar. Thick, red liquid bubbled inside. Maddie felt a pain in her chest as her eyes came to rest on a bloody lump sitting at its base.

She could hardly move her mouth to form the words. "My heart."

Gwynedd sneered as red light pulsed in the jar. Maddie put out a hand, and the splinters turned themselves on Brynna.

"Wrong again," Gwynedd said. "It's mine."

The ambassador flinched and held the chair out as a shield. "Maddie . . . " she said. "Stop."

Maddie strained against her muscles, but her body wouldn't move, and the impressions of the world in her head were gone. The Earth Sight had been pinched off like water in a knotted hose.

She shouted, "I can't!"

Gwynedd chuckled and tapped her palm against the jar. "It's no use fighting," she said. "I've had a thousand years to perfect this magic. You may not realize it yet, but your whole life has been building to this moment."

Brynna took a step forward. "Get away from her."

Gwynedd shot her a skeptical glance. "Or what?"

"This place is full of —"

"Guards?" Gwynedd asked. "I think you'll find them occupied. There's a war on, you know."

"This was your plan all along," Maddie said, gritting her teeth. "Ever since I got away from you in the woods."

"Something like that."

"Stop," Moira said. "There's no point in drawing this out. It's sick."

"Reservations, little prince?" Gwynedd asked.

"Just get it over with!"

"Little prince . . . " Maddie breathed, pulling her gaze around to Moira. "Morrow?"

"I'm sorry, Maddie," Moira said. "I didn't have a choice."

Maddie searched his expression. It was the same one he'd worn the evening they'd met. She'd grown tired of seeing it.

Her face twisted with anger. "There is always a choice."

"You'll never make it out of here," Brynna said.

Gwynedd extended a hand. "Neither will you." The wooden stakes flashed through the air, shattering the chair, and pierced the ambassador through the heart. She fell to the ground, lifeless. Maddie's mouth dropped in horror.

"Come along, Foxglove," Gwynedd said. "It's time for you to meet your maker."

Heartbeat

They went out onto the balcony. Morrow ran to the railing and looked down at the city. Soldiers and citizens crammed the market square, surrounded by Aster's soldiers. The army of Amaranth was broken, the armies of Aster were weakened, and the forces of the Erlkin would soon be closing in. It sickened Morrow to admit that his mistress's plan had functioned perfectly.

"Stand there, Foxglove," Gwynedd said, pointing to the center of the floor. "Morrow, take her things."

Maddie shuffled forward and stood. "Please," she said. "Don't do this."

Morrow did as he was told. Maddie watched him in silence.

"I'm sorry," he said.

She clenched her jaw. "Go to hell."

"It wasn't personal. I had to do it."

Her eyes narrowed as she stared ahead, unable to turn and face him. "How could you do this to me? To everyone!"

"It wasn't my fault."

"Wasn't your fault?! What a load of bullshit!"

"You have to understand!" Morrow said. "Gwynedd's blood keeps me alive. I am bound to her. I can't even think for myself. I needed to—"

She cut him off with a yell. Her eyes were full of rage and hate, and Morrow flinched away.

"Shut up!" Maddie shouted. "You're a coward and a liar, and it's pathetic! You think an apology can fix this? Nothing can!"

Morrow's shoulders drooped. "I didn't want this."

"Then you should have done something. We could have helped you."

Morrow came around in front of her. "There is no cure for me," he said. "Resisting would have meant my death."

Her black gaze bored into him. "Then you should have died."

Her eyes drove him back to the railing as he staggered away.

Gwynedd took out her knife. The stone blade caught the dim glow of the room, a shadow of orange and black. She took up a tall jar of black potion and undid the stopper. Morrow's stomach lurched as the sour, rotten smell filled the room. His mistress consumed every last drop. She cut her palms, and as hands dripped blood down the blade, it burst into shadowy flame.

Morrow heard shouts in the corridor and glanced at the door. Someone was coming. "Quickly," he said to Gwynedd.

She shut her eyes and answered, "Patience."

Morrow drew his sword and ran to the door, bracing himself against it as the light on the balcony dimmed, fading away until the moon and the stars disappeared and the only point of light was the burning glow of his mistress's stone knife.

Maddie squirmed in place, whimpering. "Gwynedd . . . please."

Morrow tried to look away but found that he could not. This was his fault. The least he could do was watch.

Gwynedd opened her robes, baring her breast as she knelt down in front of Maddie and turned the blade on herself.

"What are you doing?" Morrow gasped.

She rested the point against her chest and took a breath. "Seizing my destiny."

She stabbed herself and cut down, wincing as her skin opened. Black blood flowed out, saturating her robes as she pulled the knife down to a point below her ribs and dropped it. Green smoke burst from the wound as she pressed her hand into the bleeding gap. Yanking hard, face twisting, she wrenched her own heart out into the air.

Black magic coated the gnarled flesh like crude oil, and when the smoke cleared, the wound in her chest was gone. Maddie stared at her in slack-jawed horror. Gwynedd put her knife away in her belt, and took up the jar containing Maddie's heart.

"No going back now," she said.

She opened the jar and brought out the stolen heart. Magic flared from her palms, splitting into a thousand threads of green, red, and black. Blood pooled in the air, released from gravity as Gwynedd brought the two organs together, glistening as they beat on their own.

"Stop!" Maddie screamed. "Gwynedd, please!"

Gwynedd glanced up. "Open your robes."

Maddie wept as her hands moved and undid her clothes, tears running down her face. Morrow looked on in horror as Gwynedd pressed the hearts together, and the spell fused them into one. Light flashed, and a wave of force shook the balcony with such force that it threatened to fall from the tree.

Gwynedd held the new heart, reformed into a new, singular, otherworldly whole. Though its shape was ordinary, the feeling of power and dread that emanated from it was alien even in a world of magic.

A crash rattled against the door and Gwynedd's eyes flicked up. "Hold them!" she shouted.

Morrow was thrown aside as the balcony door shattered off its hinges and fell in pieces to the floor. Rose, Maeve, Finn, and a dozen soldiers burst into the room.

Gwynedd ducked behind Maddie, the conjoined heart burning in her palm like a muddy sun.

"Stop!" Rose bellowed.

Gwynedd thrust the heart into Maddie's chest.

Primeval

Maddie's head swam. Clouds of light and color drifted in the air. Green, orange, yellow, and red swirled around the balcony, blossoming like wildflowers in the breeze. Her body felt strange. She knew she was naked, because she could see her hands and legs and arms, but they were like clay, grown over with a patchwork of flesh, wood, and marbled stone. Long hair fell to the floor below her in a waterfall of blended colors, curling in the air and shifting across the floor. Her veins burned brighter than the sun.

She hovered in the middle of the space, toes just barely brushing the floor, while the others stared bathed in scattered flashes of flickering light.

Gwynedd stood behind her, one hand pressed into her back. Maddie felt her palm gently cupping the heart that now beat within her chest.

"What have you done?" Rose asked, sword in hand.

Gwynedd smiled. "Only what I promised. The Foxglove has been reborn, and it belongs to me." She brushed her thumb against the heart. "Let's have some privacy, Foxglove. Kill the soldiers."

Maddie shifted as her head turned. In her mind, Maddie recoiled in horror as the necks of the soldiers twisted around. She heard their bones snap and they fell to the floor.

"That's better," Gwynedd said.

Finn glanced at Maeve. "What do we do?" he asked.

Gwynedd laughed. "Indeed."

She snapped her fingers, and Maddie's head tilted to one side. Finn was thrown against the wall. His head struck the wood with a crack, and he fell to the ground, unconscious.

Maddie's arms rose, and the building began to shake. Cracks formed in the walls as the sound of splintering wood and snapping rope rocked the palace. The structure heaved and the tree tore open. The upper floors of the palace sailed away into the night, swept up in a great wind that emerged from nowhere, filling the sky with swirling leaves and broken branches.

The fighting in the city staggered to a halt. Friend and foe alike stared upwards, struggling to grasp the enormity of what they witnessed.

Gwynedd pointed at the exhausted, bloodied throng. "Them next," she said.

Maddie rotated in place. *No!* she shouted in her head. *Stop!*

Her lips were still. She strained, but her willpower disbursed into the emptiness of her mind. She had the sensation of being asleep, of fighting or running in that strange world where every step felt heavy and every blow fell weak.

She cried out as the wind intensified. Buildings crumbled and broke as green clouds formed in the sky over their heads, and the city was caught in a hurricane of dust and stone. The people threw themselves to the ground, desperate for shelter, while overhead, the birds of Amaranth and Aster were blown into the abyss, their small forms powerless against the gale.

"That's enough," Gwynedd said, nodding with cold satisfaction.

Far below, a dark mass of Erlkin soldiers emerged from the trees and moved in, marching up the steps that circled the trunk.

Rose took a step forward. "Stop!"

"Watch," Gwynedd said, "as the reign of the Faeries comes to an end."

Rose tightened her grip on her sword, and rushed at Gwynedd. The witch snapped her fingers again, and Maddie's arms flew up. Rose flung herself across the room as the invisible force that had killed the guards sprang once again into being. It held the queen, arms outstretched, flexing sinew and muscle against unseen chains.

Gwynedd looked at her with disdain. "Did you really think you could kill me that way?" she asked.

Rose looked up at her, hard defiance chiseled across her face. "No."

The sound of a bowstring snapped in the air. With a booming cry, Earnest and Kidhe came swooping down from the ravaged canopy. The ranger stood high in his saddle, firing again and again, as the wings of the great bird beat against the gale. Arrows glinted in the moonlight as they flashed towards Gwynedd. Maddie's body flew in front of the witch in a ripple of light and motion. She winced instinctively, but her eyes held themselves open as the arrows disintegrated into flecks of sawdust.

Gwynedd threw out a hand and Maddie's arm lashed out. Above, an invisible fist took hold of Kidhe and Earnest and hurled them down into the city. They struck the ground like a meteorite, and were lost in a cloud of dust.

Gwynedd took a deep breath and said, "Pitiful."

Rose stared her down. "Got you," she said, a flicker of a smile whispering across her face.

Maddie's eyes lifted as a tiny shadow descended from the sky. The silhouette of a sparrow plummeted down, emerging from behind Earnest's former place in a harrowing nose dive. Theresa stood in the saddle, crouched like a jockey. In one hand, she held the reins, in the other she gripped a long, polished spear.

Gwynedd flung her arms up in desperation, and Maddie felt her body turn. A swirling wind crashed into the air, catching the bird. Theresa leapt from the saddle and dove, continuing her deadly course as she roared with all her might.

The point of the spear missed Maddie's head by millimeters, aiming for Gwynedd's face. The weapon pressed forward through the wind, and a thin line of blood slid down Gwynedd's cheek. Theresa was held in the air, motionless.

She gritted her teeth.

"Finished?" Gwynedd asked.

"Never," Theresa snarled, wrenching her shoulders forward in a final, desperate effort to drive the spear down.

Gwynedd sighed. She flicked her wrist, and Maddie brought up her arm. Theresa yelped as she was whisked into the air. She twisted and turned, struggling to break free.

Rose cried out. "Gwynedd, no!"

Maddie's arm swept out in a brisk stroke. Theresa hurtled backwards through the air, vanishing into the darkness beyond the tree.

"And as for you . . . " Gwynedd said, turning on Maeve. "What would be a fitting punishment?"

Maddie's eyes turned and latched on to her mistress's apprehensive glance.

Maeve's body tightened as her arms trembled, and her frame began to shake. "Stop . . . please . . . " she whimpered as her hands drifted to the sides of her head and green blood began to pour from her blackened eyes.

Her sobs grew until she fell to her knees, screaming as her fingers pulled at her hair and clawed at the sides of her skull. She collapsed on the ground and lay still, barely breathing, staring dull and vacant across the floor.

Maddie watched it happen, powerless to stop it. Her heart broke as she witnessed the casual brutality, and she pounded against the inside of her mind like a prisoner in a cell.

"That was very satisfying," Gwynedd said, all but shuddering as she fixed her eyes on Rose. "That only leaves you."

Maddie's heart stopped.

"Finish her," Gwynedd said, pointing.

Maddie's arms came up.

"No," said Gwynedd. "Do it slowly." She came to stand in front of Rose. "I want to savor this."

The queen glared at her, paralyzed by the magic of the Foglove. Maddie screamed, tugging at her useless limbs in desperation as she floated across the room. She closed her hands around Rose's neck, and squeezed.

Rose choked and coughed as Gwynedd laughed. Maddie shrieked, hurling herself against the locked door of her mind.

"It's okay," Rose said, meeting Maddie's eyes with a weakening smile. "Maddie, it's okay."

Maddie wept, madly seeking some dark corner of her thoughts to hide in, but there was nowhere to go. The impassive eyes of the Foxglove stared ahead as the minutes passed, and Rose began to gag.

"It's not your fault," Rose said, chest heaving. Her eyelids fluttered shut. A final breath escaped her lips with a rattle, and she whispered, "Take care of . . . my son."

Her body relaxed, twitching until it finally went limp. Maddie shuddered, feeling to urge to vomit as the last threads of life slipped from Rose's regal form and disappeared.

Maddie stared down at her hands, quaking as she collapsed into a heap inside her mind, howling dry tears and shrieking silent screams inside a body that reacted like stone.

Courage

Morrow crouched by the railing, staring with transfixed eyes as his mistress slaughtered her enemies one by one. In another hour, Gwynedd would conquer the whole of the Veil, and Morrow knew she wouldn't stop there, not with the power of all creation at her fingertips.

His eyes strayed to the lifeless body of the queen, and he wondered if there was a point when she realized it was over. *Did you hold out hope,* he thought, *or did you know it was finished the moment the devil walked into the room?*

He looked into the burning eyes of the Foxglove and wondered what had become of Maddie. Her face was like a sun-warmed cliff, rippling beneath a waterfall of light and fire.

Can you see what's happening? Are you fighting?

Morrow didn't know Maddie well, but he knew enough to be sure that she would never stop trying.

His mistress moved across the broken remnants of the balcony, gliding over the blood-stained floor, eyes fixed on the horizon. In the distance, a bell began to toll. Midnight. The witching hour of the solstice.

Gwynedd pointed to the edge of the sky. "There," she said. "Open it."

The Foxglove reached out, dangling in the air like a divine marionette. Gwynedd stood behind her, shoulders back, chin lifted with pride as a shimmering rupture broke open where the forest met the clouds. A swirling gray mist oozed from the gap. The fog shimmered with hidden light as it poured into the forest.

Morrow thought about his mother, the ruler of the Erlkin that he once knew, before she succumbed to Gwynedd's influence. Strong, dignified, cultured, powerful . . . and gone. She had given up everything so that he could survive. What would she think if she could see him now?

His stomach turned at the thought as he stared at the oncoming storm and his mistress framed before it. Maddie told him that an apology could never fix what he had done.

Morrow clenched his fists as he got to his feet.

Perhaps there was still time.

Solstice

Maddie watched numbly, magic surging through her altered form as her power tore a bleeding slash across the sky. The World Curtain poured in through the gap, escaping the vacuum between realms as it spilling into the forest of the Veil. The clouds rolled, growing as they drew closer. The Foxglove's eyes penetrated the gloom, and through them, Maddie could make out the distant outline of a landscape on the other side: Iris, the original home of the fair folk.

The mists would remove their memories. Gwynedd, protected by the power of the Foxglove, would doubtless remain unharmed. There would be nothing to stop her from installing herself as a new ruler, and the people would never be the wiser. Only Maddie would remember, trapped in the prison of her own mind, howling for eternity as eons passed and she descended into still, silent madness.

The curtain drew nearer.

Maddie watched her future come to an end as the shroud that cloaked the world swept in to claim them.

A shriek pierced the stillness, and Maddie's head snapped around. Gwynedd fell backwards, pinwheeling off balance as she screamed. Morrow stood behind her, arms bent around her chest and neck as he dragged her back. The witch's hand slipped out from Maddie's body with a burst of light as they tumbled to the floor.

Gwynedd snatched her knife out of her belt and stabbed it into the prince's side. Morrow cried out as he struggled to maintain his hold.

His eyes rose up to meet Maddie's. "Do something!" he shouted.

Maddie felt a tingle in her arms and legs as her feet touched the floor. She tried to step back, but it was as though her body was full of cement. Her limbs were alien, and her mind rejected against them as she struggled to lift her feet and cross the floor.

"I—" Her voice broke like a sonic boom. The floor shook. Morrow let go of Gwynedd and gripped his ears. Gwynedd did the same, dropping the knife to clutch her skull as she screamed. There was blood on her hands as they came away from her head.

She snarled, "No!"

Gwynedd lunged towards Maddie, and Morrow twisted, grabbing her ankle. The wound in his side gushed. Gwynedd's hand stopped an inch from Maddie's chest.

"I can't hold her!" Morrow grunted.

Maddie staggered. A pressure grew in the space behind her eyes. Her ears filled with whispers, rising rapidly to shouts, until finally her head shook with a roar so loud that it drowned out all her senses. She collapsed onto the floor. The towering tsunami of the Foxglove's consciousness enveloped her senses and smashed her thoughts to scrambled fragments.

Until, like a bell in a quiet room, she heard her name. "Maddie."

She knew the voice, but her words had left her. She twisted her head around and saw Maeve, lying in a coma on the floor. Her eyes were bloody and glazed over, staring into an aimless abyss. Nevertheless, her mistress's thoughts found her.

"It's me, Maddie," Maeve said.

Maddie clenched her teeth and forced her mind to frame an answer. "What's happening? Why can't I see? Why can't I move?"

"It is the Allsight. You must open your mind."

Maddie squeezed her eyes shut, struggling to hold her thoughts as they threatened to tear apart. The roar in her head rose, and the sounds merged into a reverberating thrum that peaked and fell in pounding waves, pressing on the trembling walls of her psyche. She pulled her hands up and held her palms against her temples, eyes wide and drifting in the grip of a thousand migraines.

"I . . . can't," she said. "I'll die."

Maddie felt the figment of a smile brush over her face. "You are the Foxglove," Maeve said. "The Allsight cannot hurt you. It is the power of life. All life."

"But how do I control it?"

"You do not have to, Madeline Foster," Maeve said. Her voice began to fade. "It is not a part of you. It is who you are."

The noise crashed in again as her mistress's voice disappeared. Maddie looked at Morrow and Gwynedd. Blood pooled on the floor, and the prince's body sagged. Maddie saw his grip loosen as his eyes fluttered shut.

What a frustrating destiny to have, she thought. *To be born, to live, and grow, only to be lost.*

Maddie refused to believe that her life was only spare change in the pocket of magic. All the hours she'd spent building a life, agonizing over test scores, and learning who she was could not have been for nothing.

She glanced at Rose, lying on the floor. The queen wouldn't have hesitated.

I guess dreams don't get any bigger than this.

Morrow's body went slack. Gwynedd broke free and turned, reaching out to Maddie with furious intent. Maddie let go of her mind, and the vast horizon of the world pulled her apart.

Foxglove

Morrow blinked. *Am I dead?* he thought.

The world had turned white. Light filled the whole sky. As he lifted his arm, he could barely see his hand in front of his face. Every shape turned to a streak of shadow. Every shape but one.

The Foxglove floated in the middle of the room, its face a mask of quiet serenity. Its flesh and form blazed in the luminous space. Morrow could feel its massive emotion in the warmth of his chest, and his own heart resonated with it. The creature was not simply aware of him; they were one. It was him. It was . . . everything.

Gwynedd hovered, frozen in place, diving towards its body. The burning eyes of the Foxglove turned to look at her with an expression almost like curiosity. Light seemed to fold around the witch's form. An instant later, she vanished. There was no sound, only an impression of movement too rapid to be perceived, and she was gone.

The Foxglove turned to the mist and the churn rolled away, funneling backwards as though driven by an unseen, unfelt wind. It collapsed in on itself as it slithered through the gap where it had emerged. The Foxglove brought up a hand, fingers outstretched, and with imperceptible gestures, it knitted the sky together until only the smallest fleck of the rupture remained. Then, with a gentle hand, it reached up and plucked the ragged hole from the horizon. There was subtle pulse of color between its fingers as it closed its palm. When it opened, a rainbow-colored diamond tumbled to the floor. And then it turned to Morrow.

"Maddie . . . " he said, trying to shuffle back. "Can you hear me?"

It drifted forward. Morrow scrambled weakly across the floor until his back pressed against the broken railing.

"P-please," he stammered. "I'm sorry. I'll make it up to everybody, I promise!"

He swore over and over again as the Foxglove approached and leaned over him. Its luminescent hand reached out. Morrow flinched, pressing his eyes shut as he waited for the inevitable. He prayed that it would be quick, but instead of pain, a strange sensation of warmth washed over his side, reaching into his ribs and across his abdomen. It passed in an instant. Morrow remained still, frozen. When he opened his eyes, the Foxglove was back across the balcony, and his wound was gone.

Something rumbled deep within the earth. Morrow pulled himself up onto the railing and stared down as the city shook. Like a great beast rising from a long slumber, the massive roots of the city-tree broke from the ground. The great tree moved, sliding through the forest, bringing with it a mudslide of stones, brush, and soil.

Morrow felt a sudden pressure on his eyes as the forest rose up around them. The trees darkened, the air grew warmer, and a cloud of magic settled into the air like a haze of drifting pollen. The city was moving, not just along the ground but *down*, plunging through the layers of the Veil, deeper and deeper into the tangles of its most secret lands.

The light of the Foxglove then began to fade. Night fell once more, and Morrow felt his legs go slack. He coughed, breathing in the thickening magic as he slid back down to the floor. His neck felt heavy, and his head fell limp. As he looked up, the twisting vines of a thorny brier closed around the city, tightening as they wove together and locked out the sky.

Loose Ends

Maddie woke in her bed. She lifted herself off the pillows to scan the room. Confusion filled her thoughts.

Someone had dressed her in a nightgown, and she'd been washed. She stared down at her hands and arms and found them to be completely whole and normal. In fact, the only thing that felt amiss was a peculiar cold.

She brought the blankets up and rubbed her shoulders to fend off the chill, but the feeling didn't go away. It was on the inside, leeching out to freeze her limbs. It wasn't until she considered walking to her closet to find a sweater that a terrible thought alighted on the surface of her mind.

Maddie threw her blankets down and opened her shirt. The scar on her chest had turned an oily black, and it had spread. It covered her chest, running like a disease from her stomach to her neck, stretching over her shoulders. Maddie remembered what had happened as her breath caught in her throat.

Gwynedd's heart beat in her chest, fused with her own.

The last thing she remembered was lying on the floor, watching Gwynedd wrestle with Morrow. After that, there was nothing.

The door opened. Maddie pulled her clothing shut and yanked up the blankets as Ebba walked into the room.

"Maddie!" the girl squealed, running across the floor. She leapt onto the bed and buried her face in Maddie's shoulder. "I'm so glad you're okay!"

"All in one piece," Maddie said, wrapping her up in a hug.

Ebba sat back on her knees. "Nobody would tell me what happened. They just said they found you, but you wouldn't wake up. It's been three days!"

Maddie's jaw fell open. "Three days?"

"You must be hungry," Ebba said rapidly. "I'll go get you something. Soup? Broth?" She jumped off the bed. "I'll be right back. The others will want to know you're awake. Prince Finn especially. There's a lot going on, and he needs your help."

Maddie's chest ached at hearing the prince's name. She kicked her feet off the bed, feeling sick as she remembered the events on the balcony. Finn didn't know what she'd done. Despair and sadness churned in her throat. She needed some fresh air, or she was going to throw up.

"Wait. Let me get dressed," Maddie said, staggering to her wardrobe.

Ebba replied, "Are you sure? You should rest."

Maddie threw on her witching robes, careful to keep her scar out of sight, and wobbled to the door. "I've rested enough," she said, heading out into the hall. "Is everyone okay? What happened after the battle?"

Ebba followed her. "Some people are okay. A lot's happened. Are you really sure you should be up?"

"I'll be fine," said Maddie. "Please, just . . . take me outside."

The palace corridors were filled with refugees. They were tired and hungry, but they didn't look like they were injured.

"Where did all these people come from?" Maddie asked.

"The city," Ebba said, picking through the mass. "Some of them got here during the battle, but a lot came after. The buildings in town were destroyed, so Rain is keeping as many people as she can in the palace until the wardens say it's safe to go down to the ground."

Maddie tripped on someone's leg. She apologized and steadied herself against the wall. "Safe?" she said.

Ebba stopped to help an older woman off the floor. "That's right," she said. "They're not taking any chances since we moved."

"What do you mean, moved?"

They came to the palace door.

"It'll be easier to explain if you see it," Ebba said, and pushed it open.

Soft mushroom light illuminated the courtyard, where the wounded lay on the ground, bandaged and moaning as they huddled under thin blankets. The palace staff wandered among them, bringing water and small comfort, while above their heads, a towering canopy of thorny vines blocked out the moon and stars. Maddie stared up. She could hardly see the sky between them.

She asked, "Where are we?"

Ebba led her out. "Nobody knows."

"And the people?"

"We ran out of blankets and pillows on the first day, so we collected these from what's left of the city. They're still trying to figure out how much of it can be fixed, but it's a big mess. When the tree moved, it was like an earthquake."

Maddie didn't understand. *Why can't I remember?* she thought, straining.

"How did the tree move?" she asked.

Ebba hopped over a sleeping soldier. "It happened at the end of the battle. Nobody will tell me how. People are saying that something happened in the palace. Gwynedd is gone, and our soldiers captured the people from Aster and the Erlkin, and . . . " She trailed off.

"Rose?" Maddie said.

Ebba sniffled. "She's dead." Tears started running down her cheeks.

"I'm so sorry, Ebba," Maddie said, gathering the girl up into her arms. She didn't have the heart to tell her what she'd done.

"Maddie?!" someone shouted across the yard. Rain came sprinting across the crowded space, leaping over people and beds to catch Maddie up in a bear hug.

Ebba squawked. "You're squishing me!"

"After everything that happened, we were sure you would never wake up," Rain said, easing off.

"I'm still trying to figure out what's going on," Maddie said.

Rain glanced down and knelt in front of Ebba. She pointed across the yard where a line of women were washing sheets in steaming water. "I need a hand with the bedclothes," she said. "Would you go help?"

Ebba groaned. "Fine."

"Is Kidhe okay?" Maddie asked after she'd gone. "And Finn?"

"They're fine. Kidhe has a broken leg. I'll take you to him. Before you ask, Earnest is okay too. They've got him in the aviary, and they're taking good care of him. He's one of the only birds left in the city. Most of them were blown away in the storm."

Maddie's eyes suddenly sprung open. "Oh my God! Theresa?"

"Missing," Rain said with a worried look. "They found you unconscious on the throne room balcony after it was over. No one knows what happened. Rose is . . . She passed. Finn was unconscious, and Maeve is in some kind of coma."

All my fault, Maddie thought. *I should have fought harder. I should have realized before it was too late.* She felt a tear slip down her cheek. "I couldn't stop it. Rain, I'm so sorry. I couldn't do anything."

"Don't think like that," Rain said, holding her close. "It wasn't your fault. It was Gwynedd."

She doesn't know. None of them saw.

Maddie thought about confessing. She wanted to, but she couldn't bring herself to do it. They would never forgive her.

Rain led Maddie across the courtyard to a bed near the edge. Kidhe's leg was bound with cloth and a pair of long boards.

"You're awake!" he said, leaning up. He tried to stand, only to wince and slump back down.

Maddie ran over and knelt down beside him. "Stay down, please! You're injured."

He fell back onto his rumpled pillow. "It's so good to see you," he said. "I was worried you might . . . "

Maddie kissed his cheek. "I'm fine. It'll take more than a world-ending disaster to keep me down."

He chuckled, flinching as he said, "I think our camping trip might have to be put on hold."

"It's okay," Maddie said, massaging his shoulder. "I'll take a rain check."

He lay down and took a few long breaths, staring at the thorny ceiling.

"You've been all over the Veil," Maddie said. "Do you know where we are?"

"Only partly," he answered. "I've never been this deep. The magic here is so thick it's giving people headaches. My best guess is that we're in a delve. Beyond that, I have no idea."

"So, how do we get home?"

"Maddie, I don't even know how we got here."

She sat down beside him.

"I wish I knew what happened," she said. "Didn't anybody see anything?"

"There was only one other person with you in the room," Rain said, her voice dropping low. "And he's refusing to talk to anyone."

Maddie's eyes narrowed. Her voice emerged in a low rumbled as she got to her feet. "Morrow."

Same as the Old Boss

Morrow lay on the floor, bound hand and foot with thick leather cords. The palace didn't have a dungeon, and the only jails were down in the city, so the guards had removed the furniture from one of the bedrooms to keep him. A tall bucket sat in the corner.

"They're still trying to figure out what to do with him," Rain said.

Maddie stared at the Erlkin prince. He was a man again. Gwynedd's magic had worn off. His eyes were clamped shut as he slept, but even asleep, his body shook and his limbs twitched in fits of paralysis.

"What's wrong with him?" Maddie asked.

Rain shut the door. "We're not sure. I've never seen anything like it. Cedric thinks he's sick, but he doesn't have a fever, and Maeve's in no condition to examine him."

Maddie gave a grim nod as she stood over Morrow. "He told me he needs Gwynedd's blood to survive. He'll die without it." She kicked his boot, hard. "Isn't that right?" she said as he started awake.

His eyes trembled as he looked up at her, but his expression was not one of fear. He was merely resigned.

"You're here," he said. "I told them to bring you, but they said you were in a coma."

Maddie leaned down into his face. "I was."

"I was hoping I might have earned a pardon," he said, tugging at his bindings.

Cold hatred rose up in Maddie's throat. She spat and lowered herself to her knees. With one hand, she took hold of his hair and gripped it in her fist. He winced and squinted an eye shut as the darkness of the room closed in around them.

"How could you possibly deserve anyone's mercy?" Maddie said. "All of this is because of you."

He hung from her hand, twitching. "I know . . . and I'm sorry. You told me I couldn't fix it, but I tried anyway." His jaw spasmed, and he pulled in a breath. "How'd I do?"

Maddie yanked his hair. "Rose is dead, Theresa is missing, and Maeve might never be the same. What do you think?" She dropped him and stood up.

He shivered as he gave a rapid, unsteady nod. "It was the best I could do," he said.

Maddie grunted out a laugh. "Well, it wasn't good enough."

The chill in her chest spread to her arms, coating her like a layer of ice. A rising tide of malice froze in her throat, driving her to pin the man to the floor and strangle him with her bare hands.

"Are you alright?" Rain asked, touching her shoulder.

Maddie gasped and stepped back as Morrow pulled himself up to sit. His eyes studied her face, drifting to the black tendrils of her scar where they rose above her collar.

He spoke haltingly as he pointed with a shuddering hand. "You can feel it . . . " he said. "Can't you?"

Maddie pulled her collar tight.

He smiled, shaking as he relaxed back onto the floor. "It never goes away. Her will . . . It makes you do things. You don't even realize until it's too late." He forced a weak smile. "Or almost too late."

Maddie took a deep breath. "You expect me to forgive you?" she asked. "You attacked me in the woods. You held me down while Gwynedd cut out my heart. You pretended to be my friend so that you could betray me *and* the city. Thousands of people are dead. One good turn can't repay that."

He shrugged, curling into a ball against an unseen cold. "I had hoped. I didn't mean . . . "

"To violate me?" Maddie stared down at him. "You are a murderer and a coward. You deserve worse than death."

Morrow coughed as he gripped his shoulders and struggled to breathe. "You might have to settle for it," he said, wincing.

Maddie pulled her stone knife out of her robes. The blade caught the dim light from the hall.

"Maddie . . . " Rain said, taking a step forward.

"It's alright. I won't hurt him," Maddie said, waving her off. "Wait outside."

Rain drew back tentatively and left. As the door shut, Maddie pulled the point of her knife across her hand. Blood welled up in her palm, a mixture of red and black.

"You need Gwynedd's humours to survive?" she asked, thrusting her arm forward. "Well, drink up. I'll show *you* what it feels like to be held down."

Morrow's tongue flashed across his lips, but he pulled back, recoiling with every ounce of his waning strength. Maddie stepped across the gap between them and grabbed his head. He shook it, powerless as Maddie held her clenched fist above his mouth, and the blood fell in a narrow stream. Morrow's pupils dilated and his shaking stilled as it trickled down his throat.

"Now," Maddie said. "Tell me what you saw."

He recounted everything. When he was done, Maddie left the room and slammed the door.

Rain looked at her in shock. "Maddie, what did you do?"

Maddie stared down at her hand, wet with blood. She shuddered, sickened as she clutched her robes to stop the bleeding.

"Nothing," she said. "He's fine now. Where's Finn?"

"With his mother," Rain answered warily. "In what's left of her private parlor. Finn hasn't left the room in days, and we were hoping you . . . " She paused. "Well, because the two of you . . . you know. We thought you might be able to bring him out of it. His people need him. With Theresa gone, there's no one else. Some of the ambassadors are still in the city, and Delilah is already playing politics."

Maddie gave her friend a skeptical look. "How come she isn't locked up?"

"It was a legal war," Rain said. "Properly declared. She didn't commit a crime."

Maddie checked her hand. The bleeding had stopped. "That is so stupid," she said.

Rain came around in front of her. "People are starting to talk. Rumors are spreading that Finn isn't fit to lead. Cedric and I can hold things down for now, but pretty soon it's not going to be enough. The shock will pass, and someone is going to have to start making decisions. If the prince doesn't get involved, he's going to lose his kingdom."

Heir

The parlor was quiet when Maddie entered. The glowing fungus on the ceiling shed a warm light over the shadowed space. Rose lay in the middle of the room on a mound of soft, red pillows, her crown resting delicately on her head. Maddie couldn't help but notice how peaceful her expression was. She might have mistaken the queen's repose for sleep. It wasn't until she drew closer that she noticed the telltale signs of death. Her chest was motionless, and her eyes were still beneath their lids. A black cloth covered the bruises around her neck.

Finn sat beside her, head hung low, one hand holding his mother's lifeless palm.

"I don't know what to say," Maddie said as she sat down beside him.

His shoulders tensed at the sound of her voice. A tear rolled down his cheek and fell on his soiled clothes. Maddie considered putting out a hand to touch him, but fear of his reaction kept her still. She couldn't bring herself to tell him the awful truth about what happened. She pleaded with herself to try, but the words died on her tongue. No matter how desperately she wanted to bare her soul and beg for his forgiveness, the prince was on the point of breaking, and his people needed him intact.

"I tried to fight," Maddie said. "I tried so hard." She felt her own tears welling up and pulled the prince onto her shoulder.

He put a hand to his face and rubbed his eyes. "I know," he said with a sob.

A long moment passed in silence.

"Your power . . . " he said. "Can you use it? Can you bring her back?"

Maddie tightened her arm around the prince and clenched her fist. "I . . . no," she said. "I'm sorry. I don't even know how I became the Foxglove or how to become it again. I don't remember anything. But when I was . . . I think, if I could have helped her, I would have."

Finn's shoulders sank as his last hope died. Maddie remembered what it was like when she lost her father. She felt the same the pain that he was going through, the loneliness and the certainty that nothing would ever be the same. It was true; it never would be. Even after everything that had happened and all the time that had gone by, she could still remember her father's face, his smile, his voice . . . and his death. Thinking about it was like looking back on a bad dream. Finn had lost both his parents, and for all he knew, his only sibling as well.

Rose had asked her to take care of him. It was the least she could do.

She held him, cradling his head as she spoke softly into his ear. "You're not alone."

He shuddered.

"It's going to be alright," she said. "I'm here for you. I will always be here for you."

Finn collapsed with grief and wept into her robes. Maddie held on for as long as she could before she started crying too. It was a long moment before either of them spoke again.

When she finally let him go, he sat up, taking in a slow, halting breath.

"They're waiting for me, aren't they?" he asked.

Maddie shook her head. "Not really waiting."

"Damn," Finn said, wiping his eyes with a sigh. "Delilah?"

"Already positioning herself."

She stood up and took hold of Finn's hand, lifting him to his feet. She could feel the tension in his palm and the pain he was holding back as he stared down at his mother.

"I don't know if I can face them," he said. "I'm the younger brother. I worked and studied so hard, but I never counted on this. How can I replace my sister? My mother?"

"You don't have to," Maddie said. "Just do your best. It'll be enough."

The words had already left her mouth before she realized they were Rose's, and Maddie clenched her teeth to stop herself crying again.

Finn gave a forlorn laugh and said, "You really think so?"

"You've got the head for it," Maddie said, poking him in the center of his forehead. "You might even be smarter than me."

Finn blinked, stunned. "I can't believe you said that."

Maddie smirked and said, "Don't worry, I was just trying to be nice."

Finn laughed, and Maddie felt her heart ease.

"There," she said. "That's better."

Finn cast a final glance down at his mother. "I wonder what she would do if she were here."

Maddie pointed up at the ceiling. "That," she said.

Finn's eyes rose to the carving that surrounded the light.

"That's her dream," Maddie said. "She once told me that the last three children represent the city. They were her family, and they're your responsibility now. You have to protect them. If you can't think of anything else, aim for that."

"Including the kids?" he asked, smiling.

Maddie shot him a stern look. "I should slap you. You've got a long way to go before you start thinking along those lines, your highness."

He straightened his clothes, glancing for a moment at her neck. "What happened to your scar?" he asked.

Maddie looked down. "A parting gift from Gwynedd," she answered. "We can talk about it later. Right now, you've got politics to attend to."

His eyes drifted to the door. "It will be easier if you go in with me," he said. "I know how much you love state functions."

Maddie rolled her eyes. "Oh, yeah. Can't get enough."

"How do I look?"

Maddie fixed his collar. "Like a king," she said.

He gave her a skeptical look. "You're just being nice again, aren't you?"

"I am," Maddie said, giving him a peck on the cheek as she opened the door. "But don't worry. We'll make it work."

Rosewood

Maddie fingered the badge on her robes. Gold thread wove through the fabric in the shape of an amaranth flower. She was far from prepared to take over Maeve's duties, but the imagery went a long way towards getting the ambassadors in line.

Finn's first act was to appoint her royal practitioner, hoping that her status as a supernatural being would keep Delilah's ambitions in check. His crown depended on his ability to maintain a delicate diplomatic balance. There were a thousand problems to attend to, from bed space to food and water, not to mention the enormous task of getting settled in their new home.

Maddie excused herself as the discussion moved on to practical matters, and she made her way from the royal apartment where the meeting was being held to the balcony in what was left of the throne room.

The city had settled at the end of an enormous valley. The landscape swept away, scattered with patches of silver light where the moon and stars peeked through the brambles. A warm wind blew across the terrace, and Maddie shivered as it brushed against her skin.

"Maddie," a voice said, emerging in her thoughts.

She looked around, but there was no one. "Maeve?" she answered.

"It's me," her mistress said.

"But how can I hear you?"

"Some portion of the Allsight must still be with you. Search at your feet."

Maddie sifted through the rubble, and her eyes fell upon a glittering, rainbow-colored stone. It sparkled when she picked it up.

"What is it?" she asked.

"All that remains of the gateway Gwynedd used you to open. Why you did not close it completely, I do not know."

Maddie held the twinkling jewel in front of her face. "What do I do with it?"

"Keep it safe," Maeve answered. "Tell no one of its existence. We do not yet know the power that it holds."

Maddie placed the stone in her pocket. "Will I always be able to talk to you like this?"

"Perhaps," her mistress said. "Perhaps not. You are the Foxglove, Madeline. Nothing can change that. Now that you have felt its power, your spirit longs to return to its true state. You must prepare yourself for when that time comes."

"Will you help me?"

"All that I can."

Maddie's hand drifted to her collar. "I have Gwynedd's heart. I can feel it doing . . . something, but I don't know how to fight it."

Maddie felt Maeve's concern, severe and grim. "Gwynedd's essence is strong, and the spirit is malleable. In time, the feeling of strangeness will pass, and you will no longer be unfamiliar with what you have become. Your second nature will become your only nature, the old replaced by the new."

"How do I remove it?"

Her mistress's thoughts were hard as stone. "It cannot be done," she said. "I told you at the beginning: what we take in, we take in forever."

"Then what do I do?"

"Be vigilant," Maeve answered. "The change will come in ways you do not see, in the subtlest of impulses. You must deny your instincts and listen to the echoes of your true self. And trust your friends. Eventually, only they will be able to discern the difference."

A murmur of sensation drew Maddie's eyes back out into the valley, and she felt movement in the dark.

"You can feel them," Maeve's voice whispered beside her. "Creatures of the deep Veil. I think that there is more to this new land than can be seen with the naked eye."

Maddie stared, scanning the moonlight and the shadows. "Maeve . . . " she said. "As the Foxglove, why didn't I kill Gwynedd?"

"Only you would know that," Maeve answered. "But the Foxglove is more than a being. It is life, and knowledge, and empathy beyond imagining. Even in the old world, it refused to slay the enemy it was created to destroy. Gwynedd was forced to remove its understanding in order to use it to kill. Perhaps, on its own, it is not capable of it."

"That's comforting," Maddie said.

Someone called out from behind her. "There she is!"

Leoh and the others jogged around the corner. Kidhe was on a crutch, and Rain was holding a sleepy Ebba by the hand.

Maeve smiled inside Maddie's head. "Go to your friends. The rest of your questions can wait. Tonight, it is enough to be alive."

Maeve was right. They had all suffered a terrible loss, but it was important to remember the things they still had: the people, the feelings, and the connections yet unbroken. Maddie felt warmed by her friends as they surrounded her, and deep in her chest, the brighter side of her heart beat assuredly and calm.

She remembered a conversation she had with Rose. She said the Veil was a place of dreams. All she had to do was find her own. She thought about the stone in her pocket and wondered.

In a place like the Veil, what impossible dreams might come?

From the Author

I hope you enjoyed reading Foxglove as much as I loved writing it. If you don't mind me asking you for a favor, please consider leaving a review. I read them all, and each one goes a long way towards helping a book succeed. Thank you.

Sincerely,
Aaron McQueen

Also Available from Aaron McQueen

Go to www.mcqueenserialfantasy.com and sign up to my mailing list to receive a FREE eBook copy of the prequel to Foxglove, Queens of Iris.

Special Thanks to my Patreon Subscribers!

Theresa Uber

Timothy Tortal

Matthew Edmondson

Made in the USA
Monee, IL
12 February 2020